TAKEN

BOOK 2 OF THE DJINN WARS

CHRISTINE POPE

Dark Valentine Press

This is a work of fiction. Names, characters, places, and incidents are either the product of the author's imagination or are used fictitiously. Any resemblance to actual events, places, organizations, or persons, whether living or dead, is entirely coincidental.

TAKEN

ISBN: 978-0692431917
Copyright © 2015 by Christine Pope
Published by Dark Valentine Press

Cover design and book layout by Indie Author Services.

To learn more about this author, go to
www.christinepope.com.

TAKEN

CHAPTER ONE

I DON'T KNOW HOW LONG I STOOD OUT IN THE ICY air, feeling the wind whip at my hair, tears seeming to freeze on my cheeks. Overhead, the sky grew darker and darker, a bruised-looking mass of clouds building from the northeast.

It was Dutchie who brought me back to myself, stirring me out of my frozen misery. She thrust a cold, wet nose into my palm and whined, her head cocked to the side. I forced myself to look down. The dog didn't look particularly troubled, although I could tell she wanted to go back in the house. Who could blame her, with the temperature barely above freezing? Since she was a border collie mix, she had a thick coat, but it wasn't *that* thick.

Some time would have to pass before she realized that Jace hadn't gone off with those men just to shoot dinner, that he wouldn't be back by the end of the day. After all, he often disappeared for hours to go hunting, and he didn't always take Dutchie with him. Most of the time, but not always.

"Okay, girl," I told her. We did need to go inside. I had to regroup, figure out what to do next. Standing out here in the cold and making myself sick wasn't going to do either of us any good.

Before I went inside, though, I walked down to the gate and inspected the electronic mechanism that usually controlled it. As I'd feared, a few wires were hanging out of the box, which meant the gate was now basically useless. I didn't know the first thing about electronics, or soldering, or whatever else I'd need to do to fix it.

My internal voice was far more confident than I felt. *But there are manuals and all kinds of equipment here at the compound, so don't give up before you've even started.*

That sounded great. Except right then I wasn't sure I could even summon the energy to feed myself later that evening, let alone teach myself enough about wiring that I could actually repair the gate and not blow myself up in the process.

Shivering, I pushed the gate shut. It was heavy, and I had a feeling the next morning my muscles would give me grief about the way I'd just overexerted them, but closing the gate at least gave the compound the illusion of security, if not the real thing.

"Come on, Dutchie," I said, and began the weary trudge up the hill to go back inside the house. She trotted along next to me, looking a little worried, although that might have been me projecting my own emotions on her.

What in the world was I supposed to do now?

One step at a time. Up the hill. Inside the house. Close the door and lock it. The thugs from Los Alamos must have picked the lock or used the black box to open the door or whatever, because the front door lock still seemed to work. Or maybe it hadn't even been locked. Jace and I hadn't been all that careful about it lately. What was the point, with the house guarded by a nine-foot wall and an electronic gate?

And now I was—well, I wouldn't say I was exactly feeling better, but at least I wasn't inviting incipient frostbite. Around me, everything looked familiar, unchanged. The fire still crackled in the hearth, and the air was spicy with the scent of the Christmas tree that stood in the corner.

The tree. I went to it and inhaled its fragrance, reached out to touch its soft needles. Jace had brought me that tree. He'd brought it because he loved me.

That memory was all it took. The tears I'd pushed back returned with a vengeance, coursing down my cheeks as my fingers clenched so tightly on one of the popcorn strands surrounding the Christmas tree that it broke, sending soft white kernels falling to the floor.

Shit. I dropped to my knees and attempted to gather them all up. What if that was one of the strands Jace had made? I had hardly anything left of him, and now I'd just broken something that he'd touched, something he'd created with his own hands.

You don't know that, I tried to scold myself. *You made twice as many of those strands as he did, since he ate almost as much as what actually ended up on the tree.*

Unbidden, a smile came to my lips, even through the tears. I remembered him sitting on the couch, dark eyes guiltily shifting to me as at least one kernel went in his mouth for every one he strung on the thread I'd given him.

How could he be so human? Were the djinn really all that different from us, or had Jace perfected the guise of humanity better than most of them?

I didn't know, and right then, I didn't care. The only thing I knew was that I loved him, and he'd been taken from me.

Rage erupted in me at that thought, pushing away the despair. Well, that was right on schedule, wasn't it? First denial, and then anger. But I didn't want to come to acceptance, once the anger had burned its way through me. I'd never accept the way the gang from Los Alamos had stolen Jace from me. They had no right. He'd done nothing wrong, in fact had done everything he could to prevent the Dying, from having his people continue plotting to destroy humanity. And when it was clear that he'd been overruled in that debate, he'd somehow chosen me from all the survivors, had made sure at least I would be safe.

True, the djinn were responsible for humanity's demise, but not all of the elementals had participated in that genocide. It seemed clear enough to me that was a fine point of distinction the Los Alamos people didn't want to make. Much simpler to condemn all the djinn as a single monolithic group, right?

With an almost physical effort, I made myself turn away from the tree. Then I went down the hall to the guest bathroom, which was closest, so I could splash some water on my face and blow my nose.

The simple actions helped a little. Not completely, but at least I felt as if I had a slightly stronger grip on my emotions. Crying wasn't going to change anything. I wouldn't allow myself to feel bad for having a temporary meltdown, but on the other hand, I knew I had to get myself together and figure out what to do next.

It was only a little before noon. Strange how my life could be changed so utterly before the day was even half over.

As I looked down at her, Dutchie gave me a half-hopeful tail thump.

"Close enough to lunch," I told her, then went to fetch a cupful of food from the big bag of dry food in the pantry.

Feeding the dog helped me to calm down a little. Jace was gone, but I still had Dutchie to take care of, and I needed to take care of myself, too. I needed to be in the very best fighting shape possible so that when I went to rescue my djinn lover, I wouldn't have self-sabotaged by moping around and not eating, or drinking too much, or whatever else I felt like doing at that particular moment.

Although my appetite had completely deserted me, I made myself eat some leftover baked sausage and macaroni. I remembered sitting down and having that meal only a few nights earlier, recalled the way Jace and I had laughed and plotted and planned for the coming spring, how we'd realized we should make another foray to Home Depot to scoop up any seeds and other useful gardening items that the gleaners had left behind.

Well, now at least I knew who those gleaners were. The people from Los Alamos.

How many of them were there? The leader of the group had said they were trying to in-gather as many people as they could, but that meant nothing to me. New Mexico hadn't been a densely populated state even at its peak. Altogether, there were probably only a few thousand survivors of the Dying here, but how many of those humans had the vengeful djinn picked off before those few souls could make it to this supposed haven in Los Alamos?

I wasn't sure I wanted to guess, but between that and the inevitable disease and accidents that occurred after any great cataclysm, I estimated maybe a thousand were still alive. Of those, I doubted all would have made their way to that small hillside town, built on several plateaus nestled in the Jemez Mountain range. So possibly...five hundred? Six hundred?

That didn't sound like a whole lot, but it was still five hundred of them up against just one of me.

Trying not to sigh, I forced down the leftovers, ignoring Dutchie as she settled near the base of my chair and waited to see if I'd have any scraps to give her when I was done. I also tried to ignore the thoughts that swirled around in my brain, telling me that Jace had been wrong and that the Los Alamos crew was going to execute him just as soon as they cleared space on the hanging tree or whatever they planned to use to rid themselves of their captive.

Although...*could* you even execute a djinn? That is, Jace certainly felt real enough; I'd kissed him, touched him, made love to him. His body certainly seemed human, at least in every aspect that mattered to me. Some of that could have been subterfuge, but not all; when he'd given up his assumed identity of Jason Little

River, Jace still looked human, just different from the man I'd come to know.

But he'd told me of being trapped on this plane by the device the man in the glasses had been carrying, which meant Jace had the ability to move from this world to others, planes of existence I could barely begin to imagine. So maybe that body was real while he was here, but changed into something else when he wasn't on the corporeal plane?

Just trying to figure out how that could possibly work made my head hurt. I'd never believed in ghosts and spirits, psychics and channeling and all that stuff. I believed in what I could see, could touch. Well, I'd seen Jace floating above the living room floor, so I knew he wasn't an ordinary man. And I'd touched him, so I also knew he was real. Ergo, there were things in heaven and earth that certainly had never been dreamt of in my philosophy...at least not until the Dying changed the world irrevocably.

And I couldn't begin to guess where the man in the glasses might have gotten that device he was carrying. Was it djinn-made? I hadn't gotten the impression that he was in charge, exactly...the guy with the military-looking haircut had definitely appeared to be the boss of that particular group. So how were they connected?

I threw Dutchie one last scrap of sausage that I'd saved for her, then went to rinse off my plate. As I did so, my brain kept working away at the problem. The leader of the group from Los Alamos had said that Jace would be put on trial for his supposed crimes. Would it be a real trial, or at least a facsimile of one, with a prosecutor and a defense attorney and all that? Or would they dispense with the niceties, declare him guilty after a sham trial, and string him up anyway?

The thought crossed my mind that I could go to Los Alamos and offer myself as his defender. Never mind that everything I knew about courtroom procedures I'd gleaned from watching old episodes of various crime dramas. Then again, even my limited knowledge might be better than the so-called "defense" Jace would get from whoever in Los Alamos was assigned to his case. If they assigned anyone at all. Maybe they expected him to defend himself. That would go over really well.

After heading back to the living room, I pushed the curtains aside and peered out. The sky still looked lowering, but the snow, if it was coming at all, hadn't made an appearance yet. And although I'd shut the gate, I hadn't secured it. Until I could attempt to make repairs, I really should get out there and lock it up with some chain and a padlock or something.

First I made a detour to the office and woke up the computer so I could take a look at the security feed. As I'd feared, even though the cameras on the rest of the property seemed to be working normally, the one that overlooked the front gate was dark, so it had to have been disabled at the same time the main mechanism was circumvented.

Well, at least I had eyes on the rest of the compound. That was better than nothing. Also, I was able to scrounge some chain and a padlock—still in its clamshell packaging—from the storage area in the basement, and that made me feel...well, not better, exactly, but at least slightly safer.

I pulled on my coat and scarf, but not my gloves, since I needed the full use of my hands. Once I was outfitted, I went back outside, Dutchie bounding along at my heels, and headed down to the gate, which I secured to the wall as best I could by looping the chain around the steel frame bolted to the adobe. When I pulled on it, there might have been the slightest amount of give, but overall, it seemed sturdy enough. No, it wouldn't stand up to someone driving a Hummer through it, and if you were determined enough, you could probably still climb up and over the gate itself, but I thought it should deter anyone who was only out for some casual looting. If such a person even existed; for all I knew, I was taking all these precautions for nothing. The Los Alamos team had included the only people I'd seen since I'd left Albuquerque.

But having the gate locked made me feel a little better, if nothing else, and I needed to feel better. I needed to tell myself there was still hope, that this would all somehow work out in the end. Right then I couldn't see how that was possible, but when the Heat had swept through Albuquerque, I was sure I would die along with everyone else, and yet here I was.

Good enough for now.

We went back inside, and I piled a few more logs on the fireplace. A long, empty afternoon stretched in front of me. Funny how I'd never felt at loose ends when Jace was around. We'd always had plenty to occupy us. Well, in a few hours I'd have to go out and feed the chickens and the goats, make sure they had fresh water, but what I was supposed to do between now and then, I didn't know. Sit down with one of the new-looking paperback mysteries from the shelves in the office and pretend my world hadn't just ended?

No way.

I did go into the office, but ignored the paperbacks in favor of the manuals that sat on one of the shelves. There actually was a book on basic electronics, but when I picked it up and started flipping through it, my eyes wanted to cross at all the diagrams and the figures and formulas I found in it, and I felt like crying all over again. After all, there was a reason why I'd been getting my master's in English, and not in electrical engineering.

A meltdown was not something I'd allow myself, though. I made a few desultory notes about possible methods of fixing the gate, peered outside and saw the snow had finally arrived, then decided I'd better take care of the animals early before it got too bad.

The goats had already taken shelter in their shed, so I filled their trough with pellets. Their water still looked good—Jace had handled that in the morning—so I left it for now. Same thing with the chickens, although there were a few new eggs. I scooped them into my pockets before heading back to the house, dodging snowflakes the whole way. It seemed the storm had decided to arrive in earnest.

Inside it was snug and warm enough, though, and I puttered here and there, forcing myself to focus on mundane chores, such as bringing in more wood from the log room on the side of the house and stoking up all the fireplaces to combat the rapidly dropping temperatures outside. Busyness helped a little, although I couldn't help feeling the gnawing, aching sensation somewhere in my midsection, the one that told me Jace was gone and I had absolutely no idea of how to get him back.

It isn't fair, I thought irrationally. *To survive the Dying, to lose everyone I cared about, and then to lose him, too.*

Well, as my parents had been all too fond of pointing out, life wasn't fair. And right then I wasn't about to dissect the cognitive dissonance that came from knowing Jace's people were the ones responsible for the Dying, and yet still to miss him, to want him, to know that I loved him in a way I hadn't thought I could ever love anyone. My anger with him at deceiving me about his true identity had been as intense as a summer monsoon storm, but just as short-lived. Now I only wanted him back.

Sitting at the table in the breakfast nook where we'd shared too many meals hurt far too much, and so did the idea of trying to eat at that vast dining room table. I took my dinner of heated-up canned soup and toasted bread to the living room where I could eat in front of the fireplace, although even the warmth of that fire didn't seem to penetrate the core of cold at the very center of my being. Nothing could dispel that inner chill, except Jace's touch.

I wondered if I should leave here the next day, head up to Taos and see if the djinn there could do anything to help me. But no, that wouldn't work. Zahrias had said his people were unable to penetrate the veil that had apparently descended on Los Alamos, and had resorted to sending some of their Chosen to that enclave of the Immune to see what they could discover. Since none of the Chosen had returned, I had to believe that they'd either been captured as spies, or had a change of heart once they were safe and among their own kind.

No, that didn't seem right. I knew that being around the other survivors wouldn't have changed how I felt about Jace; if anything, it would have made me work harder to convince them that not all the djinn were evil. Those other Chosen must have been caught, found out. Would they also be put on trial as traitors?

I didn't know for sure. The leader of the group that captured Jace had appeared interested in convincing me to join them, and not because he seemed to think I was guilty of crimes against humanity or whatever. No, I'd seen that look on enough guys' faces at bars or clubs to know what it meant—that he wouldn't mind getting into my pants in the near future.

There was a joke. I would rather have jumped into bed with Zahrias than with that human bastard.

But his interest was still something I might be able to exploit at a later date, and it also told me that he was willing to overlook my fraternizing with Jace, as long as there was no chance of it happening again.

All right, I'd found an angle. What exactly I could do with it, I didn't know. I also couldn't help wondering if Jace had told me to stay away because he wanted me to be safe, and not because he thought I actually had a better chance of rescuing him if I was out in the world where I could find an ally, some assistance. It would be just like him to think of my safety and not his own survival.

His concern wouldn't stop me, though. He could be as noble and selfless as he wanted, but in this matter, I intended to be utterly selfish. I wanted him back. I wanted *him*. No matter what.

All right, so I was resolved to rescue him. I still needed a plan.

Scowling, I picked up my plate and bowl and took them to the kitchen, then poured my half-eaten soup down the drain. Completely wasteful, and not like me at all, but in that moment I couldn't really force myself to care. There was pallet after pallet of canned soup down in the storage area in the basement, far more than I could probably eat before it went bad.

Especially now that I was the only one around to eat it.

That thick, choking feeling, the one of despair, caught at my throat, and I grasped the kitchen counter, forcing myself to breathe. To calm down. Jace was alive for now. I had to believe that. Otherwise, I might as well lie down and die, and I wouldn't allow that to happen. Not after everything I'd already survived.

The clock in the living room chimed. Seven o'clock. And in one of those moments of pure incongruity, I realized it was Christmas Eve.

Merry fucking Christmas.

I went back out to the living room and stood there for a long moment, staring at the tree Jace had brought me. How could a djinn have known that such a simple thing would be so important to me?

Because he hadn't been thinking like a djinn. He'd been thinking like the man who loved me.

The doorbell sounded, and I nearly jumped out of my skin. At least, I thought it was the doorbell. I'd never heard it before.

My frazzled brain eventually processed the meaning of that doorbell ringing. Someone was standing outside the door. How had they gotten into the compound? Climbed over the gate? Then I decided that wasn't really the important consideration here.

Someone was outside.

And irritated, too, by the way they rang the doorbell again, then started banging on the door.

An unfamiliar voice—a woman's voice—called out, "I know you're in there, Jessica! Open the goddamn door! It's freezing out here!"

That someone was a woman, and she knew my name. What the ever-loving hell?

Before I could even stop to think about what I was doing, I crossed the living room, then hesitated for a few seconds. That could be anyone out there. Someone from the Los Alamos group, come to finish me off. That didn't sound right, though. I hadn't seen one woman in their group; clearly, they didn't seem to think women made good enforcers.

You're crazy, Jessica, I thought, just before I turned the deadbolt and opened the door. Outside on the porch stood a young woman around my age, a pretty Hispanic girl wearing a red and green Nordic-style knitted cap and a bulky red parka, both of which were dusted with snow.

I'd never seen her before.

We stared at each other for a few seconds, and then she said, "Are you going to let me in? Because you'd better, if you ever want to see your djinn lover alive again."

CHAPTER TWO

BECAUSE SPEECH SEEMED TO HAVE DESERTED ME for the moment, I opened the door a little wider and let her in. She pushed past me and yanked the cap off her head, shaking her hair so little bits of snow flew off and landed on the Navajo rug. A streak of red cut through her dark, dark hair—even darker than mine—and she had short bangs cut Bettie Page style. In one hand she held a shiny black patent leather weekender bag.

"Who—" I finally managed after I had shut the door and saw her standing in the middle of the room, giving it an admiring once-over even as she bent slightly to let her bag drop to the floor.

"Nice place," she remarked. "We were just holed up in a king suite at the Ohkay Owingeh casino in Española. This beats the hell out of that." Apparently taking pity on my complete befuddlement, the girl added, "I'm Evony Rodriguez."

"Uh, hi," I said. Then I forced myself to get a grip, even though the appearance of this strange young woman was apparently the final shock in a very long day. "Jessica Monroe."

"I know." She unzipped her parka, revealing a tight-fitting black sweater worn over a lace-trimmed cami. It seemed clear enough that this Evony had been taking a lot more care with her appearance since the end of the world than I had. Her full lips were coated with lipstick in a scarlet shade that almost matched the streak in her black hair, and her long lashes had a thick layer of mascara. "You were right where I was told to find you."

"Wait—you were *sent* here?" Suspicion sharpened my tone. "Who sent you?"

"Whoa," she replied, holding up her hands. "I'm on your side. I'm Chosen, just like you. We need to stick together, especially with those assholes from Los Alamos running around and making everyone's lives miserable."

"So you know about them?"

"Of course." Evony took her parka over to the coat tree in the corner and hung it up. Seeing it there next to Jace's winter coat made my throat tighten all over again. The Los Alamos crew had captured him when he was only wearing a fleece pullover with a T-shirt underneath. I doubted whether they cared if he took a chill or suffered from the cold. They'd probably laugh and tell him to make his own fire, since he was a djinn. I didn't think he was that kind of djinn, though. From what I'd seen, Jace controlled air, not fire. Playing with fire was more Zahrias' kind of thing.

"So if you're Chosen," I said, "where's your djinn?"

"Same place as yours," she replied, a flash of anger in her dark eyes. "Bastards from Los Alamos came and got her early this morning."

My brain skidded to a stop as it attempted to process that statement. "Wait—*her?*"

"Yeah, *her,*" Evony said. One expertly plucked eyebrow went up. "What, did you think all the djinn were straight or something?"

"I, uh—" Damn, I'd really stuck my foot in it there. Truly, the sexuality of the other djinn wasn't something I'd really stopped to think about, since Jasreel was so obviously heterosexual. Maybe I had assumed they would all be like that. And because he'd been taken from me so soon after I'd learned of his true identity, I hadn't had the chance to ask him any in-depth questions about djinn culture and society. "I guess the topic hadn't come up yet."

"Uh-huh." Evony moved closer to the fireplace and spread her hands toward its warmth. "Yeah, well, my djinn is a she. Natila."

"What—what happened?" I had to ask the question, although I'd begun to guess.

A lift of her shoulders. Evony didn't bother to turn back toward me as she said, "Same thing that happened to you. Our friends from Los Alamos showed up this morning and hauled her away. They asked me if I wanted to go with them, but I said no. I had a feeling a Mexican lesbian from Española wasn't going to do to well with a bunch of good ol' boys like that. They seemed like the type who'd try to convince me of the error of my ways, if you know what I mean."

Unfortunately, I knew exactly what she meant. Some guys seemed to view girls like Evony as projects and didn't take their sexual orientation all that seriously. Being on your own in the post-Dying world could be scary, but in some cases it might be better than the alternative.

I also guessed that she had quite a story to tell, and since she'd obviously come a long way, it didn't seem very hospitable to make her keep on talking in the living room without even offering her anything to eat.

"Are you hungry?" I asked. "Because I've got plenty of food. Nothing fancy, but—"

"Starving," she said immediately. "I came straight here and haven't eaten since this morning. And if you have anything decent to wash it down...." Pausing, she gave me a meaningful glance.

"I've got a cellar full of wine."

"No beer?"

I couldn't help smiling. "Some. There are still a few bottles in the fridge. Let me put something together for you, and then you can tell me what happened."

The family room was the coziest place in the house, so that was where Evony and I ended up. I'd already eaten my dinner, but I took a piece of bread and butter with me, along with a half glass of wine, just so I wouldn't be sitting there and merely watching as my unexpected guest plowed her way through a plate of leftover sausage and macaroni, washing it down with the last of the Kilt Lifter ale that had been sitting on the bottom shelf of the refrigerator.

Evony's story—at the beginning, at least—wasn't all that different from mine. "I was home in Española when the Heat came through," she told me between bites of sausage. "And two days after it hit, I was the only one left." Her pretty face went blank then, as if she was trying hard not to let any of the emotions from that time seep through, as if the only way she could manage to keep functioning was to push aside all the death and suffering that had surrounded her.

Any words I might have offered would have been useless, empty, so I only nodded and took a sip of my wine.

She put down her fork and drank some of her beer before continuing. "I'm not going to lie—I fucking hated Española. I was working my ass off as a waitress, hoping to save enough money that I could get out and go to Albuquerque, go to school, do something with my life. I hadn't spoken to my father for more than a year—he didn't approve of me, of my lifestyle. He thought it was just something else I'd cooked up to torture him, or whatever." Her face twisted, and she went on, her voice hardening, "So I tried to tell myself when he was gone that I didn't care, since he'd made me miserable for pretty much my whole life."

I must have made some sort of sound, because Evony glanced up from her plate and cocked an eyebrow in my direction.

"Don't bother feeling sorry for me. I'm not saying this so I can have a pity party or whatever—I just wanted you to know something of where I came from." Another swallow of beer, and she closed her eyes and drew in an appreciative breath. "Thanks for having some of the good stuff. The casino was stocked with a bunch of Bud and Miller Lite and other crap. The wine wasn't much better, but that was what Natila liked."

That revelation made some sense. If Jace had been representative of the rest of his kind, it was pretty clear to me that the djinn were definitely more interested in wine than beer. The Kilt Lifter ale had still been sitting in the fridge because he'd never bothered to touch any of it.

"So...." I wasn't sure of the best way to ask, so I just said, "Natila came to you at the casino?"

A smile. Surprisingly, Evony's red lipstick appeared to be still intact, despite her having devoured most of the leftovers I'd given her to eat. "That's right. After everyone was pretty much gone, and there was no power and no water, I figured the casino would at least have good supplies of the bottled stuff—you know how they have bottles of water waiting for you when you check into your room?"

I nodded.

"Plus, they actually had a generator, so I got that running. I had lights, and I cleared one of the refrigeration units in the restaurant of the stuff that had spoiled and kept what I could in there. It was okay. Not great, but okay."

"Weren't—weren't you scared?" I asked, thinking back to my first night alone in Albuquerque, when I was so frightened about being the only person left alive in the world...and even more terrified that I wasn't.

Her shoulders lifted, but I noticed how she didn't quite meet my eyes, as if she didn't want me to see that she had, under the quick resourcefulness and the brittle composure, been scared absolutely shitless herself.

"Maybe a little. I don't know. I had a couple of guns—found them lying in the hallway next to some dust that probably used to be the casino's security guards. That made me feel a little safer, I guess. Even so, I kept wondering when I was going to get sick, too."

Oh, how I knew that feeling. I nodded, and she went on,

"Once or twice I thought I saw people out on the street, but when I really went to look, they had disappeared. Probably we were all just trying to avoid each other so we wouldn't get sick or something." A quirk of her full lips. "Stupid, huh? Because if we'd survived that long, it meant we were all immune. But no one seemed to have figured that out yet.

"Anyway, it was maybe three or four days after everything went completely to shit, and I was out in front of the casino, wondering if it was stupid of me to keep hanging out there, whether I should pack it in and head south to Albuquerque or go over to Santa Fe, or something. Someplace where there was a chance of more survivors hanging around." Pausing, she leaned forward so she could set her empty plate down on the coffee table, then drained the rest of her beer.

"Want another one?" I asked. That would kill what was left of the ale, but I really didn't drink it, either, and I figured someone might as well enjoy it.

Evony paused to consider for a moment, then shook her head. "Better not. It's too tempting to want to drink yourself out of all this, you know?"

Boy, did I know. All day I'd been fighting the urge to get completely shit-faced—not because I thought it would help at all, but just because it might have helped me to forget, if only for a half hour or so. I nodded, a grim smile pulling at my lips. "Why do you think I only poured myself a half glass of wine?"

She chuckled a little at that reply, but sobered abruptly. "So I was out in front of the casino, and then I heard a motorcycle. Big one—a Harley Road King."

I wouldn't have known a Road King if someone ran me over with one, but I only nodded.

"Gorgeous bike, too—cream-colored, ghost flames in pale blue. Expensive. And then it pulls up and stops in front of the entrance to the casino, and the rider takes off her helmet and shakes out all this long blonde hair, and I'm just—" Evony broke off and shrugged, as if even now she couldn't adequately describe how she felt. "Well, that was about the last sort of person I'd expected to see, you know?"

Oh, I definitely knew, because I'd felt just about the same way when I first saw Jace standing outside the gate to the compound. So gorgeous, and with that goofy half-hopeful, half-worried expression on his face. I'd probably started to fall in love with him then and there, even though at the time I would never have dared to admit it to myself. Strange that this female djinn, this Natila, had been blonde. Both Jace and Zahrias were dark, and so I'd assumed all the djinn had similar coloring. Apparently not.

"I know the feeling," I said, and Evony grinned.

"Yeah, it's not really fair that they're all so...perfect...is it?"

"Not really."

She settled back into a corner of the couch, then picked up one of the pillows and kind of hugged it against her, as if for reassurance. "So she says hi to me and that her name was Natalie and she'd been staying up in Abiquiu, sketching, doing the Georgia O'Keeffe thing, when the Heat came through. That she'd waited a few days to see if any survivors would show up, but because no one did, she decided to ride down to Española and try to find people there." Evony went quiet for a moment, as if savoring the memory, her mouth curved in a small smile. "And then she gave me this look, and I knew."

"'Knew'?" I repeated, puzzled.

The smile stretched into a grin. "Let's just say my gaydar was pinging, if you know what I mean."

Now I felt like an idiot. "Oh, right."

"It didn't take long before we were together, and I was just fine with that. I'd never met anyone like her before. And I was thinking, *Hey, it might be the end of the world, but so far it's working out okay for me.*"

"So she didn't tell you who she really was?"

At that question, Evony gave me a very sharp look. "Not at first. But about a week after we met, I said something about having to go scouting for more water, since the bottled stuff at the casino was running out—no big surprise, since we'd been using it to bathe as well as drink. And then Natila got all quiet for a minute, and she told me she had something she wanted me to see. I made some crack about how I knew she did, but she just shook her head and led me into the bathroom. I didn't know what the hell was going on, so I followed her. Then she lifted her hand toward the shower, and water came pouring out of the shower head, just as if it was all working perfectly and the Dying had never happened. For a second or two, I just stood there and stared at it, and then I asked her what the hell was going on."

"And that's when she told you?" I asked.

"Yeah. Explained the whole thing. Of course, at first I didn't want to believe her—how could I believe something that crazy...I mean, *djinn?*—but there was the way she'd just made the water go on, and how would she have been able to fake something like that?"

She couldn't. She wouldn't have had to, because clearly this Natila controlled water in the same way that Jasreel had command over the air, or Zahrias was attended by dancing flames wherever he went. They were djinn, elementals. I didn't pretend to understand their powers.

"Did you freak out?" I asked. "Because I sure as hell did."

"Of course I freaked," Evony replied. "But I couldn't deny what I was seeing with my own eyes. And Natila talked me down—told me how I'd been Chosen, how I'd be safe with her and that all I had to do was trust her, and she would take care of me."

"Weren't you angry, though? I mean—"

"About what the djinn had done?" Shockingly, she shrugged, a negligent lift of her shoulders. "I mean, it was horrible, but in a way it was so big that I couldn't really wrap my head around it. Anyway, *Natila* hadn't done it. None of the Thousand were involved in making the virus or spreading it. They were the good guys. They'd tried to stop it, but there weren't enough of them to make a difference. All they could do was save their Chosen. So I wasn't angry at *her*, you know?"

Then Evony had reacted with a lot more equanimity than I had. Eventually, I'd worked past my anger, but it was something I'd had to take a day to sort through.

She seemed to guess something of what was passing through my mind right then, because she continued, "I found out a lot sooner than you did, though. I mean, it was only a week after we met that Natila told me who and what she was. Jace kept lying to you for, what, more than two months?"

"He did not—" I began angrily, and then subsided. He'd had his reasons, but the hard truth of it was that he could have told me about his true identity much sooner and, for whatever reason, had chosen not to. Actually, I knew why he'd kept his silence. He'd been so afraid of destroying the love that was growing between us that he'd purposely let me believe he was a mortal man.

I'd since forgiven him, true. It didn't change what had happened, though. Lifting an eyebrow, I pinned Evony with what I hoped was a piercing stare. "How do you know all that about me and Jace, anyway?"

"Because Zahrias knew, and I heard him talking to Natila."

I thought of the hard-faced djinn who'd come to see Jasreel, and shivered a little, despite the warmth of the fire at my back. "He visited you, too?"

Evony seemed to shut down. Her face went still, and she wouldn't quite look at me. "The day before yesterday. He came to warn us—said there were Chosen gone missing, and something was up at Los Alamos. He said we needed to come to Taos, and Natila actually agreed, but—"

"But?" I prompted, even though I had a feeling her story was going to end almost the same way mine had.

"But we didn't get out in time." She hugged the pillow again, and I realized for all her hard-faced bravado, Evony was just as scared and worried as I was. "We were packing up our stuff, which in hindsight was stupid, because we could've just helped ourselves to anything we needed from all those fancy boutiques in Taos. And that's when the Los Alamos crew showed up."

"A bunch of guys in Hummers?"

"Yeah, and that squirrelly-looking one with the funky box. I don't know what it was for, but it sure did something to fuck up Natila, because all of a sudden she got pale and couldn't breathe."

My heart squeezed then as I recalled Jace suffering the same way, how all the strength seemed to be taken from him. "And they took her away."

Evony seemed to be staring past my shoulder, at the window, although there wasn't anything to see with the curtains tightly closed. "Yeah," she said heavily. "They took her away. And then I heard her in my head, you know—"

I nodded.

"The weird thing was, all I heard was Jace's name —except she called him Jasreel—followed by a string of numbers."

"'Numbers'?" I repeated blankly.

"Yeah, numbers." She set the pillow aside. "I'm weirdly good with numbers. Not crazy advanced math or anything, but doing arithmetic in my head, remembering locker combinations, that kind of thing. I never thought of it as much more than a parlor trick, but after the Los Alamos guys left and I was alone at the casino, I went and wrote them down."

"So what were they?"

A wry smile. "Coordinates. GPS coordinates for your house, actually. It took me a while to figure it out, but once I did, I found a GPS unit at a Walmart and plugged them in. I figured since Natila had said Jace's name right before she sent me the numbers, it had to mean those coordinates were for where he was holed up. So I came here to warn you. Guess I was too late."

"It's not your fault," I said. "I mean, who would've thought those bastards would be out collecting djinn on Christmas Eve?"

"Oh, shit, is it?" Evony shifted on the couch so she could see down the hall and into the living room, where the tree Jace had brought me stood in the corner. "I sort of lost track of time when I was with Natila. Merry fucking Christmas, huh?"

Funny how her words echoed exactly what I had been thinking earlier. "Yeah. I guess the whole 'goodwill toward men' thing doesn't extend to djinn." I paused, recalling what she'd said when I first opened the door and let her in. "So what's your plan?"

A look of confusion passed over her features. "Plan?"

"Plan," I said in some impatience. "You told me that I'd better let you in if I ever wanted to see my djinn lover alive again. That kind of remark leads me to believe you must have some kind of plan."

"Uh, well...." Once again her gaze shifted away from mine, and under its coating of matte red lipstick, her mouth tightened. "I actually just said that because I wasn't sure you'd let me inside otherwise. I really don't have a plan. I guess I just figured that it would be better to have the two of us working together than separately."

Oh, for Chrissake.... I ground my teeth, pushing back the retort that lying to me wasn't exactly the best way to get on my good side. But I realized I needed to cut Evony some slack. She'd experienced a terrible loss today, just as I had, and in a way, she was right. The two of us were better off together—for safety's sake, if nothing else.

As far as what we should do next, I hadn't a clue. I only knew that staying here wasn't an option. Tonight, sure. It was snowing, and night had fallen, and I knew we wouldn't get very far. It wasn't as if someone would come along to plow the roads, and although the Cherokee could manage just fine in snow, I wouldn't risk that kind of driving without some daylight to help us along.

"Well," I said, "I suppose in the morning we'll go to Los Alamos and see what we can do."

Her eyebrows went shooting up so far they almost disappeared into her short, heavy bangs. "Are you crazy? Have you ever been to Los Alamos?"

I shook my head.

"Well, as far as I know, it's one road in, one road out. And both those roads have got to be heavily guarded, Christmas or not. If you think you can just slip in and do some scouting with no one noticing, you're nuts."

That didn't sound good. Right then I wished my family had done more exploring in that part of the state, but we'd never made it to Los Alamos. I had to take Evony's word for it that the place was as remote as she described. It actually made sense that the town would be built that way, considering its origins as the birthplace of the atomic bomb. And it made even more sense that a group of survivors would gather there, using the natural geography of the area as a way to keep them safe and protected.

"All right," I said wearily. "Then we'll have to go to Taos and see if any of the djinn or Chosen there have any more information, know of anything that might help us."

That prospect didn't seem much more appealing to her than Los Alamos. "How could they? Zahrias said the Chosen they'd sent to Los Alamos had never come back, and the djinn can't see anything because of whatever the Immune are doing to hide themselves."

"Maybe so, but we've got to start somewhere. Maybe Zahrias wasn't telling the whole truth. Maybe he was just saying what he thought Natila and Jasreel needed to hear so they'd pack up and join the rest of their kind. You don't know for sure, do you?"

For a long moment, Evony didn't say anything. Her fingers kept playing with the silver and onyx ring she wore on her right hand—Navajo work, by the look of it—twisting it around and around as she appeared to wrestle with her thoughts. At last she said, "Okay. Not because I think it'll help, necessarily, but mostly because I can't think of anything else to do."

A weight I hadn't even realized was pressing on my neck and shoulders seemed to lift itself then, and I allowed myself the first cautious sensation of hope I'd felt that day. Maybe it wasn't the best of plans, but at least it was a plan, something to do that didn't involve sitting here in the house and worrying about Jasreel.

The next day, we would take the road to Taos.

CHAPTER THREE

I GAVE EVONY THE THIRD BEDROOM, MAINLY BECAUSE I was so tired by then that I didn't feel like swapping out the linens on the bed Jace had used the night before. She didn't seem to care about the size of her sleeping quarters; yes, that was the smallest bedroom, but even so it was a good deal larger than the room that had been mine in the house where I grew up, and of course the furnishings were gorgeous, just like everything else in the house.

"Well, it's not a suite at the Okay Owingeh casino, but it'll have to do," she deadpanned, and I couldn't help grinning.

"The bathroom is next door, and there's plenty of toothpaste and soap and all that, so—"

"I'll be fine. Right now I think I just want to sleep for a hundred years."

I knew the feeling. Too many ups and downs that day, and I had no idea what we would face tomorrow, both on the road and once we got to Taos. I tried to imagine a town entirely populated by djinn and their Chosen, and failed miserably. I didn't even know how many of them were supposed to be congregated there. Well, I supposed I'd find out the truth soon enough.

"I think we should shoot for the standard eight hours," I replied. "A hundred years might interfere with our rescue attempt."

Evony shot me a wry look but only nodded, and I said goodnight and went on to my bedroom. Hearing me, Dutchie came trotting down the hall from where she'd been lying by the fireplace in the family room, then waited patiently as I stirred up a fire in the master bedroom's hearth. I thought of Evony and whether she'd be warm enough—the spare bedrooms didn't have fireplaces—but the bed she was using had an electric blanket, and I figured there would be enough ambient warmth from the fires in all the main rooms that she should do all right.

It was hard to get ready for bed, though, knowing that it would be empty when I got to it, that Jace wouldn't be waiting for me and the sheets would be cold. No, he was miles away, and I somehow doubted he would be sleeping anyplace as comfortable as this. Would it be cold wherever they were holding him, with maybe only a thin blanket to keep out the freezing chill of a snowy night? Normally, I wouldn't have worried, because he was always so warm, but whatever the Los Alamos people were using to steal or block his powers also seemed to have taken that gift from him as well. He'd been shivering when they took him away.

Oh, God, I couldn't think about that, or I'd drive myself crazy. I had to get a decent night's sleep; otherwise, we could be in serious trouble the next day. Jace had taught me a lot about driving in the snow, but even he probably would've advised staying home until the roads weren't buried in ten inches of fresh powder.

I didn't have that luxury, though. Evony and I would have to get moving as early as possible the next morning, partly to save time, and partly because I really didn't know how long the drive to Taos would take in this weather. I hated not having access to weather reports and perfectly coiffed forecasters telling me exactly how many inches of snow we were going to get and how long the storm would last. But those conveniences were gone, along with snowplows and cable TV and high-speed Internet. All I could do was hope for the best.

And, as my father always used to say, prepare for the worst.

It definitely seemed like the worst the next morning after I got out of the shower, dried my hair, and wandered into the kitchen to take a look at what the storm had wrought. It was actually still snowing, but very lightly now, feathery flakes drifting this way and that, but not accumulating all that fast. The visibility didn't seem to be too bad; even so, the drifts piled against the henhouse and the goats' shed looked several feet high.

Grimly, I set about getting the coffee going and mentally preparing myself to trudge out into all that snow to take care of the animals. I'd have to give them enough feed to last a few days and hope they wouldn't gorge themselves on all of it right away. There wasn't much I could do about that, though. I'd do my best to make sure they were cared for, but the chickens and goats needed to meet me halfway.

It was only after I'd shoveled my way across the yard and fed the animals, then dragged myself back into the house and knocked my boots clean of snow, that Evony finally made an appearance. Just like the day before, her makeup was perfect. Today the sweater she wore was bright cobalt blue, and I blinked a little at the unexpected shock of color.

"Is that coffee?" she asked, heading straight for the coffeemaker and the mug I'd set out. It was my mug, but I didn't bother to stop her. I knew better than to get between a woman and her caffeine. Besides, there were plenty of mugs to spare.

"Yes, and I have fresh eggs for breakfast, and toast. No bacon, though."

"I'll live. Cream?"

"In the fridge."

She went to fetch it, doctored her coffee, and then took a sip. "That's good. Better than what we were living on."

"The guy who built this place left some pretty awesome supplies behind."

"Apparently." She sipped again. "So what's the plan?"

I'd been pondering that very subject while I showered. Yes, it was Christmas Day, but obviously the survivors at Los Alamos didn't seem to pay too much attention to holidays. For all I knew, they were patrolling the main highway that led north from here. If that was the case, the last thing I wanted was for them to figure out that we'd left our sanctuary here in Santa Fe and were heading for Taos.

"I think we should take the High Road," I told her.

Her response was immediate. Eyebrows raised, she replied, "In this weather? Are you nuts?"

"Maybe," I said evenly. "But I doubt we'll run into anyone if we go that way, so while the road itself might be more dangerous, there's a much lower risk of interference."

Evony shook her head, eyes narrowing under their cat-eye liner and heavy mascara. "Have you ever actually *driven* the High Road?"

"No."

A sigh, accompanied by a roll of her eyes. "It's narrow. It's twisty. It goes way up high where the snow will be even worse. And I guarantee there's no one left to plow the damn thing."

"I have chains," I said calmly. Not that I was actually feeling all that calm; just the thought of heading out in this weather was giving me a queasy, fluttery feeling in my stomach, but I knew there was no question of staying put. "And a shovel, and an ice scraper. Anyway, I'm not planning on tearing through there at fifty miles an hour or something. If we go slowly, we should be okay."

To say Evony looked dubious would have been an understatement. But then she let out another breath and nodded. "Well, it's not like the main route up 84 would've been all that great, either. How long do you think it's going to take?"

I really had no idea. Digging around in the office, I'd found maps of the area, so I knew the route was not quite sixty miles. On a good day, you probably could have driven from Santa Fe to Taos in about an hour and a half. Now?

"At least half the day, I'm guessing. We'll pack food and water and other supplies."

She swallowed some more of her coffee, then said, resignation clear in her tone, "Okay. But let's have those eggs and toast first. I like to do all my crazy shit on a full stomach."

"Crazy shit" was definitely one way of describing it. "Sheer insanity" might have been another, but I just couldn't risk those men from Los Alamos discovering what we were up to. Evony and I packed our things— or rather, I packed mine, while she zipped up her weekender bag and waited for me to get ready. Enough food for two days, just in case we got stranded somewhere, and a pallet of bottled water, and then the traveling dog dishes for Dutchie and a couple of gallon baggies filled with her food.

I went out to the garage and got out the Jeep, then backed it up as close to the rear entrance of the house as I could so we wouldn't have to haul our stuff too far through the snow. Evony seemed to be keeping any further observations to herself, and silently helped me load the back of the vehicle. Dutchie, excited at the prospect of a road trip, took one last pee in the snow next to the vehicle, then jumped into the back seat without any coaxing and sat there, tail wagging.

Neither Evony nor I were anywhere close to that eager. In silence, we climbed into the Cherokee after I locked the back door to the house and made sure it was secure. Now that they had Jace, I didn't think the Los Alamos gang would be coming back here anytime soon, but that didn't mean I intended to leave the house open, an easy target for anyone who might wander by. All right, the chances of that were extremely low, given how off the beaten track it was, but in the few months I'd lived there, I'd come to love that house. I wanted it to still be okay when I came back, whenever that might be.

And I hoped—oh, how I hoped—that I'd be able to bring Jace back here soon, and we'd be able to continue with the lives the djinn-hunters from Los Alamos had interrupted.

Biting my lip, I put the Jeep in neutral and cautiously shifted into 4-Lo. The snow had stopped falling, and so I'd decided to try driving without the snow chains at first. If the going was too hard, I could always stop and chain up at the side of the road. I hoped not, though, mostly because I'd only helped my father put chains on the Jeep once, and I wasn't exactly familiar with the procedure. Maybe Evony would be of some help, but I couldn't count on that. She didn't exactly seem like the outdoorsy, four-wheeling type.

But we moved forward, the tires crunching through the snow as we slowly made our way down the incline to the front gate. The padlock I'd put there was still in place, and I glanced over at Evony. "So you really did climb over."

"Well, what else was I supposed to do?" she inquired, sounding exasperated. "It's not like I packed some bolt cutters along with a change of underwear."

Despite our current situation, I couldn't help smiling. "I guess not. Luckily, I've got the key."

Leaving the engine idling, I got out of the Jeep and went to the gate, then pulled the key out of my coat pocket and unlocked the padlock. It was a little stiff—not that surprising, considering the sub-freezing temperatures—but eventually I got it open and unwound the chain, then pushed the gate open. Afterward, I knocked as much snow off my boots as I could before getting back in the Cherokee and pulling through. Then I had to go through the process all over again to secure the property. By then, I could barely feel my toes, even with the thick socks I was wearing under my boots, but no way was I going to leave that gate standing open while I was gone. That would've looked like an open invitation to come onto the property.

I'd thought that it wouldn't be all that difficult to get down the track that eventually joined with Upper Canyon Road, but the snow had fallen so thickly that the trail's outlines were all but erased. True, there was wire fencing that delineated the property to one side, but I couldn't see it all that well. More than once I could feel the Jeep starting to slip down into the rutted gully on the side of the road, and I had to brake carefully and then steer us back so we were more or less in the center of the lane.

Beside me, Evony was looking pale under her olive skin, the fingers of her right hand clutching the "Jesus handle" in the roof above her. She didn't say anything, though, as if she knew that speaking would only break my concentration.

And I needed all of it. Eventually, we inched our way down onto Upper Canyon and the going was a little easier, just because along that street there were houses, and the snow drifts hadn't completely obscured the outlines of the road. Even so, I didn't dare go over twenty miles an hour, just in case we hit a patch of ice or something. Although it felt as if we were never going to get there, we finally did reach the center of town and then begin heading north. I took side streets, following the map, because I didn't want to get on Highway 84 at all, not even for the couple of miles it took to get to 503, which would lead us up along the first leg of the High Road.

The clock on the dashboard showed that it had taken us more than an hour just to go that far, a journey that usually only took fifteen minutes, if that. It looked like I hadn't been too out of line in saying this little trip of ours might consume most of the day.

But so far it seemed that, despite the deep snow, if I just maintained a steady pace of fifteen or twenty miles an hour, the Cherokee would keep chugging away and not give me too much trouble. I had plenty of gas; Jace had helped me siphon a bunch on our last trip to town, and so that was one thing at least I didn't have to worry about.

Evony lifted one of the bottles of water. "Want some?"

I nodded, but didn't take my eyes off the road as she untwisted the cap and handed it to me. A long pull at the water told me how thirsty I actually was, and I drank some more before putting the bottle in the cup holder and returning my hand to the steering wheel.

We'd been quiet so far, but I knew Evony and I couldn't spend the entire trip to Taos in complete silence. Anyway, a few things had been nagging at my mind, and as long as I didn't allow the conversation to distract me too much, it should help to pass the time.

"Did Natila tell you a lot?" I asked Evony then. "About the djinn, I mean."

She tilted her head slightly to one side. Along with the knitted cap, she was wearing a pair of round wire-rimmed, smoke-lensed sunglasses, giving her the look of a goth snowbunny. "She told me some things. Like, have you noticed how you heal much faster now if you get hurt?"

I nodded, recalling the way the sprained wrists and bruised knee from my encounter with Chris Bowman in Albuquerque had gone back to normal within a day. "What about it?"

"It's part of being Chosen, I guess. We heal more like djinn than regular people. And we're not just Immune—we'll never get sick again. No flu, no colds, no nothing."

"Never?" I couldn't help sounding incredulous. Not that I would turn down the chance to never suffer from a head cold again, but I didn't see how that was possible.

"Never." She'd gotten herself some water, too, and drank from the bottle she held before continuing. "Nice perk, huh? But that's not the best part."

I waited, since Evony was clearly enjoying dragging this out a little for dramatic effect. Truthfully, I wasn't sure how much better it could get than never getting sick again, or healing from bumps and bruises in what appeared to be a miraculous fashion.

Clearly not put off by my silence, she said, "I hope you like being—how old are you, anyway?"

"Twenty-four."

"Cool. I'm twenty-two. Anyway, I hope you like being that age, because that's what you'll be for the rest of your life."

Despite my determination not to take my eyes off the road, I couldn't help darting a quick glance at her after that remark. "What?"

Her lacquered lips curved up in a smile. "You heard me. You'll be—well, I guess 'immortal' isn't exactly the right word for it, because it's not as if we can't be killed, but we won't age."

"At *all*?" I was having a hard time wrapping my mind around that concept.

"Not according to Natila." Evony drank some more of her water, then said, "It sounded as if the djinn wanted to make sure their Chosen would stick around and always be the same as they were when their djinn first selected them. I mean, what's the point of picking someone to save if you're just going to watch them age and die in what seems like the blink of an eye to you?"

I supposed that made some sense. As with so many other things about that strange race of elementals, I really hadn't had time to think about it. I'd barely had a chance to get my brain around the notion of Jace being a djinn at all before he was taken from me. "So are the djinn immortal?"

Evony's nose wrinkled as she appeared to consider my question. "More or less. I mean, they certainly don't age, and Natila didn't say anything about them dying of natural causes. Not exactly. She sort of hinted that they could be killed, but I don't think it's easy. That is, according to what Natila said, if those assholes from Los Alamos think they can just round up a bunch of djinn and put them in front of a firing squad or something, they're going to find they've made a big mistake."

Just the mere thought of Jace facing down a group of grim-faced survivors holding rifles made me shudder, but if what Natila had told Evony was right, then even multiple gunshot wounds might not be enough to kill him. That knowledge should have reassured me—well, I supposed it did, a little. On the other hand, if there were people at Los Alamos who were smart enough to figure out how to trap a djinn on this plane of existence, then maybe they were also smart enough to find a way to kill one of the elementals. I knew I couldn't take that risk, that I couldn't rely on the djinns' supposed invulnerability.

Instead, I told Evony, "I guess that's something," and then was silent for a moment, slowing us down even further as Highway 503 began to climb its way out of Nambe, the first hamlet on the High Road. The snow had well and truly stopped for the moment, but the skies remained gray, and I couldn't be certain that the flurries might not start up again. Unfortunately, it didn't snow all that often in Albuquerque, and definitely not heavily like this, unless some kind of freak storm was passing through.

So far we were doing okay, though, and I prayed that being cautious would be enough to get us up and over the passes, and into Taos. Fingers still wrapped tightly around the steering wheel, I commented, "You'd think the djinn would number a lot more than twenty thousand if they're supposedly immortal. I mean, humans were overrunning the earth, and we only had an average lifespan of seventy-five or something."

A shrug as Evony stared out the windshield at the snow-covered landscape passing by. "I don't know for sure. I got the impression that sometimes they did die from time to time, for whatever reason, and that was when a new little djinn would come along. But it was rare."

"And...with people?" I ventured then, asking a question that had been hovering in the back of my mind ever since I'd learned Jace wasn't precisely human.

Evony shot me a sidelong glance from under her lashes. "Are you asking if humans and djinn can make little half-breed babies?"

"Well...." It was probably a stupid thing to ask. After all, it wasn't as if Evony and Natila would've been reproducing together, unless djinn biology was very different from ours.

"I guess they can," Evony said, her tone amused. "I mean, that wasn't going to be an issue with me and Natila, which was just fine by me. I spent enough time around my little nieces and nephews and my cousins' kids to know I sure as hell didn't want any. Screaming and poop and...no, thanks."

I decided it was better not to comment on that. Someone like my mother—or even my friend Tori— would've probably argued that Evony couldn't possibly make that kind of decision when she was only twenty-two. But if that was how she felt about the subject, then that was her decision.

"It's happened over the years, though. Not often," she went on, shooting me another one of those sideways glances. If I hadn't known better, I would've thought she'd guessed about all those nights I hesitated over my little packet of pills and wondered whether I should just quietly stop taking them. "But a few times. So if you want to rescue Jace and have your little white picket fence and two point five kids or whatever it is these days, you should be able to manage it."

"The house doesn't have a white picket fence. It has an adobe wall," I pointed out, and she only shrugged again.

"Whatever. You know what I mean."

I supposed I did. Right then the road began to climb more steeply, though, and I felt the Cherokee's tires slip. Shit. They caught before I could start to really worry, but I dropped my speed again, this time crawling along at something like ten point five miles per hour.

"Do we need to put on the chains?" Evony asked, the look of amusement slipping off her face as if it had never been there.

"I don't know," I replied. "We're doing okay right now. Besides, I don't even know where we would stop."

That was nothing more than the truth. You kind of needed a clear space to put on chains, and it was just pure, virgin snow as far as the eye could see, covering the highway, mounded slightly higher on the western side of the road because of the way the wind had been blowing. The junipers were rounded blobs with some dark green showing underneath the snow, and slightly lower bumps and protrusions that had to be rocks or smaller bushes. At any rate, there certainly wasn't a nice clear "chain up" area where we could pull off and get the chains on.

"True." She surveyed the snow-covered landscape and shook her head. "That is one metric shit-ton of snow."

Probably more than just one, I thought, but I only gave her a grim smile and continued with our plodding forward motion. What else could I do? I wasn't about to turn around...not that I was sure I could even manage such a feat, since it would've required crossing back over the deep, deep ruts we'd already cut in the snow. The best thing to do was just keep moving.

Luckily, I wasn't moving too fast, or I might have missed the turnoff onto State Road 98. The sign was half covered in snow, but I caught sight of it just in time and eased the Cherokee over, glad that at least this new stretch didn't seem too hilly. Well, the road did undulate, but with gentle rises and falls, not anything too taxing.

I didn't let myself get complacent, though, and maintained our low speed. A quick glance at the clock told me it was now almost eleven in the morning. That made me blow out a worried breath, since we'd been on the road for more than two hours and were less than a quarter of the way to our destination. At this rate, we'd be lucky to make it to Taos before dark.

The last thing I wanted was to be navigating snow-covered mountain roads after nightfall. What if we missed a turn and went off the highway? What if we plowed into an elk that had decided to amble across the road?

Yeah, and maybe the Cherokee will get attacked by a pack of wolves, too, I mocked myself, but I couldn't quite banish the worry just by deriding my fears.

Those worries did lessen somewhat as we made it along 98 without any problem, and then turned right onto 76. The highway began to climb again, but the snow didn't seem quite as thick here, for whatever reason, and I murmured a silent thank-you under my breath for that.

"Are we there yet?" Evony quipped as we passed a sign saying we were entering Truchas, whatever that was.

"No. Barely halfway."

Her grin faded, and then her eyes widened and she said, "Wait—weren't you supposed to go left back there?"

My first instinct was to hit the brakes, but I knew that would only end in disaster. Instead, I let us slow to a crawl and then came to a stop in a narrow little street bordered on either side by houses, half of which seemed to double as artists' studios, judging by the signage. "This looks like the main street to me," I said in irritation.

Without replying, Evony picked up the map from where it was lying half open on the console that separated the front seats. A frown pulled at her brows. "Well, it's the main street of Truchas, according to this map, but it's not the highway. See? It jogged to the left back there."

I could feel myself scowling as well as I took the map from her and looked where she had pointed. Sure enough, 76 lay behind us. We were on 75, whatever that was. Not anyplace we wanted to be.

"Well, shit," I growled.

"Just turn us around. It's not that big a deal."

Easy for her to say. The street was so narrow that the only way I could accomplish the maneuver was to pull into a driveway and then back out. And the snowdrifts looked awfully deep.

But sitting here in Truchas was really not an option, so I sucked in a breath and began turning the Cherokee, using the extra space in the driveway to our left to get us pointed in the right direction. All went okay until I put us in reverse so we could angle back onto the actual street. I heard a horrible grinding noise, and the Jeep shuddered but didn't move.

"Crap," I said.

"What?"

"I think we're stuck."

Evony winced. "Are you in four-wheel drive?"

"Of course I'm in four-wheel drive!" I snapped. "I've never been out of it since we left the house!"

"Oh."

She didn't offer any helpful advice after that. Telling myself to remain calm, I took my foot off the brake and gave the car a little gas. More grinding. With my luck, I was heating up the snow so it was melting and turning to ice under the tires, which would only make matters worse.

I let off the gas and shifted into neutral, letting the Cherokee idle while I thought. Maybe it was time to break out the snow shovel I'd packed in the cargo compartment so I could try to dig out the piled-up snow beneath us. Obviously, the drifts filling up that driveway had proven to be too much even for the Jeep.

Hesitating, I glanced quickly over at Evony. She was staring ahead, frowning, and didn't seem to want to meet my eyes. I could guess the reason why, too—she had an idea of what was coming next and didn't want to be the one to have to stagger out in the snow and start digging us out. Well, neither did I, especially since it made more sense for me to be the one behind the wheel. I had no idea whether she even knew how to manage a four-wheel drive.

I supposed it couldn't hurt to try one more time. If that didn't work, then I supposed one of us would have to get out and start digging. We could always flip a coin to see who got shovel duty.

Holding my breath, I took the Jeep out of neutral and into low gear, then applied as much gas as I dared. Again the tires ground against the snow and ice.

"Shit," I muttered under my breath, adding a second mental curse at myself for missing the turn-off and stranding us here.

And then—well, I couldn't say for sure exactly *what* happened, except that I felt something almost like an enormous hand shoving the rear of the Cherokee, and all of a sudden we were moving forward, leaving the snow-piled driveway behind us. I blinked, shocked at the abrupt change in our status, but recovered myself enough to apply a little more gas, getting us up to the fifteen or so miles per hour I'd been driving the entire trip.

"You did it!" Evony exclaimed, looking relieved beyond measure that she wouldn't have to get out and shovel the back tires after all.

"Uh-huh," I said.

The problem was, I didn't think I actually *did* have anything to do with getting us unstuck. That shove had felt far more like something Jace might have done. However, I knew he couldn't have, not locked up and with his powers stripped from him.

Exactly who...or what...had decided we needed a nudge to continue on our way?

I wasn't sure I wanted to find out.

CHAPTER FOUR

THE LIGHT WAS JUST BEGINNING TO FAIL AS WE came down the mountain and into Taos. And as the day died, snow started to fall once again, lightly at first, then more thickly as we headed toward the center of town.

During the last half of our drive, Evony and I hadn't spoken much. I was shaken after the incident in Truchas, my mind working at the way the Cherokee had been more or less magically freed from the snow. And Evony seemed to pick up on my unease and stared moodily out the window, only drinking water from time to time, and eventually digging a protein bar out of the supplies we'd brought with us. At least she'd been willing to take care of Dutchie, getting some food into her portable bowl and tipping some water into another container for her to drink. At the time, I hadn't wanted to stop, had only wanted to keep crawling along the mountain road at our glacial seventeen or so miles per hour. Some part of me was scared that if we paused for anything, we'd get stuck in the snow, and there might not be an invisible hand this time to give us a much-needed push.

But now we were more or less back in civilization, although here on the outskirts of town, I didn't see many signs of life. Maybe the djinn and their consorts were all holed up in the city center, in the hotels and B&Bs that clustered near the central plaza and the shops and the museums. That seemed to make more sense; I didn't know if even the Los Alamos people had the guts to come to a place where so many djinn were congregated, but if they did, the elementals would do better if surrounded by more of their kind.

Sure enough, just as Evony and I passed Quesnel Road, we came to a sort of roadblock. Well, it was really only a couple of guys sitting in the middle of the road in a Toyota FJ Cruiser, but as soon as we slowed to a stop just before the intersection they occupied, they got out of their SUV and made their way over to my driver-side window. They weren't djinn, but they were both extremely good-looking—in their twenties, like Evony and me, one dark, Hispanic or maybe Italian or Greek, the other with blond hair pulled back into a ponytail and with the burnished tan of someone who spent a lot of time on the ski slopes.

The dark-haired man pointed at my window, and I unrolled it, letting in a freezing blast of air as I did so. "Welcome to Taos, Jessica," he said, and I started, even as Evony shifted in the passenger seat and gave him an unbelieving stare. She didn't say anything, though, but instead watched the stranger with wary eyes.

"Hi," I replied cautiously. I mean, what else was I supposed to say? But if you stopped to think about it, the djinn here weren't interdicted by the device the Los Alamos people were using, and so they could've been using their powers to watch over Evony and me as we made our way to Taos. If nothing else, that would explain the "helping hand" we'd gotten back in Truchas.

"We've been expecting you," the blond stranger said. "There's a room waiting for you, but first, you need to talk to Zahrias."

That was an audience I would have preferred to avoid, at least until I'd had a chance to rest and get myself more or less together. Even though I knew the djinn man in charge of this sector had come to the house merely to warn Jace and not for any nefarious reasons that I could discern, I couldn't help the shiver of unease that passed through me whenever I recalled the harsh gleam of his dark eyes, the cruel set to his mouth. I pitied whoever he'd chosen; I would've been scared shitless if he'd been the one to come to me instead of Jace.

Despite the friendly tone of these two men, I could tell I wasn't expected to argue with Zahrias' orders. And I wouldn't. At least they'd said there was a room waiting for me—had they put one aside for Evony, too, or did they expect us to stick together, since we were currently travel companions? That could be a little awkward, for a number of reasons.

But because the Cherokee's heater couldn't really keep up with the icy air pouring through the window, and because I knew there wasn't any point in protesting, I merely asked, "Where is he?"

The blond young man turned and pointed up the street. "He's at a resort up off Kit Carson Road. El Monte Sagrado. You can't miss it."

"Thanks," I replied, although I had a feeling it would be easy to miss a lot of things in the falling dark and the ever-increasing snow. If I drove slowly enough, however, I figured I should be okay.

The strange young man smiled and slapped the driver-side door of the Jeep with a gloved hand, reminding me unpleasantly of the way the leader of the Los Alamos gang had done the same thing to his Hummer before driving off. But I refused to let my mind go there. This was an entirely different place, and an entirely different circumstance. And, from the looks of it, an entirely different set of people.

I pushed the button to roll up the window, then began driving slowly past the two men, cutting over to the opposite side of the road to get around them. They gave me the thumbs-up before retreating to the warmth and safety of their own vehicle.

Evony had remained silent throughout the entire encounter, but she spoke then. "What do you think Zahrias wants with us?"

My mind had been playing with possibilities, each one more unpleasant than the last, but I forced myself to give what I hoped looked like a casual shrug. "He probably just wants to hear what happened to Jace and Natila. If the djinn can't see past the field—or whatever it is—that one of those boxes generates, then they're going to have to rely on accounts from people like us."

"Makes sense, I guess," she said, but she didn't look entirely convinced.

Well, that made two of us.

I drove up Kit Carson, scanning the street—which appeared to have been plowed, miracle of miracles— for any signage. As it turned out, I didn't need a sign, because over on our left there was a wide entrance to the resort, topped by a portico of rough-hewn logs. The driveway was plowed as well, so it was easy enough to pull in and then park the Jeep in what clearly had been intended as the guest registration area.

Lights shone in the windows, and farther off I could see a few vehicles parked here and there. Did they belong to the Chosen, or had they been left there by victims of the Dying? You wouldn't think the consorts of the djinn would need cars to get around, not if they were hooked up with elemental beings who could simply whisk them from place to place. Or maybe not. I didn't know exactly how it all worked, since of course Jace had been doing his utmost to convince me he was just another regular mortal, and therefore I hadn't seen too many displays of his power.

Dutchie whined, and I knew I had to take care of her before I went in to see Zahrias. The poor thing had been cooped up in the car all day and hadn't complained once, but even she had her limits. The djinn leader would have to wait.

"I'm going to walk Dutchie for a bit," I told Evony, and she tilted her eyebrow at me.

"Seriously? When Zahrias is waiting for you?"

"Yeah, well, I kind of doubt Zahrias is going to come down here and clean the pee off the back seat if I make my poor dog wait any more."

Evony made a disgusted sound. "I'll walk the dog. You go see Zahrias."

"I think he wants to talk to both of us."

"That wasn't the impression I got." During the drive, she'd unzipped her parka, but now she undid her seatbelt so she could close her coat back up again. "Those guys back there were talking to *you*. They didn't even give me a second glance."

"Well—" I hadn't actually thought about it at the time, but it was true. They'd approached me, not

Evony, which just seemed weird. After all, we were both Chosen who'd had our djinn companions kidnapped.

She flapped a hand. "Just go. I'll take care of Dutchie and then come inside. Hopefully, there'll be someone around to show me where to crash."

I glanced back toward the building, to the place that looked like the registration area. It was hard to tell in the darkness and with the snow falling, but I thought I saw shapes moving inside, so it seemed as if there were people besides Zahrias around.

"Okay," I said at last. "I'll come find you as soon as I'm done."

She nodded and opened her door so she could go around and coax Dutchie out of the back seat. Not that it was much of a problem; the dog bounded outside as soon as Evony stepped out of the way. Under normal circumstances, I would have smiled at Dutchie's enthusiasm, but I found I wasn't really in the mood to smile right then. Not with Zahrias waiting for me somewhere inside the adobe edifice only a few yards away.

After tucking my scarf more tightly around my throat, I crossed the parking lot and entered the building. Almost at once, a pretty young woman with striking red hair came up to me. "Zahrias is this way," she said, pointing down the hallway to her left.

I nodded and began to follow her. Inside it was very warm, almost uncomfortably so. I pulled off my gloves and stuffed them in my pockets, then unzipped my coat and unwound the scarf I'd just tightened. As I walked, I pulled off the knitted cap I wore and ran my fingers through my hair as best I could, then wanted to shake my head at myself. Did it really matter what I looked like? I wasn't here to impress anyone, least of all Zahrias.

Despite that, I couldn't help feeling a bit cowed by my surroundings. The place was very posh, in a high-end Southwest kind of way. Gleaming dark wood floors, with thickly plastered walls and dark-beamed ceilings overhead. Original oil paintings on the walls, and furniture that looked as if it had been crafted by local artisans.

As we walked, I asked the young woman, who appeared to be around my age, "Are you Zahrias' Chosen?"

A blink, followed by a vigorous shake of her head and a laugh. "Oh, no. Zahrias doesn't have a partner. My djinn is named Dani." She smiled as she said his name, blue eyes lighting up a little. Clearly, she was very happy with whoever had selected her.

I digested her reply for a moment. So Zahrias was overseeing all these djinn and their Chosen, and yet he'd decided to remain alone, for whatever reason. Well, in a way I supposed that was a good thing. At least my worries that he'd been frightening and intimidating some poor mortal girl appeared to have been unfounded.

It was on the tip of my tongue to ask the young woman more questions—where had she come from? how had her djinn partner approached her?—but then she stopped in front of a set of double doors and said, "Zahrias is inside. He's been waiting to speak with you."

"So I heard," I said dryly. If I could have thought of any way to stall, I would have, but she was already opening the door on the right and stepping back out of the way, so I had no choice but to go in. At least she offered me an encouraging smile as I passed. Unfortunately, a smile from a stranger wasn't quite enough to put me in a more settled frame of mind.

But then I didn't have time to think about anything else, because she had shut the door behind me, and I found myself in a largish chamber that probably had originally been intended as a conference room, the sort of place where executives on retreat might gather to have a breakfast and pretend they were doing something constructive rather than simply getting away for a few days in Taos on the company dime. Now the space was mostly empty, except for a large chair and matching side table set up at one end near the fireplace, which had a blazing fire going.

Standing in front of that fireplace was Zahrias. At least, I assumed it was him; his back was to me as I entered the room, but as I took a few hesitant steps in his direction, he turned toward me, his face blank, unsmiling. Since the chandelier of heavy wrought iron overhead was switched on, I could see him far more clearly than I had on that one frightening night at my house in Santa Fe. Back then, the flickering fire- and candlelight hadn't given me a very clear impression of his features, save for the hard lines of his jaw and the cruel set of his mouth.

Now I could see that he actually was handsome enough, just like all the djinn, with the sort of heavy eyelashes that could make a man look as if he was wearing eyeliner even when he wasn't, and a firm chin and fine brow with thick dark hair flowing away from it. Unlike the time he'd visited the house Jace and I shared, Zahrias now wore a heavy quilted sort of robe over the billowing pants, although reddish-gold jewelry still gleamed at his wrists and his throat.

His feet were planted firmly on the floor, and that made me wonder if he had to make an effort to do that, so as not to scare the human.

"Jessica Monroe," he said. His voice possessed a harsh edge that Jace's lacked, although they both had rich-sounding baritones.

I forced myself to look squarely at him, even though I felt like a grubby mess in my muddy boots and jeans, my hair probably a disaster after having that knitted cap on all day. "I heard you wanted to talk to me."

"I want to know what happened to Jasreel." Zahrias went to the table a few feet from him, where I noticed for the first time a decanter of dark wine and a few glasses sat. He lifted the decanter and poured some of the wine into one of the glasses, then held it out to me. "You look as if you could do with this."

That was an understatement. My shoulders and neck were still stiff and tense from that nerve-wracking drive along the High Road, and a little muscle relaxant could be just what the doctor ordered. Even so, I shot Zahrias a wary glance, wondering what his game was. Certainly nothing I'd seen of him during his conversation with Jasreel back at the house would have led me to believe he'd be at all solicitous toward a mere mortal.

"Maybe," I allowed, taking a step forward. Then I paused. "What about Evony?"

A negligent lift of his shoulders, the red and gold brocade of his robe glinting in the firelight. "What about her?"

"Don't you want to hear her story, too?"

"I want to hear yours. I have a feeling that they are materially similar. Besides," he went on, "hers is not a mind given to much analysis. Natila could have chosen better."

That comment seemed a little harsh. Evony might not have been a Fulbright scholar, but she appeared quick and clever enough to me. However, arguing with Zahrias on his home turf didn't feel like a very good idea. I shrugged, then closed the rest of the gap between us so I could take the glass of wine from him. We didn't touch, but despite that, I could practically feel the heat radiating from his skin. Jace had always been warm, but this was different, something like a fire that seemed to burn along Zahrias' veins. Maybe it had something to do with the kind of elemental he was.

I took a sip of the wine, and, to my surprise, it tasted familiar. Possibly the djinn or their Chosen had been doing a little raiding of the La Chiripada tasting rooms as well. Either way, it was lush and velvety on my tongue, and felt awfully good sliding down. Only problem was, that wine was hitting an almost empty stomach. A protein bar and a couple handfuls of chips weren't really enough to do much good when it came to soaking up alcohol. I knew I'd have to pace myself.

"So," the djinn leader said, once he seemed to realize I wasn't going to drink more than those first few cautious sips, at least not for a little while. "Tell me what happened."

The last thing I wanted to do was relive those horrifying moments when Jace had been taken from me, but if Zahrias could offer me any insight, anything that might help me in getting Jace back, then I knew I had to relate everything I remembered.

"We were going to leave," I said. "I was just finishing up a few chores, and then we were going to pack up

and head up here. But we ran out of time. It seemed—
that is, all of a sudden Jace...Jasreel," I amended, once I
saw the way Zahrias' brows pulled together at the use
of the nickname, "couldn't seem to breathe, and then
these men burst into the house."

"How many?"

"Seven." I didn't even have to stop to think about
it. The scene was burned into my brain cells. "One of
them was holding a black box about so big"—I ges-
tured with my hands to indicate a cube roughly ten
inches square—"and seemed to be controlling it by
touch pad or something."

"What was this box?"

"I don't know. That is, I assumed it had to be some
sort of device designed to affect a djinn. It certainly
seemed to be hurting Jace." I had to stop then and take
a sip of wine to ease the sudden dryness in my throat.

Zahrias' expression darkened further, if that was
even possible. "You say 'assumed,' 'seemed.' So you
don't know for certain."

"No," I replied. I had a feeling that lying to this
hard-faced djinn was not a good idea, so I wouldn't
offer him anything other than the truth, or at least the
truth as I'd experienced it. "Whatever it was didn't
affect me, probably because I'm just a regular mortal."

"As to that," Zahrias said, "you are not a regular
mortal any longer. Not now that you've been Chosen."

Evony's revelations from the road came back to me, and my mouth went dry all over again. True, no regular mortal could heal as quickly as I seemed to now, and according to her, I would also be twenty-four in looks and vitality until the day I died...whenever that might be. So I supposed Zahrias was right. There wasn't anything normal about me. Not anymore.

But I didn't want him to see how much pondering that strange new future upset and worried me, so I said evenly, "True enough. But I guess it didn't affect me because, although I've been changed somehow, I'm still not a djinn."

He seemed to accept this, taking a drink of his wine and studying my face. It was hard not to flinch, or blink and look away. Doing any of those things would have been a sign of weakness, however, so I kept my chin up as best I could and hoped that would be enough.

It seemed to work; Zahrias gave the faintest of nods, then asked, "What happened next?"

I described the scene as best I could—the way Jace had been hauled off, the unexpected joy of hearing his voice in my mind, even though that unspoken conversation ended with him being taken away in one of the Los Alamos crew's Hummers. Zahrias listened, jaw hardening, but he didn't interrupt me. When I was done, though, he said,

"Tell me of this Los Alamos."

Despite myself, I couldn't help blinking at him in surprise. After all, he'd known for some time that the threat to the djinn appeared to originate in that mountain community. I'd assumed he must have been picking the brains of the Chosen gathered here in Taos to gather what intel he could about the place.

"I don't know what you're expecting me to say," I told him. "I mean, I've never even been there."

"But you are a native of this place—this New Mexico, as you call it?"

"Well, yes. But there are still corners of it I've never visited. Los Alamos has—had—a lot of scientists working at the labs there. I'm assuming at least one of them was Immune." The image of the man with the black box was as clear to me as if he were standing there next to Zahrias, so I went on, "That must be who the guy holding the box was. Some kind of scientist. It seemed to be his baby."

"'His baby'?" Zahrias repeated, one eyebrow lifting slightly at my use of the word.

"Well, he seemed pretty engrossed in using it. He hardly even looked around. In fact, I'm not sure he glanced up once, except to see where he was walking so he wouldn't trip over something." That *had* been strange, now that I was recalling the scene in detail. You'd have thought the man would at least have looked to see who he'd caught in his net, but apparently not.

"Have you ever heard of anything like this box? Seen anything like it?"

I shook my head at once. "Zahrias, up until yesterday, I didn't even know that the djinn were real."

His mouth compressed. "Foolish of Jasreel. He should have told you the truth immediately, and not let it go for so long. You could have been safely here with the rest of us."

Funny how I'd been thinking more or less the same thing. Hashing over Jace's mistakes—real or perceived—wouldn't change anything, though, so I only shrugged and said, "Maybe so. Anyway, no, I've never heard of a device like that. But I suppose if one of the scientists was immune, and he figured out what had happened...then I suppose it's possible he came up with a way to interfere with djinn powers somehow. I say 'somehow' because I'm not a physicist or an engineer. I have absolutely no idea how something like that would even work. Obviously it does, though, because I saw him using it. I saw—I saw what it did to Jace." On his name, my voice broke, and I raised the glass of wine to my lips and drank again. I doubted that fooled Zahrias for a second, but at least it gave me a chance to attempt to regain my composure.

He frowned, then stepped over to the table so he could pour a bit more from the bottle into his glass. Since I'd only had four or five sips so far, he didn't offer to give me any more, but only set down the bottle and turned back toward the fire, his expression settling into that same blankness I'd first seen when I approached him. At the same time, I could see those odd, fiery flickers around his head, cousins to the ones that danced in the hearth. Did they materialize when he was worried, or troubled, or were they something that came and went at their own whim, like little companion dogs?

I certainly didn't have the courage to ask.

Because he didn't seem inclined to speak further, I only stood there, growing increasingly uncomfortable as the silence stretched between us. Through sheer force of will, I kept myself from drinking too much of the wine out of the impulse to be doing something... anything.

At last he shifted back toward me. "This puts us in a difficult position. You know how several of our Chosen went to Los Alamos to gather what intelligence they could, and did not return?"

I nodded. At this stage in the game, I didn't see the point in denying that I'd been eavesdropping on Zahrias' conversation with Jace.

"You have seen this device in action, and so now I know more than I did before you arrived. What we cannot know is if it only works on one djinn at a time, or whether its power can affect a number of us simultaneously. I had thought we would be safe here in Taos, that our numbers would be enough to deter the survivors in Los Alamos, but...." He let the words die away, and although he didn't quite shrug, I thought I saw his shoulders move slightly.

"How many of you are there?"

"Fifty of those djinn we refer to as 'the One Thousand,' and their Chosen, and then myself, and you and your travel companion." Zahrias smiled, but it was thin, hardly even a baring of his teeth. "Fifty djinn with their assembled powers would be quite enough under normal circumstances. I fear, however, that these circumstances are far from normal."

Even though I still found him intimidating, at the same time I couldn't help feeling a bit sorry for Zahrias. It couldn't be easy to have thought of yourself all along as invincible, only to discover that you were actually very far from it.

I couldn't offer any words of reassurance, because I didn't have any. And I wasn't going to contemplate the utter strangeness of a desire to offer Zahrias reassurance. For a moment I was silent, turning the wine glass around in my hands, feeling the cool surface against fingers that I'd thought would never be warm again. Here, though, everything was warm. Djinn magic?

Then I said, "That's why I need to go to Los Alamos. I have to set Jace free somehow, and while I'm there, I can try to find out more about that device—what it does, how powerful it is."

Another one of those thin smiles. "Just like that? And how is it that you think you'll succeed when our own Chosen didn't?"

Good question. I paused, attempting to gather my thoughts. After sipping my wine again, I replied, "Well, for one thing, the leader of the group from Los Alamos basically gave me an open invitation. He said I was welcome to come join them if I changed my mind."

"Indeed?" Zahrias sounded skeptical, and I couldn't blame him. I probably would've sounded equally doubtful if our situations had been reversed.

"Indeed. And even if he hadn't, I'd still have to go. I can't leave Jace with them."

The djinn leader's expression shifted then, although I couldn't quite read it. Something like a flicker of amusement, or possibly irritation. Whatever that look was, it disappeared before I was able to decipher it. All he said, though, was, "Perhaps. But you cannot go tonight, so let Lauren—she was the Chosen who led you here—show you where you will be staying. And the Chosen are having a special dinner as well...it is your Christmas, I think."

Holy crap, it was. Sometime during the journey from Santa Fe to Taos, the actual date had completely slipped my mind. And Zahrias was right about one thing—I couldn't set out for Los Alamos tonight, not in the dark with more snow falling. It was probably a good idea to get some rest, one or two good meals, and then decide what to do next. If I was really lucky, the storm would pass as well, and I'd have better luck striking out for Los Alamos in the morning.

Besides, if I said I wasn't itching to meet more of the Chosen, I'd be lying.

CHAPTER FIVE

Lauren was waiting for me outside the conference room where I'd met with Zahrias. I had no idea whether she'd been standing there the whole time, or whether he'd sent some sort of silent signal to summon her.

Either way, it was a relief to be away from him, to not have to worry about the way he was or wasn't dissecting everything I said. I could tell he thought my plan to go to Los Alamos was a waste of time, but at least he hadn't attempted to talk me out of it. Not yet, anyway.

"Your friend Evony brought your things in from your car," Lauren said, leading me down a hallway that clearly led to a block of hotel rooms. "She's already set in her own room, and you're just a few doors down."

"So are all of the Chosen staying here at the resort?" I asked.

"Not all. There are a few more up the street at the Taos Inn. We were a lot more scattered around the town, using vacant houses and B&Bs and whatever was most appealing, but then Zahrias was concerned after four of our Chosen disappeared when they went to Los Alamos, so he made us all move where we would be closer together."

From a tactical standpoint, that made sense. You wouldn't want your forces spread out all over town. On the other hand, nice as this hotel was, it had to feel sort of cramped to be stuck in a single room after having a house all to yourself.

"Here we are," she went on, opening a door for me. "We've disabled the outer locks because we didn't want to mess around with key cards, but you can still lock the door from the inside."

Seeing the room that had been waiting for me, I thought I might have to revise that "cramped" judgment when it came to these hotel rooms. I had no idea how much they varied from room to room, but mine was very large, much bigger than the apartment I'd lived in over my parents' garage, and had a kiva-style fireplace in one corner, a little sitting area with a chair and love seat, and an enormous carved bed. Gazing at it, I wished with all my soul that Jace could be here to share that bed with me.

He will, I told myself fiercely. *You'll find him, and rescue him, and then you can test out that bed and see how it compares to the one back in Santa Fe.*

For some reason, though, that thought made me worried rather than hopeful. What if I couldn't rescue him? After all, it wasn't as if Zahrias had offered me any helpful advice on the subject. No, more the reverse. I could tell he didn't think I would be successful, that I was intent on carrying out a fool's mission.

Well, I looked forward to proving him wrong.

Something must have shifted in my expression, because Lauren gave me what she probably thought was an understanding smile. "It must be hard, being separated from your partner. But we're having a big dinner in about a half hour. Please come and join us. It'll help take your mind off things."

I sort of doubted that a turkey dinner would soothe my woes, but I'd already resolved to eat a good meal and get some rest, so I didn't bother to contradict her. Summoning a smile of my own, I said, "That sounds great. Where are you having the dinner?"

"In the restaurant here, De La Tierra. You can follow the signs to find it. And one of our Chosen was actually a chef down in Santa Fe, so it'll be good. Philip is awesome."

Right then, any kind of hot meal sounded awesome, especially one I didn't have to prepare myself. "Great," I told her. "I'll get myself straightened up a little, and then I'll come find you all."

"Perfect," she said, with another one of those bright, blazing smiles, then let herself out. I had no idea what her story was, and I didn't know if I'd have the time to find out, but clearly she wasn't having too many issues with being Chosen, with having a djinn lover.

Or maybe she was just one of those people who happened to be really good at hiding what she was actually thinking.

Either way, it wasn't really my problem. More pressing was the realization that all I'd brought for a change of clothes was another pair of jeans and a bulky gray sweater. I hadn't really been thinking I'd need a party wardrobe on this trip.

Oh, well. As I'd told myself earlier, I wasn't here to impress anyone. I'd packed things that were warm and serviceable. If the Chosen here couldn't handle that, it was their problem, not mine.

Someone knocked at the door as I was brushing the tangles out of my hair. I went to see who it was and nearly got bowled over by Dutchie as she went rushing past me so she could sniff around the room before coming back to paw at my leg.

"Looks like someone was missing their mommy," Evony said as she came in as well. I noticed she was holding the little backpack I used to carry all of the dog's supplies. I also noticed that she'd had time to get spruced up; her dark hair gleamed in sleek waves over her shoulders, and she'd changed into a festive red sweater just a shade brighter than the color she wore on her lips.

"More like she wants her dinner," I replied, bending down to scratch behind Dutchie's ears. After taking the backpack from Evony, I got out the dog dishes and filled one with water and the other with dry food, then placed them on the floor. Dutchie set to immediately, tail wagging.

"Speaking of dinner," Evony went on, giving my drab ensemble a jaundiced look, "you are not wearing *that* to go meet all those Chosen and their djinn, are you?"

"Well, sorry. I guess I plum forgot to pack any party clothes."

She sighed. "I figured. Let me go get you something."

"It doesn't matter—" I began to protest, and she held up a hand.

"It matters to *me*. I don't want to show up with someone who looks like something the cat dragged in."

"What, am I your date now or something?"

Her lip curled. "Don't flatter yourself."

I couldn't help grinning, and she went back out. Since Dutchie was occupied with inhaling her dinner, I went over to the window and looked out while I waited for Evony to return. There was actually more to see than I thought; snow still fell, but the lights in the garden area outside were on, illuminating the bare trees and shrubs, and the thicker, darker shapes of the pines and junipers that dotted the landscaping. It was probably very beautiful in the spring and summer, but right now it just looked bleak, abandoned. I also had to wonder about the electricity. Were the djinn powering the grid somehow? Had to be; all this couldn't be running on stored solar energy alone.

Since I hadn't locked the door, when Evony came back, she let herself in. In one hand she held a small makeup bag, while a bright kelly-green sweater was draped over her other arm.

"I don't think we have time for a makeover," I began, but she ignored me and went into the dressing area in the bathroom, then set the makeup bag down on the counter.

"This isn't a makeover," she said. "Just a quick sprucing-up. Take off that trash bag you're wearing and put this on." She tossed the sweater to me, and I caught it. I would've said that she and I were roughly the same size, although I was about an inch taller, but that sweater looked too small for either of us.

From the glint in her eye, I could tell she was poised and ready to counter any argument I might give her, so I decided it wasn't worth arguing about. Instead, I took the sweater and pulled the one I was wearing over my head, then drew on the one she'd given me. As I'd feared, it was tight. Not "I can't breathe" tight, but a lot more snug than anything I'd worn for months, even the slinky black dress I'd put on for Thanksgiving.

But I shouldn't have thought of that dress, because then I recalled how Jace's eyes had lit up when he caught sight of me, the way he'd told me I was beautiful. While I was keeping myself busy, I could stop myself from worrying about him, but if I let my guard down, like in moments such as this...well, I could feel the worry seize me again, the sharp burn of tears at the back of my eyes.

Don't, I told myself. *Just don't.*

So I managed to swallow, hard, and force the tears back to wherever they'd come from. At the same time, I twitched the sweater more or less into position. Since I was wearing jeans tucked into knee-high boots, it didn't look too mismatched. I hoped.

"Come here," Evony commanded, so I went into the dressing area. She eyed me critically and nodded. "That's a good color on you. And your hair doesn't look quite so much like home-fried crap now that you've brushed it."

"Gee, thanks," I said.

One corner of her mouth quirked slightly, but she just handed me a tube of lipstick. "Try this one. It's nice and festive."

I took it from her but looked down at it dubiously. To say I wasn't a lipstick kind of girl was an understatement. Lately, all I'd been wearing was colored lip balm, and even when I used to get dressed up, I always went for gloss. Lipstick felt sort of old lady-ish to me, unless you were going for Evony's clearly intentional retro look.

But since she obviously wanted me to put it on, and I just wanted to get done with the primping so I could get some food in my stomach, I spread a light coating over my lips. It looked garish against my pale skin, but Evony gave a satisfied nod.

"Much better. Don't suppose you packed any mascara?"

"No," I replied. Lip balm and deodorant and a toothbrush and toothpaste, yes. Makeup had been pretty far down on my list of priorities.

"Too bad." She squinted at me and then shrugged. "Good thing you have nice eyelashes anyway. I know people who would've killed for those."

I actually always had been proud of my lashes—a feature I'd inherited from my mother—but for obvious reasons, I hadn't been paying much attention to them lately. At least at the moment they'd save me from having to put on mascara, though.

"It's all in the genes, I guess," I said lightly. "Are you ready?" I figured she must be, since she looked like she was about to go out on a hot date instead of have Christmas dinner with a bunch of strangers.

"Yes." Despite her reply, she looked a little uneasy. Maybe it was just the prospect of having to face a room full of people she didn't know, but in my short acquaintance with her, Evony hadn't exactly struck me as the sort of person who was lacking in confidence.

Or maybe it was having to go meet a group of Chosen, and know that your own djinn partner was in captivity miles and miles away. I could relate to that feeling.

But I'd told Lauren I would go. Anyway, I was hungry, and I guessed that Evony must be starving, too, since she hadn't eaten much more on the drive here than I had.

I patted Dutchie on the head, told her I'd be back soon, and then closed the door behind me and went to the hall, where Evony had been waiting for me while I attended to the dog. We were both quiet as we walked back toward the more public areas of the resort, following the signs to the restaurant.

Which was already full when we got there. Evony and I both hung back a little, watching as people moved to and from an enormous buffet that had been set up on a series of long tables off to one side. Christmas music played in the background, and everyone seemed to be laughing and chatting and generally having a good time.

After so many months of only being around Jace, of hearing very little music—the real estate developer's music collection hadn't been much to my taste—the assortment of sounds seemed almost deafening. My first instinct was to duck back toward the lobby and hide in my room, and it seemed as if Evony was feeling about the same way.

But then Lauren approached us, smiling, and said, "I've been saving seats for you two. Let me take you over to my table."

Oh, thank God. Hers was the only halfway familiar face I'd seen so far, and, with any luck, her table would be somewhere tucked away to one side where we could mostly escape notice.

No such luck. It was out in the middle of the dining room, and I could feel everyone watching as Evony and I made our way over to it and took the chairs Lauren indicated. Not wanting to be obvious about staring, I'd only gathered scattered impressions of the people in attendance, but it seemed to me that the Chosen were all in their twenties and extremely good-looking. There didn't seem to be any djinn here. In a way, that made sense; I sort of doubted they were the type to celebrate Christmas. No, this party was for the mortals living here in Taos, a way for them to feel somewhat normal in a world that would never be normal again.

To my surprise, I did recognize the two people sitting at Lauren's table. They were the guys from the roadblock out on the highway, now wearing sweaters instead of the heavy parkas they'd had on while performing guard duty. Their plates were mostly empty already, so it looked as if Evony and I had gotten here later than I'd thought.

"Hey," said the blond one. "Glad to see you again. I'm Aidan."

"Hi," I said, while Evony murmured a half-hearted greeting.

"And I'm David," the dark-haired young man put in. "Have a seat."

Evony and I sat down, and Aidan picked up one of the bottles of wine at the center of the table and asked, "Red okay?"

"God, yes," Evony replied, eagerly holding out her glass.

I picked up my glass as well, and he stood and poured for us. Lauren resumed her seat on the other side of David's chair, then took her own glass, which was a little less than half full.

"So," Evony said, glancing around the room. "No djinn?"

Lauren and David exchanged a quick glance. "No," Lauren responded. "This is our party. That is, I think some of them may drop by, just to see how things are going, but they wanted this to be for us."

"It looks great," I said, even though I was a little disappointed. I wanted to see how the djinn interacted with their Chosen, what their relationships appeared to be like. Since I was still planning to leave for Los Alamos the next day, weather permitting, I knew I might not get a lot of chances to observe these people with their otherworldly partners.

But, despite my disappointment, the place really did look beautiful. Someone had set a large fir tree in one corner, and, judging by the cohesive look of the ornaments hanging from it, they had to have raided the resort's holiday decorations to trim the tree. Evergreen garlands swagged the staircase off to one side of the room, and everyone was nicely dressed. Well, why wouldn't they be? They had all the shops and boutiques in town to choose from when it came to putting together their holiday wardrobes.

"Well, I'm going to load up my plate," Evony announced. "You ready to eat?"

"I was ready hours ago," I said, and my table companions smiled. After getting up from my seat, I followed Evony to the buffet line and, as she'd so eloquently described it, began to load up. Turkey and ham and wild rice stuffing and potatoes and...well, basically the sort of meal I hadn't thought I'd ever eat again. With a small pang, I thought of the venison I'd left defrosting in the refrigerator back at the house in Santa Fe. I'd planned to make venison cutlets for Christmas Day dinner, but my discovery of Jace's true identity and his subsequent kidnapping by the Los Alamos survivors had driven those plans right out of my head.

What were they feeding him? Probably not turkey and mashed potatoes.

I bit my lip and forced myself to concentrate on filling up the last section on my plate with what looked like homemade cranberry sauce. Where they'd gotten the cranberries, I had no idea, but I supposed they must have scrounged frozen ones from the supermarket. Anyway, I told myself that bursting into tears in front of everyone certainly wouldn't solve anything, and besides, getting a good meal in me could only help restore my energy levels for the next day.

A final pause to pick up a dinner roll, and then I navigated between the tables back to where Aidan and Lauren and David were sitting. Their plates still held traces of dinner, so clearly they'd already eaten and were more or less hanging out at this point. I had to hope they wouldn't mind Evony and me eating in front of them.

She sat down a minute after I got back, her plate looking even more packed with food than mine. Clearly, worry over what might be happening to Natila was not affecting Evony's appetite.

It did feel a little strange to eat when the other three Chosen were just sitting there and drinking wine, chatting about the weather and the possibility of some skiing, but not discussing anything that I really wanted to hear. I wanted to know who their djinn were, how they had met them. How they had come here.

But maybe that was all old news to them. I had no idea how long Lauren or Aidan or David had been here in Taos. For all I knew, they'd gathered in the small tourist town not all that long after the Heat had done its dirty work, and therefore had known one another for months. From the easy way they conversed, joking and laughing, that seemed entirely possible.

They let Evony and me eat, for which I was grateful, because that way I didn't have to attempt to make conversation. Eventually, though, I'd cleared off enough of the food on my plate that Aidan apparently thought it was safe to ask,

"So, you really came here by the High Road?"

I had no idea how he knew that. My intuition told me that Zahrias had been the one to give the Cherokee the push that got us out of the snowbank, and so I supposed it was possible that the story had originated with him and made the rounds from there. I didn't know how much interaction he had with the Chosen, if any, but he could have always said something to one of the other djinn.

"Yes," I replied.

"That must have been some driving," David added, popping the last bit of the roll from his plate into his mouth.

Uncomfortable at being the center of all their attention, I could only shrug. "It wasn't so bad. I just drove as slowly as I could. It felt like it took forever, but it got us here."

"Why the High Road, though?" Lauren inquired. Her fingers were resting on the stem of her wine glass, but I noticed that she didn't appear inclined to pick it up and take a sip. From the easy way she smiled, it looked to me as if she'd already had a few. Maybe she was trying to slow down a bit.

"Jessica was afraid we'd run into those Los Alamos assholes if we took the main highway," Evony said, reaching out for one of the bottles of wine and refilling her glass.

Again, the three Chosen exchanged a glance that I couldn't quite decipher. After an uncomfortable pause, Lauren remarked, "Well, I suppose that makes sense."

I felt like I had to ask. "Have they tried to come up here?"

"To Taos?" David said, then smiled derisively. He had great teeth. I supposed they'd always stay that way, now that he was under his partner's protection. "I'd like to see them try. They wouldn't get within ten miles before the djinn blasted their asses off the face of the earth."

"But could the djinn really do that?" I asked. "I mean, with that device the survivors have—"

"What device?" Aidan asked, leaning forward and frowning. It was an expression I doubted he wore often; to me he looked almost too sunny and laid-back, the kind of guy whose biggest worry was how good the powder would be on the ski slopes that winter.

So they didn't know about that scary little box? I shot a questioning look at Evony, and her shoulders lifted. It seemed the djinn weren't exactly broadcasting the fact that the Immune from Los Alamos weren't quite as defenseless as the community here in Taos seemed to think.

"Um, the one they were using to interfere with—"

"And how are you all faring?" a new voice broke in.

I looked up to see a tall dark-haired man—djinn—pause behind Lauren's chair and lay a hand on her shoulder. She smiled up at him, but it was a very different sort of smile from the ones she'd offered the rest of us. No, this one was softer, warmer, more...bedroom-y, if that was even a word. Like she was thinking about all the things she'd like him to do to her, and she'd like to do to him. I knew that smile well enough, because I'd felt it on my own lips more than once when I was daydreaming about Jace. I knew right away who this newcomer must be, even before Lauren said,

"Jessica, Evony, this is Dani."

"It's very nice to meet you," I said politely, although inwardly I couldn't help being suspicious. I doubted it was coincidence that had made him show up at our table just as I was about to tell the other Chosen about the way their djinn might not be quite the invincible force they thought they were.

"Hi," Evony put in. From the way she didn't quite smile, I got the impression she realized as well that Dani's sudden appearance had to have been calculated.

"I am very sorry for both your losses," he said, his expression turning grave.

"'Losses'?" I repeated, then shook my head. "Actually, our partners were taken. We certainly didn't lose them, and we fully intend to get them back. Don't we, Evony?"

"Yeah," she said, dark eyes narrowed slightly.

"Ah," Dani replied, looking somewhat taken aback. "Well, that is a noble ambition. But if you don't mind me stealing Lauren away?"

She got up from her seat at once, looping her arm through his. I had the feeling her next question was asked purely for form's sake. "Will you two be all right on your own?"

"Fab," Evony said, sipping from her wine.

I was about to say we wouldn't exactly be alone, not if Aidan and David were still with us, when two female djinn approached, both of them dark-haired, voluptuous, and wearing low-cut tunics with full, filmy pants underneath, one outfit in shades of blue, the other warm brown. They offered us polite smiles, but also seemed intent on removing their partners from our presence.

And the two men appeared all too happy to go. They wished us a merry Christmas and then left the restaurant, heading off toward one of the wings of the resort where the rooms were located.

"I think we've been dumped," Evony said. Once again she reached out for the wine bottle, only this time I gave her a sharp look.

"You might want to slow down with that," I told her, and she scowled.

"Sorry, Mom, didn't think I had to worry about driving."

No way was I going to get in an argument with her right here in front of everybody. Not when I could see a few of the Chosen giving us speculative glances, as if trying to figure out how we'd managed to drive away all our dinner companions. I also noticed that no one else attempted to approach us. Maybe they all thought that losing your djinn partner might be catching, like the measles or something.

"Do what you want," I said, then pushed my plate away. There was still most of a roll and some mashed potatoes remaining on my plate, but I found I'd lost my appetite. "I want to get to bed so I can get an early start tomorrow."

She set down her wine glass. I could tell from the way her gaze darted toward me and then the windows that she was wondering if such a plan would even work, given the current weather conditions. But all she said was, "So *we* can get an early start, you mean."

Relief rushed through me. We hadn't really gotten the chance to discuss it, but I supposed that somewhere deep down I was worried Evony might want to stay here where it was safe, wouldn't want to go chasing off to Los Alamos with me. On closer examination, though, that wasn't really fair to her. She certainly hadn't given any indication that she was any less devoted to Natila than I was to Jace.

"Right," I said.

"I'll be up in a few. They were putting out some kind of pie, and I haven't had a real dessert in, well... not *since,* you know?"

I did know. Luckily, I'd never had much of a sweet tooth, except for a fierce craving for chocolate a few days out of the month. It was something I'd been able to keep indulging, since the real estate developer who'd built my Santa Fe refuge had laid in quite a stockpile of dark chocolate in a variety of flavors, including my new favorite, the kind with some chili pepper mixed in.

But pie was no inducement for me to stay at the party, and now that I'd gotten enough to eat, I could feel the weariness really beginning to set in, a dull ache in my shoulders and head. Maybe I'd take a long, hot bath before going to sleep. It was still a little early for bed, after all, and a bath would help to ease some of the knots in my neck.

"Well, enjoy the pie," I said, and headed off toward the corridor that led to my room...or rather, the room Zahrias had given me to use while I was here.

I couldn't help wondering if he planned to make an appearance at the party, but I somehow doubted it. He really didn't seem like the partying type. Truly, I couldn't imagine him doing much of anything except hanging out in that room of his and drinking wine and looking brooding, but I supposed that wasn't fair. I didn't know anything about him, except that he was in charge of this odd little community here in Taos. Had he been one of the djinn who'd conspired to spread the Heat all over the world, or was he one of the thousand conscientious objectors? But no, that didn't sound right. Lauren had flat out said that Zahrias didn't have a Chosen.

Because I was so preoccupied, I almost collided with someone who was coming down the hall toward the dining room just as I was leaving it. A pair of strong hands caught me, holding me away.

"I'm so sorry," I began, then paused as I realized the person whose hands now rested on my arms was a djinn. Like all of them, he was tall, but his hair was more a warm brown than the black that Jace and Zahrias shared.

Piercingly blue eyes seemed to bore into mine. "My fault, I fear," he said. "I was hurrying."

"And I wasn't looking where I was going." As gently as I could, I shifted so he would be forced to let go of me. A slight hesitation, and then his hands did drop away.

"You must be Jessica."

I wouldn't bother to ask how he knew that. Apparently, I was pretty famous in Taos. "Yes," I said simply.

"Aldair," he replied.

"Nice to meet you, Aldair," I said. Something about the way he kept staring at me was, to put it mildly, unnerving, so I added, "I was just going back to my room to rest, but I think there's still some dessert if you hurry."

"Ah, that," he responded. "Yes, I suppose I should check to see what there is."

I think I smiled. Then I ducked my head in a nod of farewell and hurried past him. Although I wouldn't allow myself to look back, I still caught a glimpse of the djinn in my peripheral vision. He hadn't moved toward the dining room, but only stood there, watching me.

A second later, I had to make a left to go down the hallway where my room was located, and Aldair was gone. I let out a quick sigh of relief, my steps speeding up until I was practically running by the time I reached my door.

Even after I was inside, and the lock engaged, I couldn't help feeling uneasy.

Who was this Aldair? Why had he been staring at me like that...and why did it unnerve me so much?

CHAPTER SIX

IT COULD HAVE BEEN THE LUXURIOUS BED, OR THE bath I'd taken before going to sleep. Whatever the reason, I slept much later than I'd intended, and woke up to see light peeking around the curtains in my room. By instinct, I glanced toward the nightstand next to the bed, but there was no clock radio or iPod dock. Strange.

But I had my watch, which I'd kept set according to the clock in the Cherokee, and that told me it was almost nine. Shit. Half the morning gone. True, under normal circumstances, you could make the drive from Taos to Los Alamos in an hour or so, but the weather lately hadn't exactly been normal. Besides, I realized I probably wouldn't want to go straight there from here anyway. If the survivors really were watching the highway, I'd want to leave from Santa Fe so they wouldn't think anything was out of the ordinary, that I was heading out directly from the house.

Since I'd taken that long bath the night before, I got myself together quickly this morning—a fast five minutes in the shower, just to freshen myself up, and then I was out and getting dressed. I laid Evony's borrowed sweater aside so I could give it back to her, brushed my hair and teeth, and applied some of the tinted lip balm I'd brought with me, then gave Dutchie her food and water. She'd need a walk before we headed back to Santa Fe, but I knew she could hold on a little bit longer.

While I was performing all these tasks, however, I could feel an undercurrent of dissatisfaction running through me. To be fair, I hadn't had a clear plan when I'd come here, but I supposed I'd thought I would get some kind of assistance, some kind of input. True, Zahrias had been far friendlier than I'd expected. That friendliness hadn't extended to any sort of an offer of help, though.

Well, what did you think he was going to do? I scolded myself. *He may be running the show here, but he's also a djinn who can be affected by that little device the Immune have, just like anyone else of his kind. He can't exactly drive you to Los Alamos and blast his way into the place.*

All right, that was true enough, but.... I sighed and shoved the last of my meager belongings into my bag.

Just as I was zipping it up, I heard a knock at the door. I glanced at my watch; ten minutes until ten. That had to be Evony coming along to collect me so we could get going. Dutchie thumped her tail in anticipation; obviously, she was thinking the same thing.

But when I opened the door, I saw Lauren standing outside. She glanced past me to the freshly made bed and the bag sitting on top of it, and a little frown creased her forehead. "Were you going to leave without getting breakfast?"

"Well, I ate enough last night to hold me for a while," I replied with a smile.

This time she didn't return the smile. Still with that same frown pulling at her brows, she said, "Zahrias wants to speak with you."

Maybe he'd decided to help me after all. Jace was one of Zahrias' kind, and it seemed wrong that the leader of the djinn here in Taos wouldn't offer some kind of assistance with a rescue attempt. "Okay." Then I tilted my head at Lauren. I just had to know. "What, are you his personal secretary or something?"

The frown disappeared, and she gave a small laugh—a light normal sound, one that reminded me I hadn't had much to laugh about lately. "No. Zahrias and Dani are brothers, and I volunteered to help out with any sort of administrative work he might need done." She added, glossy lips quirking a bit, "I was an executive assistant...before. So I guess I don't have it quite out of my system."

I hadn't really stopped to think about it, but in a situation like this, even with a hundred people gathered in a small area, you were bound to run into tasks that needed to be managed, messages that had to be relayed, logistics that must be worked out. "He's lucky to have you. Handy that he and Dani are brothers, I suppose."

"Yes, I suppose," she said absently. "But let's go. He's waiting."

And of course the great and mighty Zahrias doesn't like to be kept waiting. I didn't say anything, though, but only told Dutchie this wouldn't take long, then stepped out into the hall and shut the door behind me. The corridor was empty except for the two of us, and once again I wondered why Evony wasn't being included in this convo with the djinn leader.

Sunshine streamed through the windows, glittering off the snow-frosted trees and shrubs outside. It looked like a fairyland out on the resort's grounds, and I wished I had the time to go out and enjoy them, take Dutchie with me, now that the sun had reappeared.

That wasn't going to happen, though. I dutifully followed Lauren back to the same conference room where I'd spoken with Zahrias the night before. Today there was no decanter of wine, but a pot of heavenly-smelling coffee, and a plate heaped with what looked like fresh-baked muffins, blueberry and corn and carrot spice.

He was standing by the fire again, however, and gave the same off-hand nod toward Lauren, effectively dismissing her. She shut the door, and he said,

"Have you broken your fast?"

"No." My stomach rumbled a little, despite my protestations earlier that I really wasn't that hungry. I hoped that the sound of the wood crackling away in the hearth was loud enough to hide the embarrassing noise.

"Then have some coffee, and eat."

I couldn't help my eyes narrowing, just a little. Why was he being so nice? But I needed to eat, and I needed the coffee even more, so I went to the table and poured some of the steaming-hot brew into a sturdy dark green mug, then added my usual amounts of cream and sugar. All of the muffins looked delicious, but I decided on one of the corn ones—flecked with green chiles and cheddar cheese—and set it on a small plate that was sitting next to the muffin basket.

"Your plans for today?" Zahrias asked, after I'd taken a cautious sip of my coffee. I needed the caffeine badly, but I didn't want to burn my mouth.

"I was about to go back to Santa Fe, check on the house, and then head out to Los Alamos," I replied. "Thank you for the hospitality, but it doesn't seem as if you can help me, so there's no point in staying."

"You are determined in this?"

Why did he keep pushing? Did he really think I was going to change my mind? After setting my coffee mug down next to the plate with the muffin on it, I said, "Of course I am."

"Even if I were to offer you an alternative?"

That question made me straighten up and give him a very direct look. This morning he was dressed more or less as he had been the night before, in the silken robe and loose pants, although I noticed he wore none of the flashy rose gold jewelry, and his hair was pulled back into a ponytail rather than hanging loose on his shoulders.

"Alternative?" I asked, not sure I liked the sound of the word.

"Last night you met one of my people—Aldair."

"Ye-es," I said slowly. Where was Zahrias going with this? The image of the other djinn, the sharp, penetrating blue of his eyes, flashed through my mind. "We more or less bumped into each other as I was leaving the dining room."

"His is a sad case. He was one of those whose Chosen went to Los Alamos to investigate and did not return."

A little shiver began to work its way down my spine, even though the fire was quite hot. "That's too bad," I said, my tone possibly a bit too casual.

"It has been difficult for him, and for the three others who lost their partners." For the first time, Zahrias bent to take up his own mug of coffee; I was surprised to see that it wasn't black, the way Jace drank it, but doctored to a shade lighter than my own. "But then he saw you last night and realized who you were."

"And?" I asked, even though I had a suspicion where all this might be going. No wonder I'd been so uneasy after meeting Aldair.

"He would like you to be his Chosen."

Just like that. My mouth was dry, so I retrieved my coffee as well and swallowed as large a mouthful as I could without burning my tongue. Tone flat, I said, "Isn't he sort of forgetting that I already have a djinn partner?"

"A partner who is a captive."

"A partner I intend to rescue," I shot back.

Zahrias' eyebrows lifted. "And how precisely do you intend to do that?"

"I don't know," I said honestly. "But I'll figure something out. I always do."

His only response was a thin smile. "I think you would be far better off if you accepted Aldair's offer."

And maybe if Aldair wanted me so badly, he could have asked me himself, instead of having Zahrias act as his pimp. Right then, anger began to flicker through me, bright and terrible as the fire in the hearth only a few feet away.

"Oh, really?" I asked, hands planted on my hips as I shot Zahrias a narrow-eyed glare. Voice tight, I went on, "Just like that? Abandon the man I love and let the Los Alamos people do what they want with him—torture him, or...or do experiments on him—or execute him?" I paused to gather myself. Ignoring the deepening scowl on Zahrias' features, I went on, "Jace is one of your own people. Don't *you* care what happens to him?"

"What I might personally think or feel is of no import. Because of the device you described, we cannot attempt our own rescue of him." Zahrias' black eyes glittered, and it was as if I could see flames of dark orange and red gleaming within them, echoing his inner fury, raging against his impotence. "It seems that the machine does far worse than merely rob us of our powers, but also weakens us to the point of uselessness. What do you expect us to do to combat that?"

"Nothing," I said, my tone far gentler than I'd intended it to be. Zahrias—and all the djinn—probably had no experience with that sort of powerlessness. So how could I expect them to put themselves so terribly in harm's way, with no hope of success? "Which is why I have to be the one to save him, and Natila, too. I can't stay here and leave them to their fate. Maybe it's easy for Aldair to forget the person he lost. But I can't—I can't transfer my affections like that. I need to get Jace back."

For the longest moment, Zahrias said nothing, only stared at me, brows lowered, mouth pressed into a thin line. He did look very forbidding, and I swallowed, knowing that, although the Los Alamos survivors might have the means to take his djinn powers away, here in Taos I was in his territory, where he possessed his full strength, and he could do whatever he liked.

Up to and including smiting an impudent mortal, if she annoyed him enough.

But then he shook his head. "I had not expected this."

"Not expected what?"

"For you to have loved Jasreel like this, so much so that you are willing to risk your own life in an endeavor that could very well end badly for you both."

"Don't the Chosen here love their djinn the same way?" I inquired, genuinely curious. "Doesn't Lauren love your own brother enough to sacrifice herself for him?"

At the mention of his brother, Zahrias' face grew clouded again, but he smoothed the expression away almost as soon as it appeared. "As for that, I suppose you would have to ask her. They do seem to care for one another, but it is not a relationship that has been... tested...as yours has."

I decided it was probably better to let that go for now. "Well, if this is a test, then I want to make sure I pass it. And that means going to Los Alamos. I realize there isn't much you can do to help, but—"

"I can do a little." He moved away from me and stood by the window, and for the first time I could see shimmers of dark, dark blood red in his black hair as the sunlight caught it. "At least I can make your return journey go more smoothly. You have seen how the streets here in Taos have been cleared of snow?"

"Yes," I replied, wondering where he was going with this. "I figured you had some of the Chosen out plowing the roads."

A small smile as he turned back toward me. "No. The djinn of the air have blown the snow away, and those of us with the gift of fire have melted the ice from the walkways, so all can walk safely."

Well, that was handy. But even as I visualized all those djinn out on snow-clearing duty, a suspicion began to grow in my mind. "So, wait—you could've cleared the highway for me? Made it so I didn't have to crawl here for hours and hours and almost get stuck in the snow?"

"Yes," he replied, then added, "Although I did help you out of that one tight spot in Truchas, did I not?"

That answered one question...but not my others. Shaking my head, I said, "I don't get it. Why make me go through all that?"

Another one of those tight little smiles, almost mocking, but not quite. "I wanted to see how serious you were about rescuing Jasreel."

Right then, I wished I had the courage to knee a djinn in the nuts. But I didn't, so I only gave Zahrias the sourest look I could muster, then finally helped myself to the muffin I'd selected. Even with elemental intervention, I still had a long drive back to Santa Fe.

Any hope that I could go back to my room in stealth and retrieve my bag, and then fetch Evony from her own borrowed suite, was dashed before I was even halfway to my destination. From nowhere, seemingly—and maybe it was from nowhere, since an elemental could probably come and go from this plane as he pleased—Aldair appeared in the corridor, arms crossed. To my surprise, today he wasn't wearing the gaudy djinn garb of brocade robe and flowing pants, but a dark sweater and jeans and hiking boots. If I hadn't known better, I would have said he was just a regular mortal like me, one of the Chosen...except for the ghostly wind that seemed to move in the hallway and blow against my loose hair.

So, an air elemental, like Jace.

Since I couldn't really go around Aldair, I stopped where I was and gave him an inquiring look.

"You are leaving." It wasn't a question.

"Yes."

Those laser-bright blue eyes seemed to bore into me. "Without even considering my request."

Seriously? I didn't have time for this. One chance encounter where we'd exchanged fewer than a dozen words certainly didn't give this djinn the right to think he had a claim on me. "A request delivered through your leader instead of coming to me directly."

His head tilted slightly. "Would it have made a difference?"

"No, but it would have been a little more considerate."

"I don't understand. You are a Chosen without a partner, and I am a djinn who has lost his. It makes perfect sense for you to stay here with me."

Right then I began to appreciate even more the way Jace had handled our relationship. Yes, some might argue that he should have told me the truth much earlier, but at the same time, he'd given the two of us a chance to grow into one another, to appreciate the other person for who he or she was, and not what. This Aldair was acting as if one Chosen was as good as another, as long as she was to his taste.

Hands on my hips, I said, "Actually, it doesn't make sense, for two reasons. First, because Jace is still alive, only captured, and so we're still very much together. And two," I added, hurrying because I didn't want this confrontation to go on any longer than it absolutely had to, "contrary to what you might think, we mortals aren't interchangeable pieces. You can't expect us to transfer our affections in the blink of an eye. It doesn't work that way. So, if you'll let me pass—"

He didn't seem inclined to do that at all. Arms still crossed, he regarded me with a mixture of annoyance and amusement, as if all my arguments had meant very little to him. "I don't think I'm done speaking with you, Jessica."

"Oh, yes, you are." Zahrias' voice, and I never thought I'd ever be so happy to see the djinn leader. I hadn't even noticed where he'd come from, only that he was suddenly there, standing a few paces away, his arms crossed and an irritated glint in his dark eyes. "Jasreel's Chosen has offered what I believe are very cogent arguments. You will let her go. You will let her leave so she can rescue her lover."

At the word "lover," Aldair's eyes went almost to slits, his heavy lashes hiding the fierce blue of his eyes. But it appeared that he didn't want to get into an actual argument with Zahrias, because he let out a rumbling sound of disgust and then blinked out of existence, leaving the two of us alone in the corridor.

"Thank you," I said.

"Aldair can be rather stubborn. But he will lick his wounds for a while, and eventually, if he still wants a mortal, he can make another choice from those still alive in Albuquerque, or even farther south. There are probably one or two likely candidates."

Meaning someone young and attractive, I supposed. It seemed that the djinn were just about as shallow as humans when it came to that sort of thing. Now was certainly not the time to remark on their taste in partners, though, so I only said, "Well, I hope he finds someone." *Because then he can forget about chasing after me....*

"That, I suppose, is up to him. Safe travels, Jessica Monroe."

And then, like Aldair, Zahrias disappeared as well, and I was alone in the hallway. Handy trick, although it must wreak havoc on a person's notions of privacy, being able to blink in and out wherever and whenever you wanted. I wondered how the djinn culture had evolved to deal with it.

That was something I'd have to discover at another time, however. For now it was enough to finally go fetch Evony, and release Dutchie from her durance vile in my hotel room.

Time to go home...if only for a short while.

As Zahrias had promised, the High Road was cleared of snow and ice, although the drifts were piled up on either side of the highway to almost shoulder height. Evony looked at the bare asphalt with disbelieving eyes and demanded, "You mean they could've done this for us all along?"

"Yes," I said, and I couldn't even find it in me to be angry. Well, not much. Right then it was enough to be cruising along at a steady forty-five miles an hour, and to see the sun sparkling off all that lovely fresh snow. Of course, it was mostly lovely because it wasn't slowing us down, but still.

"Jesus Christ," she muttered, then pursed her mouth. "Thank God Natila wasn't so...arbitrary."

"What is she like?" I asked, using the present tense on purpose. Already I'd caught myself using the word "was" when I thought of Jace, and I needed to stop doing that. He was alive. He was still present, not past.

Anyway, Evony hadn't said all that much about Natila, not after she'd described how the djinn woman had come into her life, and I figured it couldn't hurt to learn a bit more. It would help to pass the time, although now, with these magically cleared roads stretching ahead of us, I knew we'd be back in Santa Fe before noon.

"She's...." Evony seemed to pause and consider for a moment as she stared out the window. The trees outside were still sugar-frosted with snow, although a brisk wind blowing down off the Sangre de Cristo mountains was sending fine flurries everywhere as the snow shook itself from the branches of the pines and firs. "She's fun, I guess. Back at the casino, she would make jokes about having to take baths with bottled water and eating out of cans and all that. Made everything seem not quite so hard." Another silence as Evony kept her gaze fixed on the window, although I could see her throat working, as if she'd had to swallow back some unexpected tears. "But now I just feel mad at her."

"Why?" I asked, surprised. That was about the last thing I would have expected Evony to say.

"Well, even though she told me the truth about herself pretty early on, she could've done it even earlier than that. We could've had running water from the beginning, and better food. And there wasn't really any reason for us to be hanging around Española all that time. I don't know what the hell she was thinking, especially now that I know where we could have been staying in Taos."

On the surface, those all seemed like valid complaints. However, just like Jace, Natila must have had a reason for lingering in Evony's hometown, although at the moment I couldn't figure out what that might be.

It was on the tip of my tongue to tell her as much, but another glance at the hard lines of Evony's profile, the way her fingers were clutched tightly around the small backpack she held in her lap, told me that probably wasn't such a good idea. For all I knew, she was using that anger as a shield, a way to protect herself from worrying too much. If she thought she was angry with Natila, then she wouldn't have the mental energy to grieve and fret.

"Well," I began, then hesitated, trying to think of the best way to phrase my remark so I wouldn't upset Evony, "it sounds as if she was trying to do her best to cushion things for you. I don't think she meant to make things harder."

"Maybe." She let out a breath, then shook her head. "It's just...you think you've survived the end of the world, and then you think you've finally found the perfect person for you...and then they aren't who they said they were, and...." The sentence trailed off there, but I knew what she meant. Far more than I really wanted to, actually.

But because that was obvious to both of us, I didn't bother saying anything else. Instead, I drove as quickly as I could, which still wasn't quite up to the speed limit, despite what the djinn had done to clear the roads. Here and there were still patches of ice from the snow melting off the slopes above, not a lot, but enough that I didn't want to take the curves with too much abandon.

It still felt like we were flying, though, compared to our agonizing drive the day before. And before too long we were coming down into Nambe, where I cut off on a side road to take our same stealthy path into Santa Fe, the one I had to pray wasn't being observed by the Los Alamos group. I really didn't see how they could—watching the highway made sense, but spying on every road in and out of town would be way too much for their limited manpower.

Or at least I hoped it would.

I didn't see any sign of life as we skirted the northern edge of town and then picked up Alameda, however. Here I had to slow back down, as obviously the djinn weren't about to tip their hand by clearing the roads in Santa Fe. That was the worst part—dropping to a crawl when we were so close to our destination, but I didn't have much choice.

The drive along Upper Canyon was similarly deserted, and the bright sun had melted enough of the snow that the road was icy in spots. Even the four-wheel drive slipped here and there, and I clamped down on my bottom lip and prayed we wouldn't get stuck. Zahrias had bailed us out once, but I couldn't expect him to do it again. Not here, so far away from his home territory.

Eventually, though, we did make it to the gate to the property, and I climbed out to unlock the padlock and unwrap the chain. At least today the sun was shining, although the air had an intense bite to it, and I knew I wouldn't want to remain standing in the snow for too long. I didn't have to, of course, and within a minute or two, I was back inside the Cherokee and coaxing it up the incline to the house.

Since we probably wouldn't be staying long, I didn't bother with putting the Jeep in the garage, but instead backed it up as close to the rear door of the house as I could. Dutchie pressed her nose against the window and whined softly; I could tell she knew she was home, and wanted out.

You and me both, I thought, climbing out of the vehicle and going to the rear door so I could let her out of the Jeep. Evony climbed out as well, and I unlocked the back door to the house, standing out of the way so Dutchie could go charging inside.

Nothing seemed to have been touched. It was cold, because we hadn't been there to light any fires, but the refrigerator still hummed away, and none of the digital clocks on the other appliances were blinking. Clearly, the power had held, even through the storm.

It hurt to think I wouldn't be staying here in this place of refuge Jace had provided for me...but I reflected I wouldn't have this sanctuary at all if it weren't for him. Anyway, I wouldn't be able to rest here until I brought him safely home.

"I need to pack a few more things," I told Evony as she set her weekender bag on the kitchen counter. "Not much—just a few changes of clothes. And then I need to check on the animals...." I let the words die away then as it came to me that I'd need to do something about the livestock. Leaving them on their own for a night was one thing, but I had absolutely no idea how long I would be gone this time. "Well, shit."

"What?" Evony asked. She'd started heading toward one of the cupboards, probably to scrounge a snack or something, but at my curse she turned back toward me, eyebrows raised in question.

"The goats and the chickens. If it was summer, I'd just let them all go and hope for the best, but I can't do that to them now. They'd never survive." From somewhere, a memory of glowing red eyes came to me, and I recalled the coyotes who'd watched Jace and me drive by in the Cherokee on that November night not so long ago. No, I definitely couldn't leave the animals to fend for themselves. It was almost January, and those coyotes were probably pretty hungry right about now.

"Take them with us," Evony suggested, and I blinked at her.

"What?"

"Why not? You have a trailer—I saw it out there by the garage. Maybe the Los Alamos people will be happier to see us if we bring them a little present. A peace offering, you know?"

I could have hugged her. That was brilliant. Yes, I'd be giving up the animals Jace and I had so carefully gathered and brought here, but I had to guess that the survivors in Los Alamos would be happy to get some livestock to add to whatever they might already have. Even if they'd managed to keep the lights on the whole time, and the local grocery story had never run out of power, I doubted they'd turn up their noses at an additional supply of fresh eggs and milk.

And if I succeeded at bringing Jace home, we could always go on another foraging expedition. I had absolutely no idea how many goats and chickens had been raised on local farms, but there would have to be some left around...assuming they had someplace to shelter from the cold. Anyway, I told myself that what we'd done once before, we could do again.

"That's perfect, Evony. Thank you." Of course, even as I thanked her, I began to worry about how we'd get the goats in the trailer. The first time around, they hadn't exactly been amenable, and I didn't have Jace with me to put his goat-whisperer moves on them.

But it turned out they were a lot more tractable this time, possibly because they were hoping a ride in the trailer meant they were going to greener pastures than the dead grass in the yard and the drafty little shed Jace had built for them. I had no idea what kind of facilities were available in Los Alamos, but surely someone there had to have kept horses or something. After I maneuvered the Cherokee around and Evony helped me get the trailer on the hitch—"I used to help my brother get his cars ready for shows," she informed me—we herded the goats into the trailer, and they went in more or less obediently enough.

The chickens were a little tougher, but I ended up putting plastic down in the back of the Jeep and then loading them in there. Good thing that Evony and I were both traveling light; she put her weekender bag on one side of the back seat, and I set my duffle on top of that. Dutchie would just have to be confined to half the seat. She didn't look all that thrilled about it, but since she could tell she wasn't going to be left behind, she was willing to put up with the cramped quarters. At least she was such a well-behaved dog that I wouldn't have to worry about her bothering the chickens.

As for the rest...well, the house was tightly built, and should be all right. The drip system in the greenhouse more or less sustained itself. Yes, I'd have some maintenance to do when I got back, but I thought the plants would be okay for a few days.

Or weeks. Whatever it took.

We locked everything up again and headed out. I'd thought driving in snow was hard enough, but doing it while pulling a horse trailer was doubly difficult. The only thing that saved me was following the trail I'd already broken on the way up to the property. Well, that and the sunny, clear day itself, since at least I could see where I was going.

Westward through Santa Fe, and then finally to the highway. I paused there and took a breath. Evony glanced over at me, gaze questioning.

"Are you ready for this?" I asked her.

"Probably not," she replied, and grinned. "But let's go for it anyway. The worst they can do is shoot us."

"Thanks."

She didn't stop smiling, though, and I pushed us up onto Highway 64, angling north and west.

To Los Alamos.

CHAPTER SEVEN

Oddly, the highway felt somewhat clearer than the roads. Maybe that was because it sat up high, and the wind had managed to blow some of the snow away. I doubted the open highways in this area had anything to do with the djinn, not in as exposed a spot as this.

And it did feel exposed, trundling along, never going more than twenty miles an hour or so. From time to time, I had to slow down even more than that to avoid stopped vehicles, the smaller ones almost buried in snow. I thought we would probably make it to Los Alamos before dark, even as creeping as our current pace felt, but it would be close.

After we'd pulled off Highway 64 onto 502, the road that led directly to the stronghold of the Immune, Evony finally broke the silence.

"Don't you wonder where the rest of them are?"

"The rest of who?" I asked, hands tight on the steering wheel. Right then I was really wishing that the Los Alamos crew had waited until the spring thaw to make their move and start kidnapping djinn. It would've made this whole situation a lot easier to deal with.

"The djinn." She glanced skyward, then over at me. "You know, the ones who didn't want to play nice and rescue any mortals. The ones who started this whole thing."

Damn, didn't we have enough to worry about already? "I hadn't really thought about it," I said carefully. "I guess I figured they were leaving us alone because we were Chosen, and they'd made a deal with the Thousand, the conscientious objectors."

"I suppose." Before we'd left, I'd set fresh bottles of water in the cupholders. She picked up her bottle now and cracked the cap, but she didn't drink, instead sitting there and tightening it and loosening it. "But what if they decide they don't want to leave us alone anymore?"

Despite myself, I couldn't help shooting an uneasy glance of my own upward, as if I expected to see a horde of djinn come screaming down out of the sky like a bunch of rage-fueled Valkyries. "I don't think they would do that. The other djinn—the Thousand—would never allow it."

"But there are only a thousand of them. Natila said there were twenty thousand djinn altogether. Talk about being outnumbered."

"Since when have you been such a buzzkill?" I demanded, my hands tightening even more around the steering wheel. At least focusing on driving kept me from brooding too much over her words. I had a feeling if I really allowed myself to start thinking about it, I'd seriously freak myself out, and I didn't have time for that.

She shrugged. "I don't know. I guess I'm just starting to get the heebie-jeebies. When I came to find you, I had a mission, and I guess I wasn't thinking about the whole thing. And when it was snowing, I felt, I don't know...more protected. Safer. Like those other djinn couldn't see me. Which I know is stupid, because it sounds like they can see pretty much whatever the hell they want, except in Los Alamos."

"Well, that should reassure you, then," I said. "Because none of the djinn can see anything in Los Alamos, thanks to that doohickey they have, which means that once we get there, we should be safe enough."

"Safe from *djinn*," she pointed out.

All right, that much was true. The bad djinn wouldn't be able to get to us there, but that didn't mean the mortal population couldn't do us plenty of harm if they wanted to.

I started rehearsing what I was going to say when we got there, making sure I had something of a coherent story straight in my head. The last thing I wanted was to start stammering all over the place like a guilty idiot the first time they started asking questions. I was going to say I got scared, being alone on the compound like that, and I wanted to be with my own kind. Evony had found me, and we'd decided that it was best for us to go to Los Alamos. As for our djinn lovers, well, we'd just been trying to stay alive, and had gone along with their wishes. The world had collapsed, and we didn't know what else to do. But now we'd finally realized what a mistake we'd made.

And so on.

Lying like that would feel terrible—even lying to the people in Los Alamos. It would seem like a repudiation of everything Jace and I had shared. But I would lie for the next hundred years to everyone I met if it meant getting him home safely. I couldn't worry about scruples right now. Not with so much at stake.

After we passed the outskirts of Española and began moving upward toward Los Alamos, the snow on the roadway decreased, leveling out so much that it was clear the Immune there must have been plowing it. Why, I wasn't sure, except that maybe it helped speed up any trips they might have made to go foraging. The pickings in Española wouldn't be as good as in Santa Fe, but it also wasn't nearly as far away.

And then I had to bring us to a stop just as we rounded a curve where the road split off between the 502 and the 30, because there was a barricade across the highway, with a bright yellow Hummer I knew all too well parked in front of it, and two men holding assault rifles standing there in the cold. One of them had a cigarette hanging out of his mouth; a thin line of smoke trailed upward into the cold, clear sky.

My heart began to pound, but I forced in a breath, trying the best I could to look calm as the man without the cigarette began to approach the Cherokee while his companion hung back, rifle pointed directly at our windshield. Beside me, Evony sat straight and unmoving, fingers clenched on the edge of her seat.

As the guard approached the driver-side window, he made a rolling-down motion with one hand. I pressed the button, and then tried not to gasp when I looked up into his face.

I knew this man.

All right, not really, but I did recognize him. The blond guard from the raid on my house, when they had taken Jace away.

His eyes widened behind his sunglasses, and I could tell he'd placed me, too. The gloved hands clutching the rifle relaxed almost infinitesimally, but I noticed.

"What the hell?" he began, then seemed to check himself. "That is, Ms. Monroe? What are you doing here?"

"Taking you guys up on your offer," I replied. A casual tone, but not *too* casual. If I sounded a bit worried, I wanted him to think it was because I didn't know for sure whether they would actually take me in.

A long pause. He took off his sunglasses—which weren't really necessary by that point, as the sun had begun to dip behind the mountains—and flicked a gaze past me to Evony. "Who are you?"

"Evony Rodriguez," she said. "I used to live in Española."

Again he hesitated, and then I saw him nod, as if he'd just placed her as another Chosen like me. "And what's this?" He pointed at the trailer we were towing.

"My livestock," I explained. "That is, five goats. We have a dozen chickens in the back. I stayed at the house because I didn't want to abandon the animals, but then I realized I just couldn't stay out there alone. I was hoping you might need some fresh eggs and milk."

His expression softened finally, and I realized he actually wasn't a bad-looking guy. In fact, once upon a time, if he'd come up to me in a bar and offered to buy me a drink, I doubted I would have declined. But I wasn't that girl anymore.

However, he didn't have to know that.

"We could use it," he said. "That's...generous of you, Ms. Monroe."

"Jessica," I put in, and he even smiled. Just a little, and it was gone in a flash, almost as if he didn't want his cigarette-smoking companion to see him getting too friendly.

"Jessica," he repeated. "I'm Dan Lowery. I can't leave my post here, but I'll radio ahead that you're here, and someone will meet you and show you where you can take your...goats. And then I'm pretty sure the commander will want to talk to you."

"Commander?"

"Captain Margolis. And he really is a captain," Dan added, as if he felt the need to explain further. "National Guard."

I remembered the big man with the short hair, the grim expression on his face as he'd looked at Jace. And I also recalled the way he'd looked at me. Not exactly professional, but, as I'd already told myself, with an interest I would definitely exploit if necessary.

"Okay," I said. "That's totally understandable. But—there'll be someplace for us, if you take us in?"

Another reluctant smile. "Not an issue. We've in-gathered a lot of Immune, but altogether, we're still not nearly what the population of the town was before the Dying."

No, I supposed it wouldn't be. I doubted there would ever be a town or city again that could get anywhere close to its pre-Dying population. Housing wouldn't be an issue for a long, long time.

I told him, "That's good to hear," and he nodded and stepped away, calling out to his companion that we were coming through.

The other guard stubbed out his cigarette, then climbed into the Hummer so he could pull it just far enough out of the center of the road that we'd be able to squeeze by. The entire time I was maneuvering past him, I kept expecting him to step on the gas and ram us or something, prevent us from going farther up the hill, but he didn't. We moved along without incident, then continued our climb into Los Alamos.

And it was quite a climb. Even though intellectually I'd known that the town was perched up in the Jemez Mountains, I hadn't really understood what that meant until we were twisting and turning up the two-lane highway, the trailer rattling along behind us, complete with some irritated bleats of protest from the goats inside. No wonder the Immune had chosen this place—this road would be dead easy to defend, and from what Evony had said, going out the back way wasn't any better.

At last the highway emerged onto a plateau, and the road widened into four lanes. Snow was piled high to either side of us, but the street itself was clear. Well, not entirely clear. Stopped directly ahead were two SUVs with light bars on top and some kind of blazon on the side, clearly law enforcement vehicles.

Knowing the drill a little better now, I slowed to a halt and waited as a man and a woman wearing dark uniforms with heavy parkas over them emerged from the first SUV and began walking toward us.

"Go directly to jail," Evony quipped. "Do not pass Go—"

"Very funny. The guard said the commander would want to talk to us, so I guess this is his way of guiding us in."

"Looks very welcoming."

I shot her a sour look but didn't say anything, mostly because I really didn't want the two approaching officers—or whoever they were—to hear us squabbling. Better to sit tight and wait to see what happened.

This time I rolled down the window right away. The woman peered in at us. I noticed the way her hand rested on the sidearm at her hip. "Jessica Monroe?"

"Yes," I replied, although I couldn't help wondering who the hell else she expected me to be.

"Step out of the vehicle, please," she said. "Your companion, too."

This really didn't feel good, but there wasn't much I could do about it. As I'd loaded my belongings into the Cherokee, I'd contemplated bringing along a couple of handguns, and maybe one of the rifles. I'd decided against it, though, worried that the Immune would get the wrong idea if they discovered a cache of weapons in the vehicle. And now, as Evony and I got out, and the male officer peered in the back of the Jeep to see the chickens there, along with Evony's weekender bag and my duffle, I was glad we were unarmed. Provoking a confrontation over a few guns would definitely be the wrong way to get started in Los Alamos.

"Officer Ortega here will take the livestock to a safe place," the female cop said.

Wait, what? Dan Lowery had made it sound as if I'd be the one driving to wherever the goats would be sheltered. And if they thought I'd let this Officer Ortega take off with my dad's Cherokee....

Then I saw again the way the female cop's right hand rested on the gun at her belt, and I realized getting in an argument about the Jeep probably wasn't that great an idea.

"Okay," I replied. "But can I get my dog out of the back seat? She goes everywhere with me."

To my surprise, the hard set of the woman's mouth softened slightly. "No problem. Go and get her."

I nodded and went over to the rear driver-side door of the Jeep, then opened it. Dutchie jumped right out, tail wagging. Since I was there anyway, I also retrieved Evony's and my bags, and carried them back over to where she and the female officer were waiting.

"Let me see inside those," the cop said.

Knowing any protests would be useless, I backed away a foot or so. The woman knelt and unzipped first my bag, then Evony's, and poked around in each of them. Since there wasn't anything more incriminating in there than toiletries and a few changes of clothes, she quickly closed the bags back up and got to her feet.

While she was occupied, her companion had gotten behind the wheel of the Cherokee. It hurt to see him slowly drive it off, but I forced myself to stand there and let it go. Los Alamos wasn't that big a town; I'd locate the Jeep again if they didn't seem too eager to give it back to me when I needed it.

"Your dog have a leash?" the female cop asked.

I nodded and pulled Dutchie's collar and leash from where I kept them coiled up in the outer zippered pocket of the backpack that held the rest of her supplies. These days, I really didn't bother with either of them, and the dog gave me a curious tilt of the head as I snapped her collar on. But again, it wasn't worth getting into an argument over.

"Okay," the officer said. "Come on, and I'll drive you over to the justice center."

Evony's eyebrows went up at an alarming angle. "Are we under arrest?"

Not even a quirk at the corner of the woman's mouth. She looked like she was probably in her early forties, with brown hair pulled into an intricate French braid and cool gray eyes. If she hadn't been a cop before the Heat struck, she'd still been...something. Maybe ex-military.

"No, you're not under arrest. But it's a hike up to the center, and the commander wants to talk to you ASAP. So let's go."

Evony and I exchanged a glance, then silently gathered up our bags and obediently followed the cop over to her SUV. She opened up the back so we could dump our bags in, and indicated that we should get in the back seat. Dutchie got the place of honor, riding shotgun, and, to my surprise, I saw the officer reach over to scratch behind my dog's ears before she slipped her key into the ignition. Dutchie, indiscriminate ho that she was, gave a big doggy smile.

Brat, I thought, but my inner amusement faded as we began to move, heading into the heart of town. Here, too, the streets were all plowed, the sidewalks shoveled. And I saw what appeared to be normal signs of life—vehicles on the street, almost all of them trucks and SUVs equipped with four-wheel drive; cars actually parked in the lot of the local Smith's grocery store; even a woman out at a park with a couple of kids, watching as they hurled snowballs at one another.

Kids. These were the first children I'd seen since the Heat swept through the population. There had to have been some children among the Immune, but I hadn't come across any in Albuquerque, and of course the djinn were preoccupied with their Chosen, so no children in Taos, either.

Well, I guess that means the djinn don't have any pedophiles among them, I thought, then wanted to shake my head at myself. But it was true. They obviously gravitated toward Immune who were young and good-looking, but that certainly wasn't a crime.

I could tell Evony was watching, too; her gaze was focused on the world outside the window, intent. However, her expression appeared to be very blank, for her. Not that I could claim to know her very well, not after only a few days in one another's company, but in general she seemed to wear her moods on her face. Was this glimpse at an almost normal world upsetting her somehow? Or was she just merely trying to practice her poker face for our interview with the commander?

That was an interview I could have lived without. Then again, I'd managed to face down Zahrias and lived to tell the tale, so I should be able to survive an encounter with a mere captain easily enough. Maybe. In the end, Zahrias had turned out to be—well, I wouldn't go so far as to call him an ally, but he was certainly far less scary than I'd imagined him to be.

We pulled off onto a side street, then into a parking lot that backed up to a large modern-looking building of brick and glass. Considering how rundown in appearance a lot of the municipal facilities in Albuquerque had been, I was a little surprised to see how nice this place was. It looked as if someone had had money to throw around in Los Alamos, small as it was.

"Go ahead and bring your bags," the officer instructed us. "You'll be getting your housing assignments here as well."

"'Housing assignments'?" Evony echoed. A flicker of worry passed over her face, and I could tell she was thinking we were going to get stuck in some kind of barracks apartment, something left over from the time when Los Alamos was Atomic City and they were building the Bomb here.

"The commander didn't want things to turn into a free-for-all with people squabbling over who would get which house, so now all newcomers have housing assignments." The female cop opened her door and got out, and so Evony and I followed suit, with Dutchie leaping across the driver's seat in her eagerness to follow us.

Again the cop flashed one of those incongruous smiles. In general, she seemed pretty tough, but I could tell she must be a dog person.

"But there's plenty to go around," she continued, handing me the trailing end of Dutchie's leash once I'd reclaimed my duffle bag from the back seat. "At the worst you'll get a townhome, but I think there are still a good number of regular houses available."

"That sounds fine," I said. "Very generous, actually."

A nod, and then she told us, "This way."

We followed her inside the building, which was just as clean-edged and modern on the inside as it was on the outside. There were a good number of people here—an older woman sitting at the desk in front, and then more men and women in uniform. Just how many people did they have in their police force, or whatever it was? Way more than you'd think the current population of the town would require, from the looks of it.

The female cop led us past the reception area and to an elevator. No worries about the power being on in Los Alamos, clearly. I wondered how they were doing it. Solar? Wind? Whatever its source, it seemed to be doing the job.

Once we reached the second floor, we headed down a hallway to an office suite, where a woman, casually gorgeous with long dark-honey hair, sat at the receptionist's desk. She smiled when she saw us, a contrast to our hard-faced escort. "Are these our newcomers?"

"Yes. Captain Margolis said he wanted to see them right away?"

"So he did. I'll send them in. Thanks, Nancy."

Nancy. The name didn't seem to fit the female cop very well, but I wasn't going to worry about it now. She gave us a sort of half-nod, then headed back toward the elevators, leaving us alone with the receptionist, or whoever she was.

"Do you mind if I watch your dog while you talk to Captain Margolis?" the woman asked. She was very pretty, so pretty that I wondered why some djinn hadn't snatched her up as his Chosen. But she did appear to be a few years older than I, and that could have been part of the reason. I hadn't seen anyone in the group in Taos who looked older than twenty-five.

"Sure," I said, handing over the leash. "Her name is Dutchie. I don't know how much work you'll get done with her around, though—she's kind of an attention whore."

"That's okay." She leaned down so she could scratch Dutchie behind the ears. "She's a beautiful dog. I'm Julia, by the way—Julia Innes."

"Nice to meet you," I said, and the words didn't feel that far off from the truth. She seemed pleasant enough, especially in contrast to Nancy, the poker-faced cop.

"And you're Evony, right?" she asked, looking past me to Evony, who stood there with her hands wrapped around the handle of her weekender bag.

"Yeah, that's me."

Julia blinked, seeming a little put off by the brittle reply. But then she straightened and essayed another smile. "Welcome to Los Alamos, both of you. Go on in—it's that door over there."

She pointed to a door on the other side of the reception area, which was decorated with high-quality photographs of the Los Alamos area, mountainscapes and images of pine forests and snowy hillsides. I really wished I could have loitered there for a few more minutes, chatting, just so I could have maybe gotten a bit more information out of her about Captain Margolis and what he really wanted from us.

That clearly wasn't going to happen, though, and so I gave Dutchie one last pat on the head and then went over to the door, Evony right behind me.

You can do this, I told myself, wrapping my fingers around the handle and pulling the door open. *Just sell it, and sell it good.*

The office was a large one, with a big desk of dark oak and matching bookcases along the walls, all filled with legal-looking books. I had a feeling the office had once belonged to the local assistant D.A. or someone along those lines, but obviously he didn't need it anymore. A silvery laptop lay closed on the desk, and next to it was a stack of papers and a walkie-talkie. One window overlooked the street outside, and standing by that window was Captain Margolis.

He turned as Evony and I entered, a smile on his features that was about a hundred times less believable than the one Julia Innes had worn. Now that I was facing him in a much less turbulent environment than the one when he and his men had abducted Jace, I was able to get a clearer look at him—big and broad-shouldered, although with a bit of a gut straining over his belt, dark close-cropped hair, features regular enough but stopping short of actually being attractive.

Or maybe he would have been attractive to someone else, someone who didn't hate him quite so much.

"Ms. Monroe," he said, then hesitated, his gaze barely moving past me to Evony before it returned to settle on me. "And Ms. Rodriguez. I have to say I was a little surprised to hear that you'd come to Los Alamos."

"Well," I began. I'd resolved to do the talking, but now I realized that wasn't entirely fair to Evony. But out of the corner of my eye, I could see her shake her head slightly, and I took that to mean she was just fine with me being the spokeswoman. "I know I told you that I didn't have any intention of coming here, but—"

"But?" he interrupted. He stepped away from the window and went over to his desk but didn't sit down behind it, instead electing to lean up against its front, arms crossed as he stared at me. His eyes were dark, and set too close together.

"But I didn't like being there alone. It was—well, it was a little scary, if you want to know the truth." There, I'd made my false admission. So what if it made me sound like a helpless female? I *wanted* him to think I was a helpless female. Then he wouldn't expect much from me.

"Alone?" Again he glanced at Evony, and this time his mouth twisted slightly. "Even though you had Ms. Rodriguez there with you?"

His tone held the faintest hint of a leer, as if he had visualized some hot girl-on-girl action between Evony and me, even though he had to know I didn't exactly swing that way. Or maybe that was just his way of attempting to put me off-balance.

"Only for a couple of days," I said. "She was frightened to be left alone, too, and when I told her how you'd said it was okay for me to come here to Los Alamos if I ever changed my mind, well, she wanted to do that, too."

For a few seconds, he didn't respond, but just stood there, watching us. Or rather, watching me. After that last dismissive glance at Evony, she might as well not have existed for him. Maybe in a way, she didn't. She wasn't interested in men, and therefore he had no interest in her. Whereas I...

...well, I was fresh meat, in a manner of speaking.

"Besides," I went on, thinking my flimsy story needed a bit more ballast, "there was someone prowling around the house. The cameras caught movement, but I couldn't see for sure who it was."

Margolis' gaze sharpened on me. "Did they try to break in?"

"No, but they pulled on the padlock on the gate. I had to lock it up that way after—well, after your men got in the first time. But for all I knew, whoever was prowling around planned to come back with a set of bolt cutters and let himself in. I couldn't take that risk."

"Didn't you have guns at the house?"

"Yes, but I'm not a very good shot," I lied, giving him what I hoped was a realistic shrug. Maybe I couldn't exactly drill a hole in a dime at fifty yards, but in general, if I shot at something, I hit it. The commander didn't need to know that, however.

"And I've never shot a gun at all," Evony put in. "Well, unless you count video games."

The look he sent in our direction after her contribution to the conversation was positively condescending, and I forced myself not to react. I wanted him to be condescending and macho and therefore, hopefully, blind and unaware.

Then he nodded, pushing himself up from the desk so he could move toward us. He put a hand on my shoulder in a gesture he probably thought was intended to be reassuring, but instead just made me want to take a bath.

"Well," he said, "I can see why you girls would want to take refuge out here. Truth is, the world isn't safe. We've had a lot of the Immune gather here, and they're good people, but there are still others out in the wild who see the collapse of society as a good thing, who want to take advantage of anyone they come across. You wouldn't have stood a chance, not in the long run."

"So," I replied, attempting to look as big-eyed and concerned as I possibly could, "you'll let us stay?"

"Of course I will. It wouldn't be Christian otherwise." His fingers tightened on my shoulder, and I tried not to shudder.

"Welcome to Los Alamos."

CHAPTER EIGHT

AFTER THE INTERVIEW, HE HANDED US OFF TO Julia, saying she'd take care of us, that he had a meeting at the labs he had to attend. What they were doing up at the laboratory facility, I had no idea, but I guessed it had something to do with those hideous little boxes, the ones that effectively destroyed the power of the djinn.

"I've got a nice place over on Alamo Road," Julia told us after firing up her computer and flicking through a few screens. The minute I'd showed back up, Dutchie trotted over to me, tail wagging, and I took her leash in one hand. I trusted her to stay put, but it felt more polite to keep her close by until we left the office. "Sara Garcia was staying there, but then she moved in with Jim Michelson. Three bedrooms, so there's plenty of space for the two of you. That is...I assume you'll want to stay together?"

"Yes," I said firmly, even as Evony put in,

"Yeah, we're staying together, but we're not *together,* if you know what I mean."

Julia didn't bat an eye. "No, of course not. That is, I assumed, since Jessica was with...." At that point she did break off, looking a little flustered, and I filed her reaction away mentally to follow up later. It seemed clear enough that she knew something about Jace's and my relationship, which made me wonder if he might be right in this very building somewhere. It was the justice center, after all, so possibly there were jail cells located here as well.

I knew I couldn't ask. No, I'd have to spend some time with these people, convince them that I was one of them, before I could even begin to inquire about Jace. Still, Julia Innes' friendly expression gave me some hope. Maybe she would be sympathetic, once she knew the truth. In the meantime, I'd have to pretend I was oblivious to my djinn lover's fate, that I'd seen the error of my ways.

"Anyway," Julia went on, recovering herself, "Lindsay cleaned it up before she moved out, so it should be ready to go. I'll take you over there now."

Evony and I murmured our thanks, and Julia picked up the handset from the phone on her desk before pressing a few buttons. "Hannah? It's Julia. I have to drive the new arrivals to the house on Alamo Road. The commander is at a meeting at the lab, so it should be pretty quiet up here. Just keep an eye out for me, could you? Thanks."

She hung up, then gave me an inquisitive look as I stood there, goggling at the phone.

"What is it?"

"That," I said, pointing at the telephone, one of those multi-line deals you'd see at your doctor's office or something. "Just...you using the phone. It's like...it's like it never happened."

As usual, I didn't have to explain what I meant by "it."

"Oh." A shrug, followed by, "Well, with the power on, it's really not that big a deal. This is just an internal system. Obviously, the outside lines don't work, because we don't have anyone we could be calling, you know?"

"So there's no one else?" Evony asked. "No other survivors?"

Julia had bent down to retrieve her purse from the bottom drawer of her desk. As she straightened up, the pleasant expression she'd been wearing abruptly disappeared. "There was a group of survivors down in Las Cruces. A couple hundred of them, from what they told us. They'd gathered there from the surrounding areas. We were talking with them on the ham radio, trying to set up a way that they could get up here safely and join us. And then...nothing."

A chill went over me, because I had a sinking feeling what that radio silence might have meant. "Nothing?"

"We lost contact. No replies to our calls. We argued for a while about whether we should send a team to see what had happened, but we only had the one device at the time, and it wouldn't have been safe."

By "device," I figured she must have been talking about the little black box the man had been carrying when the Los Alamos team captured Jace. So did that mean they had more than one now? They must, or I had a feeling they wouldn't have made their foray out to my house in Santa Fe. One to take with them to capture a djinn, and another to stay behind in Los Alamos and protect them from the rest of the vengeful elementals, the ones who hadn't bothered with any foolishness about the "Chosen."

And I realized then what must have happened to the survivors in Las Cruces. They had no such protection, and the djinn must have wiped them out. Just another stop in their worldwide destruction tour.

It looked as if Evony had come to the same conclusion, since her expression had turned fairly grim, for her. "Anyone besides that?"

"We were in contact with two other groups— Colorado Springs and Flagstaff. They've both gone dark." Julia's full mouth tightened, and then she pulled a set of keys out of her purse, saying, "Come on. Let me show you where you'll be living."

I could tell she didn't want to talk about it anymore, and I couldn't blame her. Just the thought of those small groups out there, coming together, struggling for survival, only to be wiped out by the kind of enemy they couldn't possibly fight, made my stomach clench. To those djinn, we humans weren't worthy of any kind of consideration. Just insects to be wiped out so they could enjoy a pest-free world. It made me wonder why Jace and the rest of the Thousand were different, how it was that they could see humans were worth saving, that we deserved the same love and consideration they would show to members of their own race.

Maybe I'd never know for sure. It could simply be a difference in temperament, an openness, a tolerance that the other djinn, the evil, destructive elementals, didn't share.

I hoped I'd someday have the chance to ask Jace.

Evony and I followed Julia out of the office and to the elevator, which we took to the first floor. She waved at the receptionist there and led us through the rear entrance to the building, one which opened on a staff parking lot. Waiting there was a big black Suburban, the kind you tended to see in films and TV shows being used by government agents. Evony took shotgun, while I climbed into the back seat so Dutchie could sit beside me. I hoped Julia wouldn't mind a bit of dog hair on the upholstery.

As she backed out of her parking space, she said, "We're closing in on five hundred people now. Los Alamos used to have a population of a little more than twelve thousand, so we're far from full, but we're not completely empty, either."

"Are you expecting more?" Evony asked.

A pause, and then Julia replied, "After what happened in Las Cruces...I don't know. Maybe stragglers who come in by ones and twos. I think anyplace people were gathering in a group, they attracted too much attention. But we're still holding out some hope that there might be a few more who've been hiding as best they can."

There wasn't much either of us could say in response to that, and so Evony and I were both silent as Julia drove us through the snow-plowed streets of Los Alamos. She turned off the main road and headed into a residential area of modest but well-kept homes. The sidewalks here also seemed mostly cleared, and some of the driveways had vehicles parked in them, more trucks and SUVs.

"We'll let you settle in tonight, but after that you'll need to come back to the justice center and get your work assignments," she went on.

"Uh...work assignments?" I ventured. That didn't sound like much fun.

"Oh, yes...everyone works here." She turned again, skirting the edge of a park, this one deserted, the playground equipment still dusted with snow. "We do our best to match you up with something you did... before...but we all have to pitch in. So what did you two do?"

"I was a waitress," Evony said.

A little silence. Then Julia said, her tone almost too bright, "Well, that'll be helpful. We've opened a couple of the restaurants here as gathering places, although we're still working on getting them up to speed. Do you know anything about cooking?"

"No."

Another pause. Julia gave a quick glance back over her shoulder at me before returning her attention to the road. "What about you, Jessica?"

"I was getting my master's in English, so I was a T.A. for a couple of lower-division courses." In other words, completely useless.

Julia didn't seem to think so, however. "Oh, that's great to hear. We have eight kids in Los Alamos now, ranging from nine to sixteen. We've been doing our best to keep up with their schooling, but none of the survivors here were teachers."

"Well, I wasn't really a teacher, either," I began, but she just shook her head.

"More so than any of us. It would be a great help to have someone who knows what they're doing."

"Maybe," I said, my tone sounding reluctant even to me. "That is, I could help with English and history and that kind of thing, but please don't expect me to teach them trig."

"No, we have Miles for that...if we can tear him away from the lab."

"Who's Miles?" Evony asked.

"He's a scientist at the lab. The only scientist now, unfortunately." Julia fell silent for a few seconds, as if deciding how much she really wanted to tell us. "You'll meet him eventually, I suppose, although he doesn't socialize much."

If this Miles was the person I'd seen holding the black box, then I could understand him not getting out too often. He had the appearance of someone who only seemed marginally aware that a world existed around him. And if he was the only surviving scientist from the government labs here, then that meant he had to be the person who'd invented those djinn-damaging boxes. How, I had no idea, but who knows what they'd been working on up at that facility....

My musings were interrupted by Julia pulling into the driveway of a small freshly painted one-story house. I couldn't help gaping, simply because sitting in that driveway was my Cherokee, sans horse trailer, goats, and, presumably, chickens.

I must have looked pretty gobsmacked, because Julia laughed and said, "When I told Hannah I was bringing you here, she radioed the men who were taking your goats over to the horse facility and let them know where they could drop off your car. You look surprised...did you think we were going to keep it?"

Somehow I remembered to shut my mouth. "Um, well...."

"It's okay. We've commandeered a lot of similar vehicles over the past few months, but never anything that actually belonged to someone. Anyway, let me show you your new place."

She got out of the Suburban. Evony and I followed suit, bringing our meager luggage with us, Dutchie in the rear, tail wagging at the prospect of exploring someplace new and exciting. The front walk was a little icy, but I managed to keep my footing as we made our way to the front door. Julia produced a key from her purse and let us in. It was very cold, and she went at once to the thermostat and pushed it up.

"All-electric house," she explained. "We're trying to stay out of the ones with gas heating because we haven't gotten the natural-gas lines working yet."

I paused in the living room and surveyed my surroundings as Evony went on to the dining room and set her weekender bag on the table there. The carpet looked a little worn, but it was clean, and the furniture was the sort of simple stuff you'd see being sold in inexpensive groupings at your local big-box store. After the luxury of the house Jace had found for me in Santa Fe, it didn't look like much. But it was definitely better than nothing.

I let Dutchie off her leash, and she started sniffing around. Luckily, I knew she was very well-behaved and would wait until I took her for a walk or let her out in the backyard before going potty, no matter what kinds of interesting smells she might find in the house.

One thing I did notice was that there didn't seem to be any personal touches anywhere—no family photographs sitting on the mantel of the brick fireplace, or houseplants, or anything like that. I raised an inquiring eyebrow at Julia.

She seemed to understand my question, saying, "We try to go through the houses and remove any personal items that belonged to the former owners—photographs, legal documents, that kind of thing. We need the housing, but we don't want to be intrusive, if you know what I mean."

I did. Yes, the people who'd once lived here certainly didn't need the place anymore, but that shouldn't give us survivors the right or permission to go pawing through their things.

"The clothing is taken to the local Goodwill, which we use for pretty much the same purpose—sorting items and then displaying them so they can be reused. We don't charge anything for them, though."

"You don't?" Evony asked, coming back into the living room. "How...socialist...of you."

This time, Julia didn't smile. "Well, we're not too worried about money right now. Captain Margolis and

I are working out a barter system, or at least a system of hours worked in exchange for certain items, but it's still in the preliminary stages. There are plenty of clothes to go around right now, though. With food, everyone gets a certain ration. I'll explain all of that when you come by tomorrow for your formal work assignments."

That was so not what I'd thought I was signing up for when I formulated my plan to come here, and I got the same impression from Evony, judging by the eye roll she gave me. I had to hope Julia wouldn't notice it. If she did, she showed no reaction that I could see. But then again, I didn't know her at all, so I had no way of knowing how good she was at hiding her feelings.

"You'll probably get a bit more in the way of rations, just because you contributed your goats and chickens, and that's going to help everyone. In the meantime, though, you should probably come down to Pajarito's. I'll get you settled with some dinner."

"Pajarito's?" I asked.

"It's one of the local restaurants." She shook her head, as if correcting herself, and went on, "That is, it *used* to be one of the restaurants here in town. We've sort of resurrected it as a hangout because it's centrally located and looks nice, and when we're in there, well...." It wasn't quite a sigh, but she let out a little breath, looking wistful. "Well, I guess we sort of pretend that nothing has changed. There are a couple of people who like to cook and prepare different things every night, depending on what's available. I just thought you might like to eat there tonight, meet a few people, especially since there really isn't any food in the house yet except some dry cereal. You can get some regular supplies later, including anything you need for your dog."

This Pajarito's place sounded like it could be...well, maybe not precisely fun, but at least a place where Evony and I could meet some more of the locals and get a better feel for exactly what was going on here. With Julia as our guide, it should be fairly safe.

"Okay," I said. "That sounds like fun. What time?"

"I'm off shift at six. Pajarito's is on Trinity Road—here, let me draw you a map." She pulled a small notepad out of her purse and swiftly drew in the major streets, and then traced a line from the house to the restaurant. I must have raised an eyebrow at her or showed some other sign of surprise, because she said, "I've been doing this for most of the new arrivals, so I've gotten familiar with the town pretty quickly."

"So you're not from here?" Evony asked, leaning past me to look down at the sketch Julia had just made.

"No, Albuquerque." She didn't seem to want to elaborate, so I didn't press her on the subject. If I were lucky, maybe she'd open up later. I'd really like to hear her story, how she'd gotten out of the city. When I was making my escape, I really hadn't seen anyone else. Then again, Albuquerque was a big place, and of course

I had no idea how long she'd stayed there before beginning her own trek northward.

"Anyway," she went on, "I've got to get back to the office. If you need anything, well, you'll need to stop by to ask for it, since the phones aren't working, but I think you should be set. There are clean linens in the hall closet, and the water is on, and if something does come up, let me know when you see me in a few hours."

"We will," I promised, and she smiled and said goodbye, then let herself out.

The door shut, leaving Evony and Dutchie and me alone in our new home. Temporary home, of course. I was only planning to be here long enough to find out where Jace and Natila were being kept, then come up with a plan to get them out. After that, well, I supposed it would be back to Taos. I ached to go back to Santa Fe, to the home Jasreel and I had made together, but returning there would be foolish. The chances of being recaptured were far too high. We would have to depend on the safety in numbers that Taos promised.

"Home sweet home," Evony remarked, looking around.

"It's fine," I said, my tone a little more severe than I'd intended, most likely because I'd been unfavorably comparing the place to the Santa Fe house, which wasn't fair. Before the Dying, I would have killed to have a house like this, instead of that tiny apartment over my parents' garage where I'd been living.

"Oh, I know," she replied. "I mean, I was living in a shitty duplex before. I can't complain. So let's go check out the bedrooms and fight over who gets the master."

We ended up flipping a coin for it—I still had some change in my wallet, money that would probably never get spent—and I lost. To her credit, Evony didn't crow too much, but I could tell she was feeling a bit satisfied that things didn't always go my way.

Right then I wasn't sure they really did. True, I'd been getting more attention than she had since we came to town, but some of it—namely from Captain Margolis—I could have done without. And it seemed as if she was content to let me take the lead in things, so how else did she expect it all to shake out? Maybe that was uncharitable. I really didn't know her all that well, except I could tell that she'd had a pretty tough time before the Heat came along. Losing Natila just when it probably seemed as if life was finally going her way had to have been a terrible blow for Evony.

In the meantime, the secondary bedroom that had ended up as mine was small but clean, with a double bed, a nightstand, a dresser, and not much else. I hung up my sparse wardrobe in the closet or put it away in drawers, depending on what it was, then took my cosmetic bag and set it under the sink in the hall bathroom.

Not that I didn't take Julia's word for it, but I went ahead and turned the tap on and off, just to be sure.

Yes, the water really worked, and had decent pressure, too. Showers shouldn't be a problem. All the comforts of civilized living, really, and I knew I should be grateful for them. It was a lot easier to think straight when you were clean and warm and well-fed.

Speaking of which....

I got out the bag with Dutchie's things, including her supply of dog food, and headed into the kitchen. It was small but, like everything else in the house, clean. Someone seemed to have put a little more love into this room rather than the rest of the house; the countertops were tile, the floor laminate, and the cabinets appeared to have a fresh coat of varnish on them. It looked to me as if the previous owners had planned to spruce up the place and had started with the kitchen.

Thinking about that, about who those people might have been, only saddened me, though. They were gone, along with so many others, and I didn't know if anyone would ever finish putting this house together. I supposed the supplies to do so were still out there in the stores, if anyone could get past the basics of survival to worry about such things, but....

Dutchie came padding into the kitchen then, and I was glad of the distraction, glad that I could pet her and tell her what a good girl she was, and then get some bowls out of one of the cupboards so I could pour her some fresh water and feed her. It was a little early, since by then it wasn't even five o'clock, but she'd never had her lunch.

"And then we'll go for a walk, okay?" I told her, and she lifted her head from her bowl long enough to wag her tail and show me she thought that was a great idea.

"Really?" Evony said, appearing in the doorway. Her hair was brushed and her lipstick freshened, so I could tell what she'd been doing to occupy her time. "Do you think that's a good idea?"

"Why not? We've got to get to know the neighborhood sometime, don't we?"

"I suppose. I just didn't think you were going to go all suburbia on me."

I leaned against the counter and crossed my arms. "I'm not. But we have to blend in and act normal, right? So walking the dog seems like something people would do in a new house."

There was a window over the kitchen sink, so I pushed the curtains out of the way and peered out. Immediately outside was the side yard, with some dormant rosebushes in a brick planter, and just beyond the roses a wooden fence. A slightly larger, two-story house stood next door, but from this vantage point I couldn't tell whether it was occupied or not. The blinds were shut, and no smoke rose from the chimney. It would make our lives a lot easier if it turned out the houses on either side of us were empty, but I couldn't count on that.

Since Evony still didn't look all that convinced, I said, "Think of it as reconnoitering. But you don't have to come along if you don't want to."

"Yeah, I'll stay here, thanks. Trudging around in the snow and slipping on the ice, just to walk a dog, doesn't sound like much fun."

I didn't think it would be all that bad. Someone had shoveled the sidewalks around here, and I'd just have to do my best to avoid the ice.

At hearing the "W" word, Dutchie came over to me and whined.

"That's right, sweetie—we're going."

Evony only shook her head and headed out to the living room, while I paused to pick up my coat from where I'd draped it over one of the dining room chairs. The sun was up—barely—but I knew it was still right around freezing outside.

Once I was bundled up, Dutchie and I went out the front door. I didn't bother to lock it; the house key was still lying where Julia had left it on the dining room table.

Frigid air touched my face, but it felt good to breathe it in, to move down the sidewalk and watch Dutchie's tail wagging frantically as she got ready to explore a whole new neighborhood. The house to my left, the one I'd seen through the kitchen window,

didn't have any cars parked in the driveway, reinforcing my hunch that it was empty, and neither did the
one on the other side. Directly across the street, however, was a big two-story with a Chevy Avalanche out
front and smoke rising from the chimney, so someone
definitely occupied that one. For all I knew, they were
watching Dutchie and me as we progressed along the
sidewalk, but there wasn't much I could do about that.

I began mentally rehearsing my story again, just in
case someone did come outside, but apparently they
weren't in the mood to brave the cold just to meet their
new neighbors, and the street remained deserted. We
hadn't gone far before Dutchie took care of business,
so to speak, and I took one of the biodegradable waste
bags off the roll I'd put in my pocket and picked up her
mess. At least that way if anyone was spying, they'd see
me being a responsible citizen.

During the whole time—well, the whole ten minutes we were outside, anyway—I did my best not to
think about Jace, about how he had to be hidden somewhere here in town. The justice center seemed the most
logical place, but there could be others. For all I knew,
they had him secreted away somewhere in the labs so
they could perform tests on him or something....

No. I shut that thought down before it could progress any further. Not that I would put it past this Miles
person or Captain Margolis, necessarily, but stressing
myself out wasn't going to help the situation any, and

in fact would only make it worse. In less than a hour I'd be going to meet a bunch of the locals, and I had to be on my best behavior. I couldn't ask any pointed questions or show too much interest in the Los Alamos group's captive djinn, or I'd be finished before I even got started. I had to make myself believe that Jace and Natila were fine for now. Well, as fine as they could be, locked up somewhere. But whole and healthy at least.

I came back to the house and stamped off what little snow my boots had managed to collect, then let myself inside. Evony was sitting on the couch in the living room, flipping through a six-month-old copy of *InStyle*. Apparently the people who'd gone through and cleared out the house hadn't thought the magazine was personal enough that it required removal, possibly because I didn't see a subscription label anywhere on it.

"Getting ready for your beach look early?" I asked, and she grimaced.

"I wish. I wish it was safe to just go around without worrying about mad scientists or crazy djinn or whatever. Just me and Natila on her Harley, heading for the coast. I'd stick my toes in the Pacific and never look back."

That did sound inviting. I'd never been to California. I asked Evony if she had, and she shook her head.

"Are you kidding? The farthest west I ever got was a trip to the Grand Canyon when I was ten." She tossed the magazine on the coffee table and stood up. "Please tell me you're going to change before we go back out."

I unzipped my parka and went to hang it in the coat closet. "Why should I? It's not like I'm going to Pajarito's to pick up guys or something."

"So what? *You* know that's not why you're going, but *they* don't have to know that. We're the new girls in town. We need to make a good impression. I'll loan you my green sweater again."

It probably wasn't worth wasting time arguing about. "Fine," I said. "But I'm doing my own makeup."

"Deal." Then she hesitated, eyes narrowing. "You did bring some makeup, didn't you?"

"Yes." Not much, but some. Even I wasn't so naïve as to think a little sprucing up wouldn't be in order. After all, I didn't know who I was going to have to sweet-talk to get what I wanted.

Because believe me, I had every intention of getting the one thing I wanted from this town.

Jace.

CHAPTER NINE

Apparently, Evony was satisfied with the job I'd done, because after giving me a critical once-over, she nodded. "You clean up pretty good, Monroe."

"Why, thanks, Rodriguez."

She grinned, and we went to put on our coats and get in the car. Whoever had dropped it off at the new house had left the keys in the ignition; clearly, auto theft wasn't something we'd need to worry about here. Then again, why would it be? Everyone who needed a vehicle had already been provided with one.

I spotted a few cars going the opposite direction as we headed into town, and none around us, so it seemed as though most people preferred to eat at home if possible. Julia had indicated that the woman who'd lived in our house before us had moved in with someone else, meaning that the members of the Los Alamos group were beginning to pair up and start new relationships. I supposed that was a good thing. It showed people were moving on, thinking of the future. They must have had a good deal of faith in Captain Margolis' leadership abilities, or at least in the devices this Miles person had invented. I wondered how many of those boxes he'd made so far. Just another bit of knowledge to dig up, if possible.

The restaurant was located in a shopping center, so we didn't have to park on the street. And even though I'd seen people passing us as they went home for the evening, I still counted about a dozen cars in the parking lot here, meaning there had to be a decent-sized crowd at Pajarito's.

I swallowed. It had been bad enough to walk into that crowd of Chosen in Taos. At least they were friendly, or more or less on my side. Here, if these people knew anything at all about me and Evony, then they'd know we'd been with a djinn before coming here. I had to pray that they'd buy our somewhat abrupt change of heart.

Then I spotted Julia's black Suburban and felt a little better, knowing that she was already here, and, if my brief acquaintance with her was any indication, thoughtfully saving us a table. I slung my purse over my shoulder and got out of the Cherokee, while Evony did the same. Once or twice I slipped on a patch of ice as

I made my way to the restaurant door, but I did manage to get there without going ass over teakettle. That would've been a really auspicious start to the evening. Those djinn had the right idea, using the fire and air elementals among them to make sure that all the walkways around Taos were clear. Unfortunately, I had a feeling that even useful djinn wouldn't be too welcome here in Los Alamos.

Taking a breath, I wrapped my fingers around the handle of the door and pushed it inward. A rush of warm air hit my face, overlaid with the welcome scents of food cooking—garlic and butter and a few other things I couldn't identify but which made my deprived stomach growl. As I made a quick scan of the restaurant, trying to ignore the curious and sometimes hostile looks shot in my direction, I spotted Julia Innes sitting at a booth along the far wall, in a nice inconspicuous corner.

Well, it would've been inconspicuous if Evony and I hadn't had to cross the whole place to get to that booth. I strode forward, my chin up, and forced myself not to make eye contact with anyone. At my side, Evony did more or less the same, although I got a challenging vibe radiating off her, something that seemed to say, *You want to fuck with me? Go right ahead.*

Please God that no one would take her up on it.

We made it to Julia's booth without anyone saying anything or stopping us. I blew out a breath of relief as

I dropped onto the empty seat, Evony sliding in next to me.

"I see you found the place okay," Julia said. She had a glass of white wine in front of her, but no food.

Thank God there was booze. I knew I was going to need it.

"Oh, yeah," I replied. "Your map made it easy."

"I went ahead and ordered us some truffle fries," she went on, smiling. "Obviously, we can't maintain exactly the same menu that the original restaurant had, but the fries were a favorite, so we've managed to keep them available so far."

"And the beer, looks like," Evony said, her gaze resting on the line of taps at the bar.

"That, too. I think they'd gotten in several shipments right before the Heat hit, so we were stocked to begin with, and then our foraging teams picked up more stuff when they went out to Santa Fe."

"All the comforts of home," I remarked.

"We do our best. Speaking of home, how is the new place?"

"It's great. Thank you so much for getting us placed so quickly."

Julia looked pleased and opened her mouth to reply, but right then a girl around Evony's age, maybe even younger, came up and asked what we'd like to drink. She kept shooting inquisitive looks at us as she took our orders, mine for a glass of malbec, Evony's for some Lumberyard ale. I thought I knew what those glances were all about—she wanted to get an eyeful of the two women who'd supposedly had djinn lovers. Thankfully, though, she didn't say anything on that subject, but only told us she'd be back in a few minutes with our drinks. Most likely Julia's presence there had kept her from really attempting to pry.

"I noticed the houses next to ours seemed to be empty," I began, and she nodded.

"Yes, they're both on natural gas for their central heating, so we haven't placed anyone there yet. We're working on getting that straightened out, but right now we have enough inventory that we're doing okay."

"It must be a logistical nightmare, having to juggle everything," I said. Thinking of Lauren in Taos, the former executive assistant, I added, "Were you an admin or something before? Because I don't think I could manage what you do."

For some reason, the compliment didn't seem to please her. Julia tapped her finger on the base of her wine glass, her gaze not quite meeting mine. "I was a paralegal at a busy law firm. So I'm sort of used to juggling fifty things at once, all of which have to be done right now."

"Margolis a pain to work for?" Evony inquired. Judging by her tone, she already had her own ideas on that score.

"He's...demanding," Julia allowed. "But I understand why. We're not having to start exactly from scratch here, but it can be tough getting people to fit in and do what the community needs."

Including conscripting me for teaching duty. I really wasn't looking forward to that. Never mind that I'd had vague plans to go into teaching once I was done with my master's, mostly because what the heck else was I supposed to do with a master's degree in English? But those plans had been to teach high school, not the lower grades, and Julia's comment that there were kids ranging from nine to sixteen hadn't exactly filled me with confidence. Well, I'd worry about that tomorrow when I went in to get my work assignment. Stressing about it now would only ruin my evening.

"I suppose it would be tough." Evony's expression wasn't exactly thrilled, either, and I had a feeling she wasn't looking forward to ending up here at Pajarito's or one of the other eating establishments they'd kept open here in town, serving drinks and food to people who'd been doing far more interesting things than waiting tables all day. Well, maybe she had some other skills that could be put to use. We hadn't had much of a chance to discuss the situation.

Speaking of servers, the girl came back right then with our drinks and set them down, then flitted back to the kitchen and returned with a huge plate of heavenly-smelling fries. I inhaled the aroma and thought maybe Los Alamos wouldn't be so bad after all.

"You can get something more substantial after this," Julia said. "But I figured the fries would be a good place to start."

I had to agree with her on that one. Evony reached for the same fry as I did at the same time, and we both laughed as we withdrew our hands and selected a different one. They were marvelous, sprinkled with parmesan cheese and drizzled with truffle oil.

"I can see why you kept those on the menu," I said, after I'd eaten a couple and then taken a sip of my wine. It wasn't nearly as good as the fries, but I was willing to overlook its shortcomings, just because of the effect it would have on me. Some of the tension began to leave my shoulders as I drank some more malbec.

"Good, aren't they?" Julia had also helped herself to a few more swallows of her wine, and she, too, looked a little more relaxed than when Evony and I had first sat down in the booth. Despite my comparing her to Lauren, Julia and Zahrias' Girl Friday back in Taos really weren't that much alike. Lauren seemed sunny and cheerful to the point that I had to wonder whether she'd been a pageant girl once upon a time, whereas there was something sad and closed-off about Julia, despite her smiles and welcoming attitude.

"They're awesome," Evony said. She lifted her pint glass and saluted the two of us. "Here's to the beer never running out."

"Well, I'm more of a wine drinker, but I'll drink to that anyway." Julia clinked her glass against Evony's, and then against mine. "Captain Margolis thought it was important for the community here to have this sort of place to come to if we want. Helps to maintain an atmosphere of normality."

My estimation of the commander rose a notch. All right, I still hated him for taking Jace away, but at least he didn't seem to be quite the tyrant I had expected.

"Very forward-thinking man, Captain Margolis," Evony said, gulping back more of her beer. She probably needed to slow down, or she'd be finished with that pint long before I was done with my much more modest glass of wine.

Then a shadow seemed to fall over our booth, and I looked up to see two large men standing there, both wearing unpleasant smiles on their faces. Something about them seemed vaguely familiar, and I thought they might have been among the crew that had seized Jace several days ago. I hadn't had any real interactions with them at the time, not the way I had with Dan Lowery, and so I couldn't be positive as to their identity. Even so, I felt myself stiffen, my fingers tightening around the stem of my wine glass.

Their appearance had put Julia on alert, too; I could see the way her jaw tightened and she took in a breath, almost as if bracing herself for some sort of confrontation.

"Well, look who's here," the one who was standing slightly closer to our table said. "It's our two little djinn-fuckers."

I couldn't say that kind of comment was completely unexpected, but even so I felt my gut clench and my heart begin to pound. Beside me, Evony choked on the mouthful of beer she'd just swallowed.

"There's no need for that, Mitch," Julia said, her voice quiet enough, but underlaid with a trace of steel. "Jessica and Evony have had a change of heart. They're with us now."

"Oh, yeah?" Mitch inquired, rocking back slightly on his heels. From his reddened eyes and the general air of blurriness that accompanied him, I guessed he'd had more than a few beers to drink. You'd think they'd have the sense to stop serving someone when he went over the edge, but maybe whoever was pouring the drinks didn't have the nerve to say no to one of Margolis' enforcers. "That still doesn't change what they did."

"Actually, I think it does." Julia's tone didn't alter one bit, and she stared up at Mitch as if she wasn't a bit worried that he probably outweighed her by at least a hundred pounds. "You ever done something you regretted, something you tried to fix later?"

"Uh...." He frowned, as if trying to work that one out. I had a feeling he wasn't the sharpest tack in the box even when he wasn't drunk. Then his gaze sharpened just a little. "Well, maybe. But nothing like that."

In another situation, I might have thrown a "to err is human" quote in there, but I had no idea how this Mitch person would react to a remark like that. It was probably better to keep my mouth shut and let Julia handle this.

She said, "We're just trying to have a quiet meal here. If all this is okay with the commander, then it should be okay with you, too."

Obviously, Mitch hadn't considered that side of the argument, because he glanced back at his compatriot, who shrugged, then stepped forward, leering at Evony.

"Hey, sweetie, now that you've given up that djinn bitch, how about you let a real man show you how it's done?"

Without blinking, Evony responded, "Sure. If you see a real man anywhere around here, send him on over."

Oh, shit. The second guy, who was probably almost as drunk as Mitch, tilted his head slightly as he attempted to process her remark. Then his brows lowered, and he said, "You think you're pretty cute, don't you? Well, you're not going to have the ice queen here around to protect you all the time."

"Butch," Julia said, still in that clear, quiet tone. "That's enough."

"We'll say when it's been enough. You shouldn't be sticking up for these bitches—"

"Back off, Butch," came a new voice, and I looked past the two rednecks to see Dan Lowery approaching, a scowl to match theirs darkening his face. "You're making a scene."

"So what?" Mitch said. "We're only saying what everyone else in here is thinking."

Dan paused next to our booth. He wasn't as bulky as the other two men, but an inch or so taller, just enough so he could stare down at them as he stood there, arms crossed. "I kind of doubt that. And anyway, if Captain Margolis is letting the girls stay, then he must be all right with them being here. What he probably won't be all right with is finding out how you've been treating them. Know what I mean?"

At that implied threat, both Mitch and Butch seemed to noticeably deflate. "We were just kidding—" Butch began, and Dan cut in,

"Well, I kind of doubt Jessica and Evony thought it was funny. So you should probably just go back to your own table."

They hesitated for a few seconds, exchanging hangdog looks, and then they slouched off, grumbling under their breath. By some unspoken agreement, Julia slid over on her side of the booth so Dan could sit down.

"Sorry about that," he said. "Mitch is all right until you get about three or four beers in him, and then he gets mean. But now he'll have a couple more, and he'll swing back to being all friendly before he passes out somewhere."

"Margolis is going to cut him off if he isn't careful," Julia said, then picked up her glass of wine and took an over-large swallow. It seemed as if that exchange had shaken her just as much as it had shaken me. Even though the two guys were gone, and we had Dan here as a buffer in case they decided to come back, my heart didn't want to stop pounding.

"Well, that's between Mitch and Captain Margolis, I guess." Dan shifted in his seat and flagged down the waitress, then ordered a Guinness. "Hope you don't mind me horning in like this."

"Not at all," I said, my voice shaky with relief, while Evony added,

"We'd never turn away a knight in shining armor."

He chuckled at that, but I noticed the way his gaze shifted immediately from Evony to me, and I felt my cheeks grow warm. In other circumstances, I probably wouldn't have minded the attention, but now it was just a reminder that I was here for Jace, and only Jace.

Julia seemed to notice the tension, because she said, "Have some fries, Dan. I think you've earned them."

A chuckle, but I noticed he didn't say no. He reached out and snagged a few of the truffle fries, munching on them in silence until the waitress came back with his stout.

I waited until he'd taken a long pull at the beer before asking, "Do a lot of people feel that way? About Evony and me, I mean."

From the way he hesitated, I could tell he really didn't want to answer me. A quick flicker of his hazel eyes under the thick dark blond lashes in Julia's direction, and she shrugged. Then he said, "A lot? I don't know. I mean, you just got into town, but even so, word spreads quickly enough. It goes a long way that Captain Margolis welcomed you here, because most people are willing to follow his lead."

"But not all of them, apparently," Evony said, her tone sour. She drained the rest of the beer in her glass, then sighed. "Should've ordered another one while the waitress was still here."

"No problem," Dan told her. He raised his hand and flagged down the server, told her Evony needed another drink, and thanked her as she hurried off to the bar.

"Wow, you really are a knight in shining armor."

"Not really. Stacy and I have known each other since Albuquerque. We met just a few days after...you know."

Oh, did we know. Those hellish days when the Heat burned through the population had begun to turn hazy and dark in my memory, though, like a bad dream you've tried very hard to forget. Even so, I wanted to hear what it had been like for other people, for those who'd had to find their own way out of the mess, the ones who didn't have the guiding voice of a djinn guardian to lead them to safety.

"So are you...." I let the words trail off, since I had a good idea that he wasn't with Stacy, but I didn't know what else to say.

"No," he replied, and I felt rather than saw his gaze rest on me, since I had glanced down and was pretending to be focused on swirling the wine still left in my glass. "She was scared and alone. I guess some guy had tried to attack her, and she ran away. I had to convince her I wasn't going to do the same thing, but then we looked out for each other after that. A few days later, we ran into a bigger group of survivors. Margolis' group. That's how I met Julia."

"So you were with Margolis from the beginning?" Evony picked up a truffle fry and popped it in her mouth.

"Almost," Julia said, although I could tell she wasn't thrilled to be revisiting this part of her past. "After my—well, once I was alone, I waited a day. I kept thinking help had to arrive, even though deep down I knew that wasn't going to happen, that if anyone was going to show up and provide some assistance, they would've done it before then. There wasn't any electricity, no phone service. My townhouse complex was completely deserted. I had a vague idea of trying to head downtown to the city center, since I thought if there was anything left, that might be where people were gathering. I didn't get even a quarter-mile before I ran into Richard Margolis and his group. He already had about twenty people with him."

The number surprised me. I wondered how Margolis had managed to get together such a large group so soon after the Heat had done its work. But, whatever my personal feelings about him might be, I could tell he was a force of nature. Maybe those survivors had been drawn to him the way iron filings were drawn to a magnet.

"Let me guess...they were all hot chicks," Evony said sourly, and Julia gave an unwilling laugh.

"Not really. The group was about fifty/fifty men and women, and they even had a couple of kids with them. Laurel, who's ten, and Oliver, who's nine. You'll meet them tomorrow, Jessica."

Dan lifted an eyebrow at that, and Julia explained how she intended to put me to work as a teacher, since I'd been a T.A. at UNM. He looked impressed, and I felt myself blush again. This was getting ridiculous.

Stacy arrived with Evony's replacement beer and asked if we wanted more food. Since I didn't even know what was available, I hesitated. Dan said, "They have burgers tonight, and chicken enchiladas, right?"

"Yeah. And zucchini lasagne if you don't want meat."

Eating meat wasn't an issue for either Evony or me, so we both ordered burgers, while Dan and Julia asked for the enchiladas. Stacy made a note of everything, inquiring if the rest of us wanted a second round of drinks, which we all did. Frankly, even with Dan sitting with us, I still felt a little on edge, and I wondered if ordering more wine was such a good idea. Too late now, though.

Evony got right back on track after Stacy left. "So how many people did you have by the time you left Albuquerque?"

Julia and Dan looked at each other, and he shrugged while she said, "Not quite a hundred. We commandeered a bunch of SUVs and trucks, and headed north. Margolis had gotten hold of a ham radio and started searching for other survivors, and he made contact with Miles Odekirk in Los Alamos. There were about sixty survivors with him, and he told us it would be safer if we came here, since this town is so defensible."

"Was that an issue so early on?" I asked, surprised. "I mean, how did he know?"

"At that point, I don't think he wasn't really talking about the djinn, just the possibility of some survivors not exactly being upstanding citizens. By the time we got here, though...." Julia reached out and snagged a fry for herself, although I got the impression she did that more to stall than because she was really all that hungry.

"What?" Evony's eyes were intent on Julia's face, and I guessed she had posed the question to see whether the other woman would really answer it.

"Well, he'd started to formulate some theories, that's all." Julia shrugged, and I could tell from the way she wouldn't really meet Evony's gaze that she didn't intend to elaborate.

All right, so it seemed as if Julia's willingness to play hostess and answer our questions did have its limits. Fair enough. I supposed if I were in her position, I probably wouldn't be discussing how our one and only scientist had not only managed to figure out that supernatural creatures were behind the Dying, but had actually come up with a way to stop them, or at least keep them at bay.

Evony seemed to pick up on that, too, because she dropped the subject and instead reached for her beer.

An awkward silence fell. I drained the rest of the wine in my glass, since I knew more was on the way. Then I asked, "What about you, Dan?"

He appeared taken aback. "What about me?"

"What did you do...before?"

Unlike Julia, who seemed particularly disinclined to discuss her past, he relaxed, saying, "I was a personal trainer."

Well, that explained the muscles, which were obviously enough even under the hoodie and T-shirt he wore. "No shit."

A grin. "No shit. And an Eagle Scout once upon a time, believe it or not. Margolis thought he'd hit the jackpot with me, especially since he was having to herd a bunch of former office workers through the apocalypse."

At that remark, Julia gave him a pained glance, and he added quickly,

"No offense."

"It's okay," she said, appearing to relent. "We *were* a bunch of office workers, for the most part. I mean, wasn't that what most people were before all this happened?"

Especially survivors from a place like Albuquerque. Even though we were in New Mexico, it wasn't exactly the wild, wild west.

"So you came up here to Los Alamos," I prompted.

Dan said, "Yeah, we came up here, and Margolis more or less took over. No one seemed to mind—it wasn't as if he was turning people out of their homes, after all. We cleared out enough houses for us all to have someplace to live, and then we got on the ham radio and started broadcasting, urging any survivors who could hear us to come to Los Alamos, that we had power and food and housing. And they did come."

"At least until a few weeks ago," Julia added. The strain was clear in her voice as she went on, "We had a steady trickle for a while, always a few people a day, sometimes as many as fifteen or twenty, traveling in groups. But around mid-December, they just stopped. That's when we lost contact with Las Cruces as well."

I didn't say anything. There was no need to. As much as I loved Jace and wanted him free, I couldn't defend the actions of the other djinn, the ones who thought human beings were lower than insects. Those djinn were murderers, plain and simple, even though they probably looked on themselves as exterminators. The problem was that Julia and everyone else here in Los Alamos thought Jace and Natila and all the djinn in Taos who had saved their Chosen were just as bad, and I didn't know how I could ever begin to convince them otherwise.

You don't have to right now, I told myself. *You don't even know where Jace is being held yet, or where Miles Odekirk keeps those damn boxes of his, or...or, well, much of anything at all.*

That wasn't exactly true, though. I now knew approximately how many people were living in Los Alamos, and I knew they had power but no phones, and I knew they were an island of safety in a sea of darkness. And whatever I had to do in order to save Jace, I couldn't compromise their fragile refuge. I couldn't leave them open to an attack by the dark djinn, the ones who wanted all humans dead.

Our food arrived, and Julia shifted the conversation to more innocuous topics, like how the power had never gone out here in Los Alamos, and so the frozen and refrigerated food at the grocery store and the various restaurants around town had never been compromised.

"It helped a lot," she said. "Plus, we foraged everything we could from the abandoned houses. There was some waste, of course, just because there were only a few hundred of us, and food here for thousands of people, but we were better off than most survivors."

"That's for damn sure," Evony remarked. "I was living off cocktail peanuts down there in Española for a while."

Everyone chuckled, which I'm sure was what she'd intended by the comment, and then we all fell silent for a while so we could eat. It was a more companionable silence, unlike the awkward one from earlier in the conversation, though, and I realized then that I liked these people, or at least what I'd seen of them so far. Yes, Julia clearly wasn't ready to open up about whatever it was that she'd left behind in Albuquerque, and Dan's apparent interest in me could turn out to be problematic. For now, though, I told myself to be grateful that Evony and I had been given a welcome here, even if it wasn't an open-armed one from the entire population.

Baby steps. And the next one after this would be attempting to find out exactly where they were keeping their captured djinn.

CHAPTER TEN

I WASN'T GIVEN THE CHANCE TO DO ANY NANCY Drew sleuthing, however, because the next day Evony and I went to see Julia at the justice center so we could officially be given our work assignments.

"We can always use servers at the restaurants, and also people to help with stocking the supermarket, keeping track of the food supplies," Julia told Evony, whose expression was an odd mixture of mulishness and resignation. "But if there's anything else you can do—"

"I can work on cars," she offered.

Julia blinked in surprise, and I shot her a startled glance myself. Evony certainly hadn't mentioned that particular skill set to me.

Seemingly amused by our shared astonishment, she said, "My brothers were always wrenching on their cars.

Custom cars were a big thing in Española. I can swap out a radiator with the best of them. Although I'll admit I don't know as much about all the computerized crap on the newer cars. We had classic muscle—Camaros, Impalas, a Barracuda. That kind of stuff. Still, a brake pad is a brake pad, you know?"

"Of course," Julia replied, typing away furiously as she apparently was updating Evony's information in the database. "This is great news. We didn't have any mechanics—a few people who can change oil, that kind of thing, but nobody with much specialized knowledge. Do you mind if I put you on shift at the motor pool?"

"Not at all. Anything's better than getting beers for assholes like the gruesome twosome from last night. I have a feeling they're ass-pinchers."

Her expression didn't change—not really, except for the slightest compression of her lips, here and gone so quickly that I could barely detect it—but I could tell Julia was not thrilled by the profanity. "That's great. Thank you, Evony. We're using the auto repair shop on Knecht Street. It's not too far from here, but I'll have someone drop you off."

"Maybe they should take me home so I can change first," Evony said, looking down at herself. She was wearing one of her tight sweaters and a pair of dark jeans with boots, not exactly the sort of attire designed for crawling around under cars.

"No, I don't want you ruining any of your good clothes. You can pop by the Goodwill store first and see if you can find something that will work."

Evony didn't seem too put out by that suggestion. It would give her a chance to do some "shopping," even if it wasn't for anything terribly interesting.

"And Jessica, we've been tutoring the children in the library. It's more central, and it seemed silly to put them in a classroom when there's so few of them."

"Eight, right?" I said. On paper, that didn't sound like a lot. But I still wasn't looking forward to keeping eight kids of various ages and interests and skill levels occupied.

"That's right." The smallest shadow of a smile appeared on Julia's features, as if she had noted my reluctance and was somehow amused by it. "Nora Almeida has been tutoring them, but she'll be glad to have a pro take over. Still, she'll walk you through it. And it's not really that bad—we only have the tutoring sessions from nine to noon, so it's not as if you'll have to keep them occupied for an entire school day."

Well, thank God for that. I could probably survive three-hour increments, even if some of the kids turned out to be hooligans. Then I was ashamed of myself for expecting the worst when I hadn't even met the children in question. These were kids who'd lost their families, their entire world. I should be glad of being provided with the opportunity to give them a little stability.

Only...I wouldn't, not really. I was only planning to be here long enough to find Jace and Natila, and then I'd be gone. Unfortunately, the most impactful lesson I'd teach those kids would probably end up being one about abandonment.

I'd just have to worry about that when the time came, though. When Evony and I had come to the justice center this morning, we'd been escorted straight upstairs to see Julia. We certainly hadn't been given the chance to do any snooping around, not even to look at the building directory to see if there were jail facilities located anywhere inside. And it wasn't as if I could pop on the Internet to do some investigating of my own....

"That all sounds fine," I said firmly, hoping that Julia hadn't noticed the way I paused before I replied. "Can I walk there from here?"

"No, you'd better drive." She opened a desk drawer and pulled out a car key fob, then handed it over to Evony, addressing her next words to her. "Since you two are going to be working in different sections of town, I figured you might like to have your own transportation. There's a Toyota truck down in the parking lot that's yours. The red one with the off-road package."

Evony's eyes glowed at the prospect of having her own wheels. "Thanks, Julia. I appreciate it."

"No problem. I'm glad we had something available you could use. I'll call over to the motor pool to tell them that you're coming, but if you have any questions or concerns, just let me know. Oh, and I've set both of you up with vouchers at the grocery store and at the restaurants around town, so you don't need to worry about that, either."

I admired the way Julia could be so brisk and efficient, so cool, as if she was merely setting up a typical job placement for someone, not trying to fit square pegs in round holes after the Dying had effectively destroyed the ways we used to all categorize ourselves. For all I knew, this was her own way of coping, of pretending the world was still normal.

With a wave of the key in her hand, Evony bade us goodbye and then headed out to the elevators. Giving a slight nod of satisfaction, Julia turned back to me. "Nora is with the kids at the library now, but I already told her you'd be over there this morning, so she's expecting you."

Great. No way of backing out of this. I told myself it was for Jace and to stop being such a baby. Besides, they were just kids. What was the worst that could happen?

On second thought....

Smiling, Julia said, "You'll do fine. It's a pretty relaxed atmosphere. And we scavenged a bunch of workbooks and lesson plans from the schools in town, as well as software, so it's not like you have to make it up as you go along." Her expression grew serious, the smile fading. "Mostly, we just want to make sure the few children who did survive will still get an education, even if it's not exactly like what they would have gotten at an actual school. It won't take much for the world to start slipping back into the Dark Ages, and we're doing everything we can to prevent that."

Now that I stopped to think about it, I realized Julia was probably right. At first I'd been focused only on surviving, and even after Jace came into my life, we still put all our energy into keeping our little compound going, on making sure we had enough to eat and a warm house to sleep in. I only opened a book when I needed to research something practical, like making sausages or cheese. It would be so easy to forget everything we'd spent thousands of years developing and instead only look toward the next meal, or, projecting a little further, the next harvest.

If we allowed that to happen, then the djinn would really and truly have won.

My voice firm, I said, "I'll do my best."

The smile returned. "I know you will."

It was a short drive from the justice center to the library, but just far enough that walking would have been asking a bit much, especially since I could see clouds moving down from the north and east, the wind picking up. I didn't have a firm grasp on the weather in this part of the world, but it looked as if those clouds might be bringing more snow with them. Having the Cherokee at hand instead of walking just seemed far smarter.

Like the justice center, the library was a clean, modern-looking building. The sidewalks had been cleared here as well, and out in front was a flagpole where the American and New Mexico flags still blew bravely in the wind. Even though I knew this Nora person and the children were waiting for me inside, I couldn't help pausing there for a few seconds so I could gaze up at those two flags. I'd thought of New Mexico as an entity off and on since the Dying, but honestly, I'd been so focused on my own problems that I hadn't had much time to think about what was happening in the rest of the country. Were we even a United States anymore, or just isolated islands of civilization struggling to survive?

And what if Los Alamos is the only one? I thought then. *What if no one else had any way of protecting themselves, and now they're all gone?*

That notion was so depressing that I had to shut it down right away. I was on edge enough already; I didn't need to meet my new students with my thoughts roiling with visions of city after city, town after town, falling to the djinn onslaught.

Pulling in a bracing breath of the cold air, I headed to the front entrance of the library and let myself in. The interior was also modern, sharp-edged, but softened by wood-paneled ceilings overhead. One wall consisted mainly of windows that let in a breathtaking view of the Jemez Mountains, now all covered in snow, clouds dropping to obscure their peaks.

Off to my right, I could hear voices—children's voices, and I took another breath and then headed in that direction. As I came around the stacks, I saw an open area with tables with iMac computers sitting on them. Most of the computers were in use, but at another table, one that was clearly intended as a study spot, a little black-haired girl of about nine or ten was buried in a book, mouth moving slightly as she read.

At that sight, I couldn't help smiling. I'd done the same thing when I was a child, and it had taken my mother years to break me of the habit.

Standing off to one side was a dark-haired woman who appeared to be in her mid-forties, a little plump but with a pretty face. She saw me come in and approached immediately, one hand held out, even as all the kids seemed to stop what they were doing and peer around their computers—and in the case of the sixteen-year-old, who looked tall and gangly even while sitting down, to lean expertly back in his chair so he could catch a glimpse of me, one foot hooked around the leg of the table to prevent him from falling over backward.

Feeling all those eyes fixed on me was not exactly the most comfortable sensation, but I tried to ignore them as I smiled at the woman and took her hand, then said, "Hi, I'm Jessica Monroe."

"I'm Nora," she replied. "And here's your class—Matt Fellowes, Laurel Garcia" —the little girl with her nose in the book looked up briefly— "Oliver Mills, Jasmine Torres, Donnie Strickland, Kathleen Elliott, Kristina Caldwell, and Ben Sanchez."

All of them said "hi" with various levels of enthusiasm, while Matt, the oldest, remained leaning in his chair, a smile playing at one corner of his mouth. He wasn't a bad-looking kid, with a mop of sandy hair that needed cutting, but I could tell he was probably going to be a pain in my ass.

As for the rest, in that moment they were just a blur of names and faces, but I hoped I'd get them sorted out eventually. Or maybe not; with any luck, I wouldn't be here in Los Alamos long enough to get to know them all that well. That sounded cold even as the thought passed through my mind, but I reminded myself that I wasn't here to educate the next generation. I was here to save Jace.

"Hi," I responded. "Nice to meet all of you."

A couple of the girls giggled. Nora said, "Okay, back to work while I talk to Ms. Monroe."

They all did obey, even Matt, although he straightened up slowly, as if to show that he was only going back to the computer because he felt like it and not because of anything Nora Almeida had said.

She noticed, I could tell, but she didn't acknowledge him one way or another. Smart. My mother always used to say that paying too much attention to those kinds of kids was playing right into their hands and reinforcing their bad behavior.

We moved a few paces away to a spot where we were partly obscured by the book stacks but where Nora could still keep an eye on the kids. "As you can see, it's quite a group. Mostly they work on the computers, and all you have to do is keep an eye on their scores and see where they're doing well and where they need some help. At the librarian's desk, we have the teacher's editions of the actual books we're using, and then the master software loaded on that computer, so it should be pretty self-explanatory."

"How do you keep track of it all?" I asked. It seemed like a daunting task, monitoring all those different grade levels and subjects at the same time.

"Well, Miles set up some software for me to do that, but I'll admit it was harder to figure out the software than to just keep paper grades for them, so that's what I've been doing. It's all in the ledger in the upper right-hand drawer."

Miles again. So it appeared he did take some time out from inventing djinn torture devices to help around the community. I nodded, since I wasn't sure what I should say.

Voice lowering, Nora went on, "We're just trying to do our best by them, poor things. It's hard enough for us adults to adjust to this world, but these children? Their losses seem so much worse than ours." She had to stop herself there; her dark eyes were suspiciously bright, and I saw the way she swallowed, hard.

My own voice soft, I asked, "You had children?"

She nodded. "Two. They're gone. My husband... gone. Everyone. I actually wanted to take in both Laurel and Oliver, but Captain Margolis decided that with so many of us having lost children, it would be better if only one child was placed in each household. I can't replace Laurel's mother, of course, but I want to make sure she knows she's safe, and loved."

My chest constricted, thinking of how all these kids had somehow survived the Heat, alone in a new and terrifying world. It had been scary enough for me, and I'd had Jace to help me through it, even though at the time I hadn't known who—or what—he was. But these children, with their families gone? I couldn't begin to imagine.

"I'll take good care of them," I assured her. Maybe I wouldn't be in Los Alamos all that long, but I would make sure to do as good a job as I could while I was here.

Nora smiled. "I know you will."

And really, except for a few muttered remarks calculated to be just below my level of hearing, even Matt was well-behaved enough. I looked in on what they were all doing so I could familiarize myself with their various levels of education, and then rounded out the morning with a spirited discussion on Pluto being demoted from planet status and why or why not everyone thought that was a good idea.

At noon their "parents" showed up to take the kids home, except Matt, who went whizzing off on a skateboard. By then the skies were overcast, the air heavy with the promise of snow, and I hoped he'd make it to wherever he was going before the storm really hit.

I was heading to the Cherokee and deciding whether I should attempt to get groceries, or take the lazy route and go back to Pajarito's for lunch, when the familiar yellow Hummer pulled into the parking lot. Stiffening—I hated the sight of that thing—I stopped where I was and waited.

It wasn't Dan who stuck his head out of the SUV, though, but his cigarette-smoking companion. He didn't have a cigarette today, though, and his demeanor seemed a good deal more official than when I'd seen him pulling guard duty out on the 502.

"Ms. Monroe, Dr. Odekirk would like to talk to you."

Ms. Monroe? The formal address seemed odd when contrasted with the person who had delivered it, a young man only a few years older than I was, his over-long hair combed back away from his face and held in place with an impressive amount of hair product. I had a feeling the phrasing was Dr. Odekirk's, not this guy's.

And what the hell did Miles Odekirk want with me? There was another interview I'd just as soon avoid. Hedging, I said, "I was just about to get lunch—"

"You can do that afterward. Follow me—I'll guide you in."

He sounded friendly enough, but I knew arguing would be pointless. Miles had sent the guard down here to fetch me, and if I attempted to put up any more roadblocks, well, I'd probably get dragged into the Hummer and taken forcibly to the lab. At least if I followed in the Cherokee, I could make it look as if I was going by my own free will.

Acknowledging defeat, I said, "Okay," then went over to the Jeep and started it up. The guard turned his Hummer around and headed back toward the street, and I followed.

I hadn't yet been to the labs, but I had a vague idea of where they were located, out toward the west end of town. We dropped back down to the main thorough-fare, Trinity Road, and then drove for another five minutes or so, until we went around a curve and came up on a guard shack, one that seemed to be occupied. However, the person inside just waved us on through, and we wound our way through the campus, past a large parking structure, now almost deserted, and past more large buildings, most of them with conspicuously absent signage.

At last we pulled into a lot with a lone Subaru Forester parked in it. The Hummer took a space next to the Subaru, and I parked my SUV beside the Hummer. The guard got out and waited while I grabbed my purse from the passenger seat and slid out.

"This way," he said, pointing to an entrance close to where the two wings of the building intersected in an "X."

I didn't have much choice but to head where he'd indicated, all the while taking furtive glances around me. Not that there was much to see; the guard and I were the only two people around, or so it seemed, and the building itself had clearly been designed for function rather than beauty.

We walked down a long hallway, our footsteps echoing off the linoleum, until the guard stopped at a door that looked like pretty much every other door along that corridor. "He's in here," the man said. "Go on in—he's expecting you."

Of course he was. Not that the guard was the most reassuring of company, but it still felt as if it would have been better for him to show me in. But since he clearly didn't intend to do that, I just nodded, put my hand on the doorknob, and let myself into the room.

I didn't know what I'd been expecting—some crazy lab full of equipment I couldn't identify, a whiteboard covered with symbols, like I'd seen in just about every show and movie that included a mad genius scientist—but that didn't describe the room I was in now. No, it looked like an oversized conference room, with a rectangular table and a dozen chairs, and a blank wall where maybe they could have projected images for a presentation. Sitting at the end of that table was Miles Odekirk, an iPad lying in front of him.

He didn't rise when I came in. He only said, "Sit there, please, Ms. Monroe," and pointed at the chair to his right.

In silence, I traversed the space and then seated myself, placing my purse on the empty chair next to me. Once I'd done that, I forced myself to cross my hands on the tabletop and meet his watching gaze.

It was hard, being this close to him. The last time I'd seen Miles Odekirk, he'd been manipulating that device of his so it nearly choked the life out of the man I loved. For just the briefest second, I wondered what he would do if I lunged across the table and latched my fingers around his throat, squeezed until I got him to agree to free Jace and Natila.

But I knew I'd never do anything that crazy. He was a tall man, maybe right around six feet or a little over, but slender, with the pale, soft hands of someone who'd probably never done a day of manual labor in his life. Despite his lack of muscle tone, I didn't know if I could successfully subdue him, and the consequences of trying and failing were too awful to contemplate.

Instead, I forced a casual note into my voice as I asked, "What did you want to talk to me about, Dr. Odekirk?"

He picked up the iPad; it looked as if it had been open to some sort of notepad program, but I wasn't sure. An iPad had been on the list of things I'd wanted but couldn't really afford, back in the day, and so I didn't know much about how to use one.

"I wanted to talk to you about this djinn. Jasreel."

My mouth went dry. "Um...what about him?"

"You spent some time with him, from what I understand." Any other man would have probably injected a leer into his voice when making such a statement, but Miles Odekirk seemed curiously uninterested in that aspect of my relationship with Jace.

"Yes," I said. If I stuck to "yes" or "no" answers, then possibly I could avoid giving Odekirk anything he could use against Jace...or me.

"What sort of powers did he exhibit around you?"

So much for the binary solution to answering his questions. I knotted my fingers together in my lap and replied, "I never saw him exhibit any powers."

That seemed to surprise the scientist. At least, one of his eyebrows went up behind his glasses, and he started typing on the iPad's screen, although I couldn't see what he was writing down. "So to you he seemed like an ordinary human being?"

"Yes."

"How long did you cohabit?"

My cheeks burned, but I said, as calmly as I could, "Around three months."

"So you're saying in that time you saw absolutely nothing that made you think he was anyone except who he told you he was?"

I reflected that Dr. Odekirk sounded as if he'd watched a few too many courtroom dramas. Then again, he didn't seem much like the TV type. It was probably coincidence that his methods of questioning were so similar to those of a district attorney.

"I didn't see anything at all."

"But when we collected this Jasreel, it seemed obvious enough then that you knew he wasn't an ordinary man. What changed?"

Well, hell. I wracked my brains, trying to remember exactly what I'd said to Captain Margolis and his men, but that scene was such a tumult of sound and fear and the echo of Jace's voice inside my mind that

I couldn't recall what I might or might not have said. Coldly, I replied, "The night before you broke into my house, Jasreel had a visitor, another djinn. I overheard them talking."

"What were they talking about?"

"The other djinn was telling Jace—Jasreel—that it wasn't safe for us to stay in Santa Fe."

Some more typing. Then Odekirk looked up at me, blue-gray eyes appraising behind the rimless glasses. "Why would he say that?"

I didn't blink, but only stared back at him and said, "I think you know why."

For a second, he didn't react. Then he laid the iPad down on the tabletop and fastened me with a stare that made me feel like a virulent bacillus he was examining under a microscope. "Ms. Monroe, for someone who claims to have rejected her association with this djinn and wants only to be a member of this community, you don't seem to be very cooperative."

Shit. *Shit*. Thinking frantically, I said, "Sorry. I just figured you'd know Jasreel was being warned because the other djinn had found out about that—that box of yours. The one that controls them."

"It doesn't *control* them," Odekirk corrected me. Then he seemed to stop himself. "Precisely how it works is neither here nor there. When the other djinn came to your home, how did he appear?"

"I don't know how he got there. He was already in the living room, talking with Jasreel, when I woke up and heard them."

Something that might have been a sigh emanated from the scientist's throat. "No, that's not what I asked. What did he look like? What was he doing?"

Oh. Feeling like an idiot, and hating Odekirk for making me feel that way, I replied, "He also looked like a man, maybe a little older than Jasreel. Dark hair and eyes. Both of them were wearing these baggy pants, and—"

Odekirk held up a hand. "You can spare me the sartorial details. Was there anything unusual?"

"They were both floating a foot off the ground."

That seemed to please the scientist, because he typed something else into his notes. "So...floating above the ground. Anything else?"

I really didn't want to give any more details than that, but I also knew I was walking a fine line here, one that teetered between providing enough information so that Odekirk would think I was being a good little citizen and definitely wasn't on the side of the djinn, and giving something away that could potentially hurt Jasreel and Natila in the long run.

Well, I figured Zahrias could probably take care of himself, so I offered, "The visiting djinn had what looked like flames dancing around his feet, and more around his head. But he didn't burn. It was the weird-est thing."

That got me an actual smile, or as close to one as Miles Odekirk could probably produce. "That is because this djinn you saw was an elemental who can control fire. Just as Jasreel can control the air—or at least he could if his powers weren't being held in check."

Jasreel can. Odekirk had spoken of Jace in the pres-ent tense, which meant he really must still be alive. I hadn't allowed myself to entertain the thought that he might be dead, but even so, the worry had been far, far back in my mind, buried so deep I could pretend it didn't exist. Well, most of the time, anyway.

But I also didn't know how best to respond to the scientist's latest pronouncement, so I only managed a flat, "Oh," and then waited to see what he would do.

Which was nothing. He didn't type on his iPad, or fiddle with his tie—yeah, the guy was wearing a tie under his lab coat—or anything. Just sat there, look-ing at me with those pale eyes of his. All right, they weren't *that* pale, not a Chris Bowman level of freaky or anything, but something about the way the light reflected off his glasses made Odekirk's gaze feel not quite human.

At last he said, "Did you ever see Jasreel suffer any kind of an injury?"

Uh-oh. "No," I replied, the word sounding way too strangled. I coughed.

"Nothing? Not a single scrape or bruise, even though he was performing some rough work around your homestead?"

How the hell Odekirk knew about that, I had no idea, but I figured that wasn't really the thing I should be focusing on right now. In saying that I'd never seen Jace hurt by anything—except that infernal box the scientist had invented—I was telling the simple truth. Then I reflected maybe it would be a good idea to embellish that truth. Just a little, nothing too extreme, but enough to let Odekirk know that hurting or killing a djinn wouldn't be all that easy.

"Nothing," I said firmly. "At the time, I didn't think that much about it, but I saw one of the goats kick him in the leg once, and he didn't even have a bruise."

The scientist didn't look too thrilled by that particular piece of intelligence. Brows pulling together, he made some more notes on his iPad. "Any other incidents like that?"

"Um...he splashed some boiling water on his hand in the kitchen when he was straining pasta. His skin didn't even turn red." *There...I hope that keeps you from trying to torture him with burning cigarettes or red-hot pokers or whatever.*

"And you still didn't think that was strange?"

I shrugged. "He put some cold cloths on it right away, so I suppose I figured he'd treated the burn quickly enough that it didn't have any lasting effects."

Silence for a moment as Miles Odekirk kept typing away on his iPad's screen. At last he set it down. However, he'd closed the notepad app before doing that, so I couldn't see anything of what he'd written. Then he just sat there, staring at me, while I forced myself to remain still, to keep my gaze fixed on his, my expression neutral. Wasn't that a sure sign someone was lying—to glance away, to look off to the side? At any rate, I had no intention of making things that easy for him.

Then he said, "What precisely are you doing here, Ms. Monroe?"

Don't look away. Don't swallow. Don't blink. Voice steady, I replied, "The same thing as all of you, Dr. Odekirk. Trying to survive."

Another long pause. I could hear the clock on the wall behind him ticking away, but I wouldn't let myself glance up at it. That would be a clear sign of unease, wouldn't it?

He was actually the first to blink. "Yes, Ms. Monroe. That's what we're all trying to do." His shoulders seemed to slump, and then he added, "That's all for now."

"I can go?" I asked, confused by his sudden offer of a reprieve.

"Yes." The glint returned to his eyes. "Just don't go too far."

"Not planning on it," I said. Then, seized by a sudden devilish impulse, I went on, "I was going for lunch at Pajarito's. Would you like to come with me?"

The look of shock that passed over his thin features was so severe, you would've thought I'd just suggested skinny-dipping in the semi-frozen Rio Grande. After a second or so, he seemed to recover himself and said evenly, "Thank you, but no. I have work to do here."

"Then I'll leave you to it," I told him in blithe tones, and reached over to retrieve my purse. As I stood up, I said, "Have a nice day, Dr. Odekirk."

Now his gaze was steady enough, although I couldn't begin to read his expression. "You as well, Ms. Monroe."

I let myself out, but I couldn't relax even then, because the guard was waiting outside. "This way," he said, leading me back to the exit. It seemed clear enough that they weren't about to allow me the opportunity to wander around the facility unescorted.

Just as well. By that point, I didn't think I was up to it. I got into my Cherokee, backed out of the parking space, and headed toward the guard shack and the main road, the yellow Hummer leading me the whole way.

And then I finally remembered to breathe.

CHAPTER ELEVEN

THE DAYS PASSED QUICKLY AFTER THAT. MILES Odekirk didn't ask to see me again, and I had to make myself focus on tutoring the children, while at the same time attempting to see or hear anything that might give me a hint as to where Jace and Natila were being held. But I wasn't able to get any definite confirmation, and I knew I didn't dare ask any questions. Evony and I were slowly being assimilated into the makeshift society in Los Alamos, and the last thing I wanted to do was attract any unnecessary attention. That meant I also couldn't make any inquiries about the Chosen who'd been sent to spy on the community here. Again, I heard nothing about them. Certainly there was no evidence I could find that any of the people I met had once been Chosen. Possibly those four were being held in the same place as Jace and

Natila. It seemed to be the only explanation that made any sense.

To my surprise, Evony seemed to have really hit it off with the two men she worked with in the motor pool. One, Shawn Gutierrez, had been a firefighter, and was still on call in case any emergencies arose around town, and the other man, Brent Sutherland, used to be an HVAC technician. They really took Evony under their wing, to the point where they'd actually faced down Butch and Mitch when they'd tried to get snarky one evening at Pajarito's.

"Shawn is one hot tamale," Evony told me wistfully. "Almost makes me wish I were straight."

At that comment, I'd raised an eyebrow at her. We were in the kitchen, having coffee and toast before getting ready to start the day. "What, are you thinking of switching sides? What about Natila?"

Evony sighed and stirred some more milk into her coffee. "No, I'm not 'switching sides.' It doesn't work that way. And of course I want to find Natila. The problem is, we don't know where they're holding her."

No, we didn't. I had my suspicions; by then we'd been in Los Alamos for almost two weeks, and I'd gotten a lot more familiar with the town. However, there were two places where I wasn't allowed to wander freely: the labs and the justice center. Either Jace and Natila were secreted somewhere in the labs so they could be experimented on more conveniently, or there were holding cells someplace in the justice center. It made sense that they'd have some sort of facility for keeping prisoners there. Just because it made sense, though, didn't mean I'd been able to confirm the existence of those cells for myself.

I nodded somberly, and after that Evony excused herself so she could go finish getting ready for work. She didn't really have set hours the way I did with tutoring the kids, but lately she'd been spending up to eight hours a day at the motor pool. Just the day before, she'd earned brownie points with Captain Margolis because she was able to accurately troubleshoot and fix an issue with one of the traction-control sensors on his Hummer.

And I—well, I was doing okay with the tutoring. My fears about the kids giving me trouble had all been in my mind; even Matt more or less behaved himself, and things hummed along smoothly enough. Really, I thought they were glad of the structure those hours of schooling provided, which gave them something to focus on other than the way their world had changed forever.

The whole time, however, I could feel myself getting more and more tense as each day passed and I was no closer to finding Jace. I almost wished Miles Odekirk would summon me for another bout of questioning, simply because there was always the chance that he might let something slip, but he didn't appear to require any more information from me.

But then I finally had something go right. I stopped by the justice center to see Julia and make a requisition for more supplies for the children...and was escorted directly to her desk so I couldn't go roaming about... and found her almost buried in paperwork and more than a little exasperated. Apparently the commander liked to flex his muscle by issuing memo after memo and demanding daily reports from the people he had working immediately under him...namely, Julia.

"Do you want some help?" I asked her. "I mean, I'm only putting in about three hours a day with the kids, plus a little more here and there to keep up with the grading. But most of the time my afternoons are free."

She tucked a piece of hair behind her ear and sat back in her chair. Even though I knew she had to be dying to have someone pick up some of the load, she still asked, "Do you have any office experience?"

"Well, not per se, but I spent a summer doing filing and stuff for the law office where my friend Elena's dad was a partner. And I'm pretty good with Word and Excel."

A nod, but she was quiet for a moment longer, obviously considering whether it was safe for her to take me up on my offer. At last she said, sounding hesitant, "We handle some sensitive material here. That means you have to be discreet. Can you manage that?"

Her tone was neutral, but I understood what she was really asking.

Can I trust you?

The correct answer was that no, she couldn't, because I was only offering to help so I could spend more time in the justice center and as a result, I hoped, finally track down whether or not Jasreel and Natila were being held there. And I had to ignore the pang of guilt that went through me at that thought, because I did like Julia a lot, despite the way she still seemed so closed off about the life she'd left behind in Albuquerque.

Problem was, I liked her, but I loved Jace. There really wasn't much of a contest.

I faced her and nodded, my expression as open as I could make it. "Yes, I can manage that. Really, I want to help. You shouldn't be so buried all the time. It's not fair."

Something in the set of her shoulders seemed to relax slightly. "Thanks, Jessica. Truth is, I could use an assistant. So...let's give it a try. Can you start each day at one? That'll give you time to get lunch before you come over here."

"That'll be perfect," I replied, trying not to sound too excited. If I got to spend part of every day at the justice center, surely I'd dig up something eventually.

"All right. You can start tomorrow." That seemed to be the end of the discussion, as she gave me a quick smile and turned back to her computer.

And that was how I began my tenure in the commander's office. He really did seem determined to chew his way through every ream of paper left behind in the justice center, whether by generating reports or by coming up with flyer after flyer to be distributed throughout the community—telling people what to do if they smelled a gas leak, mandating which parts of the forest surrounding the town could be used for firewood, assigning waste details and clean-up crews and so much more.

The tasks Julia gave me to do were busywork, but I didn't mind too much. For one thing, after I'd been there for three days, I did make the all-important discovery that there really were holding cells in the justice center's basement. They were listed on the directory, and since I was now allowed to move around the building, distributing flyers and collecting reports, it wasn't that hard for me to sidle past the listing by the elevator one day and take a quick peek. All right, so that was one suspicion confirmed. It didn't get me any closer to actually getting inside, though; none of the errands Julia sent me on went to that part of the building—by design, I was sure.

Still, it was better than nothing, and I began devising plots that would allow me entry to the holding cells. Problem was, I knew none of those plans would work. I'd be stopped before I got within fifty feet of the tiny jail. And although Evony was glad I'd made that much progress, she told me to be careful.

"You're not going to help anyone if you do something stupid and get yourself caught, chica," she said, and I could only agree with that morose sentiment. Well, I supposed my being caught trying to get close to the djinn would help Miles Odekirk, since it would confirm his suspicions about me. But that wasn't really the end result I was aiming for.

My patience finally paid off, however. After I'd been assisting Julia for a little more than a week, an afternoon came when she asked if I could take over for her at the desk for a few hours.

"Sure," I said automatically, and asked, "Um... why?"

She seemed tense, but then she smiled a little. "I need to cover for Nancy for a few hours. She's not feeling well, and her relief is up in the forest, cutting wood."

"Oh." Nancy was the hard-faced woman who'd first escorted Evony and me here to the justice center, and it didn't exactly take Sherlock Holmes to deduce that her job probably included pulling guard duty at the holding cells. And so Julia would be acting as her backup? Interesting.

I had to wonder whether she'd done this before, whether she'd spoken with Jace and Natila at all. The thought sent a flare of anger through me, just because Julia knew I'd been with Jace and most likely would have wanted to hear something about how he was faring. Or maybe not—maybe I'd done such a good job of convincing her I'd firmly thrown in my lot with the humans that she'd assumed I didn't care about his current condition.

Either way, the important thing was that sometimes Julia had to play guard, or at least was trusted enough to do so. It might be an angle I could exploit in the future, if I could only figure out how.

"Just for a couple of hours," she reassured me. "Then Tony will be back. And maybe we could grab something to eat afterward?"

It was her way of softening the request, which would keep me in the office way past the time I usually left at around four-thirty or five. I didn't mind; we'd eaten together a few times, but always in a group that included Evony and maybe Shawn or Dan or even Nora Almeida, if she could find someone to watch Laurel, and after all that, Julia still hadn't contributed much that was personal to the conversation. If it was just the two of us at dinner, maybe I could get a little more out of her.

"That sounds great," I said, smiling, and she thanked me and disappeared soon afterward, going downstairs so she could take over for Nancy.

The commander wasn't in that afternoon; he'd gone off for yet another of his visits to the lab. What exactly he did while he was there, I had no idea. Were he and Miles Odekirk concocting new ways to utilize the djinn-suppressing technology the scientist had invented, or merely discussing strategies for using what they already had? Who knew? I still had no idea how many of those boxes existed, although I had a feeling there had to be at least two, or they would never have felt safe taking one away from Los Alamos to trap Natila and then Jace. That would have left the entire colony of survivors unprotected.

I settled myself at the desk, figuring it would be fairly quiet since Captain Margolis was out and we were getting past the end of most people's workdays. That was one holdover from the time before—Los Alamos seemed to run squarely from nine in the morning to five in the afternoon, except for the three restaurants, which stayed open until nine. Well, Pajarito's sometimes was open later than that, especially on Friday and Saturday nights. Again, people wanted to cling to that schedule, for that shred of normality that dictated you worked during the week and then went out on Friday and Saturday nights.

And then there was his voice in my mind, that voice I'd secretly feared I would never hear again.

Beloved.

The pen I was holding fell from suddenly nerveless fingers. I sat stock still at the desk, then ventured, *Jace?*

Yes, Jessica. I am here.

Tears sprang to my eyes, but I knew I couldn't let them fall. That was far too risky, as someone could still come up to the office, even as late in the day as it was. *Oh, God, Jace—I was so worried—*

I know, beloved. But I am all right.

You're sure?

Yes. Confined, but alive. As is Natila.

A relieved breath pushed out of me with a *whoosh*, and then I bent over to pick up the pen I had dropped. *So how is it you're talking with me only just now? I've been working in this building for a week—*

The device they have controlling the two of us is usually set at a level much higher than it is at the moment. When it's operating at full strength, it is difficult to breathe, let alone reach out to you the way I am now.

God. I clutched the edge of the task chair where I sat, the burlap-style material rough under my fingertips. The memory of how he'd been gasping for breath when they took him away was never too far from my mind, and it rose again now. To think that they'd perpetually kept him in that state for weeks was enough to set my stomach roiling.

That's...horrible, I managed at last.

It is unpleasant, true. But the woman who has come to watch me—

Julia, I supplied.

Yes, Julia. She has lowered it slightly. At the current level, it still interferes with the majority of my powers, but I can breathe...and I can reach out to you, beloved, since you are not so far away. A pause, and then he asked, But are you well? They haven't hurt you?

No, I replied at once. *I've convinced them that I had a change of heart, that I don't want anything to do with you. And so I've been living here pretty normally, more or less. Evony and I have a house together and everything.*

He didn't ask who Evony was, and I assumed that was because he already knew. A long pause, followed by, *And have you?*

Have I what?

Had a change of heart?

Of course not! I lied so I could stay here and figure out a way to free you. I would never give up on you, Jace. Never.

Another of those hesitations. Then I felt a—well, it was hard to describe, but it almost seemed as if a wave of warmth passed over my body, as if Jace had somehow managed to gather up the energy of his love for me and send it outward, rising through the floors of the building so that it could warm me and comfort me. I shut my eyes and breathed in, fancying I could almost detect the delectable scent of his skin. In that moment, I realized how much I truly had missed him. I'd pushed away the longing and the need because I had to function on a daily basis, but feeling him again now, I knew I would do whatever it took to get him out of that damn cell and away to someplace safe.

I have to get you out of there. Can you tell me something about the place where they're keeping you?

Beloved, I don't want you to risk yourself.

But I want to risk myself. They have no right to keep you there. Fine if they want to go hunting the bad djinn, the ones who are out there killing off everyone else they can find, but—

His mental voice seemed to alter subtly. *You know this for a fact?*

Julia said they'd lost contact with the other survivors. There were some in Las Cruces, and also in Flagstaff and L.A. But they haven't heard anything for weeks now.

He seemed to sigh. *Ah. I had hoped that perhaps, at the end, they would change their minds. Clearly, I was being too much of an optimist.*

Clearly. Since I didn't want to dwell on what might or might not be happening to the survivors who weren't under a djinn's protection, or safe here in Los Alamos, I said, *It's horrible, but it still doesn't give the people here the right to keep you imprisoned, or Natila. You saved me, and she saved Evony, just as all those other djinn saved the Chosen we met in Taos.*

You went to Taos? He sounded sharper now, and I wondered why he would be upset that I had gone to the djinn stronghold. After all, he'd intended to take me there himself, but had been intercepted by Captain Margolis & Co. before he could do that.

Yes. I didn't know what else to do. I thought maybe someone there would help us, like Zahrias.

Zahrias? The name was followed by the mental equivalent of a chuckle. *Zahrias is not much in the habit of helping mortals.*

I crossed my arms and scowled, even though I knew Jace couldn't see me. *Actually, he was—well, all right, not kind, exactly, but he did take good enough care of us while we were there. In fact, he wanted us to stay, and said we would be safe in Taos.*

Of course, I was leaving out the part where Zahrias urged me to stay so that Aldair would have a new Chosen. I'd refused, so what did it matter? Even so, I thought it better not to mention the other djinn. I had a feeling that wasn't the sort of thing Jace really needed to hear right then.

I am surprised to hear that. A pause, and then, with a flicker of amusement in his mental voice, *Perhaps Zahrias was overcome by the spirit of Christmas.*

I couldn't help smiling, although I quelled the expression quickly, since I didn't want anyone who might walk into the office to see me sitting there and grinning like an idiot at nothing. *I kind of doubt that.*

But I will admit that he wasn't quite as scary as I expected him to be.

Let's hope he never hears you say that. I think he'll be quite disappointed in himself.

"Ms. Monroe?"

Startled, I looked up to see Captain Margolis coming in through the office suite's double doors. Shit. Talk about your crappy timing.

And, just as suddenly, I felt Jace's touch slip away from my mind. It was like having a warm blanket you'd wrapped around yourself torn away, leaving you exposed to the freezing night air. Somehow I managed not to react, even summoned a smile as I said, "Evening, Captain Margolis."

He paused by the desk and gave me one of those looks I hated, not quite a leer, but close enough that it still made my flesh crawl every time he did it. I'd intercepted quite a few by now, but verbally at least he'd been extremely polite, maybe because Julia had always been around.

Now, though, she was several floors below me, and I didn't even know how many people were still left in the building. The clock on the wall said it was now a quarter after six. There would be a skeleton staff, of course, since there were always a few guards around if nothing else, but that didn't mean any of them were patrolling this particular floor at the moment.

"So," the commander said, "what keeps you with us this late?"

"Julia," I replied promptly. "She had to cover for Nancy, and so I'm covering for her. I think Nancy's relief should be coming in shortly, though." That was a lie, since I didn't know for sure exactly when Tony was expected to take over his shift at djinn-watching duty. But it was now full dark, so he had to be back down off the mountain, if nothing else. Probably off dumping his load of fresh-cut lumber before coming back to the justice center. I had a vague idea that they were using the gymnasium at one of the local schools to store all the logs before they were parceled out to the community, but I'd never been there and didn't know for sure how far away it was.

"Ah." Margolis just stood there for a few seconds more, staring down at me. I tried not to fidget, since I knew part of his game included putting people off-balance so he could feel more in control of a situation, but it was difficult. Everything in me wanted to glance away, to pretend I had something I needed to look at on the computer screen. But since I hadn't actually been using the computer when Jace reached out to me, that would just look like exactly what it was—a move of desperation so I wouldn't have to maintain eye contact.

At last, though, he smiled another one of those hackle-raising smiles, then said, "Keep up the good work," before heading into his office. He didn't shut the door, though. That would've been too easy.

I allowed myself to release a tiny sigh of relief, one that no one could have heard even if they'd been standing right next to me, and then went back to the draft report Julia had left for me to proof. Her writing was actually close to flawless most of the time, but even she had the occasional typo or dropped word. But at least it gave me an excuse to look as if I was occupied with something useful, and whatever the commander might have been doing in his office, it didn't seem to include coming back out to check on me. Maybe he'd decided that he'd baited me enough for one day.

About twenty minutes or so later, Julia reappeared. Her expression was her usual one of unruffled calm, but something about the way she moved told me she was feeling tired. Watching over the djinn didn't seem to give her any pleasure—if anything, the opposite.

But of course she didn't make any comments on that subject, only offered me a smile and asked, "How does the report look?"

"Fine." I held up the piece of paper so she could see that I'd only made one or two marks on it. "Really, I doubt anyone else would have noticed either of these little mistakes."

"Maybe." Her gaze seemed to shift toward Margolis' open door, and I saw her square her shoulders. "I need to check on the commander, but after that we can head out to eat. I don't know about you, but I'm starving."

Actually, I was fairly hungry by that point, too, since I generally had a little snack when I got home. I nodded. "I'm ready to eat."

"This won't take long."

She headed into his office, and I heard their voices a moment later. They were speaking low enough, however, that I couldn't tell exactly what they were saying. Whatever it was, it didn't seem to be urgent, since she came out soon enough.

"The commander has a few more things he wants to work on, but he said it was all right for us to head out."

"Sounds good." As I was getting my purse out of the desk drawer, though, I couldn't help wondering what his reaction would be if he told us we needed to stay on, and I said no way, that I needed to eat. After all, this wasn't exactly a normal manager/employee relationship.

But he wielded the ultimate power in this community, and I had a good idea what his response would be if anyone tried to step out of line or shirk their responsibility. You couldn't get fired, but you could get turned out from your nice safe house and sent back into the wild to take your chances with the dark djinn if you turned out to be a troublemaker.

Come to think of it, that was probably a lot worse than merely getting a pink slip.

"Want to just meet at Pajarito's?" Julia asked once we were safely in the elevator. "That way we can both head straight home from there."

I agreed that it sounded like a good plan, and we went to our separate vehicles and drove the half-mile or so to the restaurant. Snow hadn't fallen for a few days, so the streets were fairly clear. I still took it easy, though, just in case the dark spaces between the street lamps were hiding patches of black ice. To save energy, half of the street lights had been decommissioned, so the town wasn't nearly as bright as its planners had originally intended.

But I pulled into the parking lot without incident, and saw Julia's Suburban slide into its own space a few seconds later. Luckily, Evony wouldn't be too worried about me; we couldn't send texts to inform each other of our whereabouts, but we'd decided early on that we wouldn't worry about making sure to always have dinner together. She went off with Shawn and Brent sometimes, and occasionally I worked late, so if one of us wasn't home by six-thirty, the other person made their own arrangements, and made sure Dutchie was fed and walked. No, it didn't exactly cover a situation where one or the other of us might be in some kind of trouble, and something less innocuous than working overtime was our reason for being late. After almost a month here, though, we'd realized the likelihood of any real emergency coming up was fairly low.

Well, except that now I know where Jace and Natila are, I thought, getting out of the Cherokee and picking my way carefully across the parking lot. *Which means that sooner rather than later, I'm going to be doing my best to bust them out of there.*

That would have to wait until I could work out some sort of plan. In the meantime, I'd have to act as normal as possible around Julia. I couldn't let on that I'd experienced something life-changing that afternoon—I'd heard Jace again, knew at last that I wasn't hanging on to false hope.

She smiled as we met at the door. "Good thing it's a Wednesday, or we'd have a hard time getting a table at this time of night."

"What's so special about Wednesdays?" I asked, giving a quick grin at Stacy, who led the two of us over to a booth in a corner. It did seem as if the restaurant was pretty sparsely populated at the moment.

A lift of her shoulders. "Some of the guys have organized a darts league. They meet every Wednesday night at the youth center. It sounds like they also raid everyone's beer supply to keep things going, so I'm not sure how much they're hitting with those darts. But I suppose it gives them something to do, although I'm surprised more people don't turn up Thursday morning with an assortment of puncture wounds."

I grinned. "Sounds like it could be fun." At least, I supposed it might. I'd never played darts, but the weather was too cold for any kind of outdoor team sports, and Los Alamos didn't have a bowling alley.

"As I said, it keeps them off the streets."

Stacy came by then and let us know what was being served that night—burgers or white chili—and we both opted for the chili, and a couple of glasses of white wine to go with it. After Stacy had left, Julia leaned back against the padded booth wall behind her and let out a sigh.

"Rough time guarding...who *do* you have down in the jail, anyway?" I asked, hoping my tone was all innocent speculation. "Mitch Kosky, driving drunk?"

At that question, she straightened, then crossed her arms and gave me a very direct look, one that made my heart beat a little bit faster. Eyes still fixed on mine, she said,

"Jessica, I think you know *exactly* who we're holding down there."

CHAPTER TWELVE

MY BREATH STRANGLED IN MY THROAT. I JUST
stared at her, at the wry smile touching the corners of
her mouth. Finally, I managed to get out, "Uh...excuse
me?"

Julia's head tilted to one side, but she couldn't reply
right away, as Stacy showed up with our glasses of wine
and set them down. Apparently not noticing the tension
at the table...or possibly ignoring it...she said, "Chili'll be
right out."

"Thanks," Julia and I both responded at the same
time, and off Stacy went again.

An awkward silence fell. Julia picked up her glass
of white wine and took a sip, staring at me expectantly
the entire time. Not knowing how I should respond, I
wrapped my fingers around the stem of my own glass,

but I didn't drink any of it. Right then, I was wishing I'd ordered something a little stronger.

At last I said, "I don't know what you're talking about."

"Oh, I think you do. You've done a good job of faking everyone else out, but I can tell your heart isn't in what you're doing here. It feels to me like you're biding your time."

Jesus. My hands wanted to shake, but I wouldn't let them. No way could I let Julia see how much she'd rattled me. I did lift my wine glass then and take a swallow, more to give me time to gather my thoughts than because I really felt like having that glass of chardonnay. It tasted sour in my mouth...or was that just nerves?

"Really, that's not it at all. It just takes me time to, I don't know, relax into a new situation."

Her blue-gray eyes were fixed on me. She had heavy dark lashes, a lot darker than her hair, but she didn't have roots, so she had to be one of those lucky blondes who didn't have fair lashes as well. Fingers tapping on the base of her wine glass, she said, "It's okay, Jessica. I don't blame you. For the record, I don't agree with holding...those two. They're not the ones to blame for the situation we're in. But let's just say I kind of have the minority opinion around here."

It was my turn to slump against the booth and stare at her. Right then, I was pretty much certain something must have gone wrong with my hearing. Otherwise, that would mean Julia Innes didn't believe every single djinn was completely evil...that she might turn out to be the most unlikely of allies.

"That's...surprising," I said eventually, then swallowed some more wine. "I take it Captain Margolis doesn't have any idea as to what you actually think on the subject?"

"God, no." Her lips pressed together for a second. Then she went on, "He's not the type who cares to hear about anyone's opinions but his own, so I don't offer mine, unless it's something to do with how I manage the office. He will actually listen to me when it comes to that sort of thing. But trying to convince him that it's unjust for us to hold those two? As they used to say, fuggedaboutit."

The word I was looking for was gobsmacked. That about summed up the way I felt as I continued to stare at her, not really believing that those words were coming out of her mouth.

"The funny thing was," Julia continued, "*he* was looking very quiet and sad when I came in this afternoon. I knew that device of Miles was hurting him. I hate that. They don't need to crank it the way they do, since a much more tolerable level is still effective at blocking a djinn's powers, but everyone else who pulls watch duty seems to regard it as their own piece of personal revenge."

I must have made some small, despairing sound, because she glanced away from me then, as if embarrassed by the actions of her fellow survivors.

"So I turned it down, and then he got the most—I don't know how else to describe it—beatific look on his face. I could've said it was just the relief from the constant pain, but it was more than that, wasn't it?"

Somehow I managed to nod. "We—we could communicate. Just for a few minutes, because then Margolis came in, and that was the end of it. But at least—at least I knew Jace was still alive. I'd kept hoping, but I didn't have any proof. Not until then." Tears began to sting at my eyes, and I blinked, willing them away. Having a meltdown in Pajarito's, even on a slow night, was not a good way to avoid unwanted attention.

Silence for a few moments then, during which Stacy showed up with our bowls of chili and some fresh-baked rolls. Julia thanked her, while I made a show of drinking some more wine so it wouldn't look odd that I wasn't saying anything.

Once she'd determined the coast was clear, Julia said quietly, "You really do love him, don't you?"

"M-more than anything."

She went still then, her expression wistful, sad. "You're lucky." Without looking at me, she spooned up some of her chili and ate a mouthful.

I hesitated, feeling as if she might be finally on the verge of discussing her past with me, and worried that if I pushed or asked the wrong question, she'd clam up again. And also, I sort of wanted to go over and give her a hug, both for her unexpected support of my relationship with Jace, and because she looked as if she could use one.

But I didn't, mostly because there was no way to do that sort of thing while sitting across from someone in a booth in a restaurant. It would have also attracted way too much notice, which was something I knew neither one of us wanted.

"You didn't...have someone like that?" I asked, my voice tentative. I seemed to recall her making a very oblique reference to a "we" when she and I first met, but she'd never said anything like that since, in contrast to a lot of the other survivors, who seemed to invoke the memories of their lost loved ones quite often, as if to keep those memories from beginning to fade away. It was harder to keep your anger alive if you had started to forget.

"Not like that," she replied, then drained the rest of her wine. A lift of her hand, though, and Stacy was back over at our table, carrying two little carafes with refills for both of us. Neat trick.

"Then...like what?"

Julia's expression hardened. "Let's just say that not everyone is angry with the djinn for wiping the board clean, so to speak. For some of us, it was like a 'get out of jail free' card."

I blinked at her, again not sure I was hearing her correctly. "You mean, you're glad they killed all those people?"

"No, of course not. It was terrible. Horrible. It's just...." She let her sentence die away into silence as she reached out to pour more wine into her glass. "In my case, they did me a favor. I was too scared to leave and didn't see any way out. Then the djinn just sort of... took care of it."

It didn't take a master's in English to read between the lines of that particular story. Julia's was an old, sad one, the kind of thing my father had seen way too often. He always said the domestic abuse calls were some of the worst.

"Your husband...hit you?" I asked, barely above a whisper.

She shook her head at once. "No. That is, one time. The problem was, I knew it wouldn't be only the one time if I stayed. It was a question of when, not if. And he wasn't my husband. He was my fiancé. Sort of made it worse, in a way. I mean, we weren't tied together legally. But he was one of those smooth-talking, controlling types. And I was stupid."

"You are not stupid." Hell, no. Julia Innes was one of the most capable women I'd ever met. Unfortunately, as my father had said more than once, being with an abuser had nothing to do with how smart or capable you were. It was all about having someone in your life who was trying to control you, who knew how to push all the right buttons. That was another reason why I'd felt so stupid about my ex-boyfriend Colin cheating on me. I should've seen the signs. At least he wasn't abusive, just...indifferent.

"I do feel stupid. I had a condo, one I'd bought with my own money after busting my ass for five years as a paralegal. He told me to sell it, since I was moving in with him anyway. So I did, and I put the money in our joint account."

"He *spent* it?" I asked, aghast, my mind going to the obvious conclusion.

"No." Not looking at me, she said, "It wasn't about the money with him. He was a lawyer. He had plenty of money. He just didn't want me having anything of my own. The one time he hit me, it was because I'd gone shopping for a car without him." Her hand went up to her cheekbone, as if feeling the spot where her fiancé had hit her. Still staring down at the tabletop, she added, "The Heat came along only a few days after that. And Julia's little problem was solved."

"I'm sorry."

Her shoulders lifted. "He went early, and I was glad he was dead. And then I was guilty for feeling glad, especially when it turned out almost everyone else was dead, too. I didn't mind the hand of God coming down to smite Ian, but I certainly never wanted anyone else to get hurt. I didn't have too much time to brood over it, though, because then Captain Margolis came along, and I could concentrate on living from day to day, on helping the other survivors." At last she raised her head and gave me a weary smile. "So there's my dirty little secret. It's far worse than yours."

"I don't think you can beat yourself up too much for that," I said gently. "I mean, I probably would have felt the same way if I'd been in your situation."

"Ah, but you wouldn't have been in my situation. I've been watching you, Jessica. You're tough. The first time a guy like Ian tried to pull that kind of crap on you, you would have walked out." She ran her fingers up and down the stem of her wine glass, gaze still not quite meeting mine. "But I don't have that kind of strength."

I hated to see her continuing to rake herself over the coals for something that really wasn't her fault. In a way, she was giving this former fiancé of hers power still, even though he was months dead. "You can't blame yourself. My father was a cop, and he saw way too much of this kind of thing. He always said abusers were crafty and clever, and way better at manipulating people than they had any right to be."

"Sounds like you were lucky in your father. Mine was an abusive bastard, and I always swore I'd never be like my mother." Another one of those tired little smiles, so incongruous when contrasted with the polish of her appearance. Unlike most of us survivors, who went around in jeans and boots and sweaters and jackets more notable for their warmth than their sense of style, Julia almost always wore skirts, albeit with high-heeled boots. You could take the girl out of the law office, and all that. "And then Ian came along, and I got trapped right in the same goddamn cycle."

"I think you would've left," I told her. "You just ended up not having to make that decision, because of the Dying."

"I appreciate your confidence in me." Despite those words, her expression appeared far from convinced. Lowering her voice, she added, "And I won't tell anyone about—about *him*."

"Thank you." I could tell she wanted to leave the subject of her past for now, so I asked, also in an undertone, "Do you know how many of those devices Miles has made so far?"

She hesitated, eyes flicking up toward me, slightly wary now. "Why?"

"I think you know why."

Another long pause, her manicured nails tapping on the tabletop. "I don't want anyone to get hurt."

"Neither do I," I said at once. It was the simple truth. Just because I wanted to get Jace out of here didn't mean that I intended to leave a trail of destruction behind me. "Really, I've got nothing against anyone in Los Alamos. I'm sure they thought they were doing the right thing when they took Jace and Natila. This isn't about revenge."

"That's...noble."

"It's the truth." Then, as her expression still appeared to be more than a little dubious, I added, "Well, okay, if the opportunity arose to give Captain Margolis a little grief, I might not pass it up."

Her lips compressed. "I can't blame you for that."

I'd been wondering exactly what the nature of their relationship was. "He hasn't...." I began, then stopped myself. Did I really want to force her into making revelations she'd rather were kept hidden?

But to my surprise, one corner of her mouth gave an ironic lift. "God, no. That is, I'm sure he wanted to, but that was one area where Ian actually turned out to be useful. When Margolis tried to put a move on me, I told him I was mourning my fiancé, and he let it go. I'm certainly not trying to defend his behavior, but at least he's not into forcing women. I think he'd prefer to think of himself as some sort of post-apocalyptic Don Juan."

Shuddering, I took a sip of wine in an attempt to get the bad taste out of mouth. "Yuck."

"That about sums up my feelings on the subject. Some people aren't quite so picky, but it's their choice. Or maybe it's not much of a choice when it comes down to getting a nicer place to live and a better food allotment."

Somehow that seemed even sleazier than out-and-out seduction. "Seriously?"

She shook her head—at my naïveté, probably. "Why else would someone like Stacy be living in what used to be a half-million-dollar house? She's a nice girl, but she didn't have any real skills to contribute to the community. Not like you and the tutoring, or Evony with the car-repair know-how. By all rights, you should have the nicer house."

"But—" I wasn't a complete idiot; I understood that all sorts of sordid sexual crap used to go on in the workplace all the time, a good deal of it much worse than putting out so you could get a nice big house handed to you on a silver platter. "But he's old enough to be her father!"

"Since when has that stopped anybody? Besides, not all of us were lucky enough to be with lovers who looked like Greek gods or something." She paused then. "Well, actually, maybe not Greek, in your case. Native American gods, I guess."

I shot her a pained look, mostly because I didn't know how exactly I should be reacting. Anyway, there were a whole hell of a lot of intermediate steps between Richard Margolis and Jace when it came to looks. Dan Lowery, for instance. He was very attractive, although I hadn't noticed Stacy paying any particular attention to him. Did Margolis expect fidelity from his conquests, even though he himself was running around like a dog in heat? I had to hope for everyone's sake he was using condoms.

But I didn't mention Dan, mostly because I'd never seen him pay any particular attention to Stacy, either, whereas he was on the verge of being just a little too friendly with me. If I brought him up at that point in the conversation, I had a feeling the best I could expect from Julia was a very knowing look, and I did not want to go there right then. Or at all, if possible.

"Maybe," I allowed. "And I don't want to judge anyone."

"Good." She sat up a little straighter, then said, "Three."

"Three what?" I asked, confused as to where that had come from.

Her eyebrow went up at an ironic angle, and then comprehension dawned as I went back and picked up an earlier thread from our conversation. There was my answer. Miles Odekirk had somehow managed to build three of those goddamn boxes.

"Does he—does he use all of them at once?"

"I don't know. There's the one at the justice center, obviously. And I think he has one deployed on the edge of town to extend the coverage they provide."

So the field each device generated had its limitations. "Do you know what the range of the boxes is?"

"Not exactly. I think it depends on how high it's dialed up. The higher the setting, the smaller the field."

"You think they'd take that into consideration when they're playing their little torture games with it," I said bitterly.

"Oh, I'm pretty sure Dr. Odekirk's had words with a few of the guards, but it doesn't seem to make much of a difference. And now that he has three of them online, he's not as concerned about it, I suppose."

Julia's tone was subtly disapproving. Whether that disapproval stemmed from the way the guards were treating Jace, or Miles Odekirk's apparent indifference to their cruelty, now that there were enough devices to adequately protect the town, I couldn't be sure.

I sat back in the booth, considering her words. She'd been fairly open with me, but I didn't know if I was brave enough to ask her whether she would help me free Jace and Natila. It was one thing to believe the community's treatment of their djinn captives was unfair, and quite another to risk everything she'd built here on what I had to admit to myself was a long shot. Also, Evony and I had someplace to go. I knew Zahrias would give us a place to stay in Taos, if we managed to make it there. But Julia was no one's Chosen, and although I would certainly plead her case and ask that she be given sanctuary, I couldn't guarantee that Zahrias or the other djinn there would be willing to take her in.

"I can practically hear the gears turning from over here," she remarked, picking up her glass of wine.

"That bad?"

"Basically." She sipped some chardonnay, then set down the wine glass and gave me a very direct look. "I can't promise you anything, Jessica. I was watching the two of them today because of a fluke, but I don't get guard duty very often."

The two of them. I'd been wondering if I should ask if the missing Chosen were being held along with Jace and Natila, but Julia's comment seemed to indicate that she'd only been guarding the two djinn and no one else. Instead, I inquired, "Margolis doesn't trust you?"

"I'm not sure it's a matter of trust, more that he's got plenty of people willing to play soldier, and my talents are better utilized elsewhere. Or at least I'm pretty sure that's what he would say if I asked to babysit the djinn on a regular basis."

Captain Margolis' purported views on the subject didn't surprise me, but the tone of Julia's remark did. I hadn't even needed to ask the question—she knew what I wanted. Unfortunately, it didn't seem as if she was in a position to give it to me.

"And there's probably no use in appealing to Dan," I said, half to myself, but Julia picked up on the comment immediately.

"Um, no. In general, asking a guy who has a thing for you to assist in a jail break for your current lover isn't recommended."

"Dan doesn't have a thing for me."

She cocked an eyebrow. "Have you spent five minutes around him? He's always staring in your direction with this moony expression on his face, but trying oh, so desperately to look casual. We might has well all be back in high school."

Right then, I kind of wished I was back in high school. All the angst of those years felt like a cakewalk compared to where I was now. Voice steady, I said, "I think you're exaggerating just a bit."

"Mm-hmm." But maybe she could tell I was starting to get annoyed by her pursuit of the topic, because she abandoned the subject, saying, "All I know is that if you're going to try something, it shouldn't wait too long. Miles isn't going to stop building those devices, and the more he has, the harder it will be. Luckily for you, they're not something he can just whip out in a few days, or even a week. But he is getting faster at it. Practice makes perfect, I suppose."

"Great," I muttered. I had a sudden vision of one of those damn things being handed out to everyone in Los Alamos, creating a field so vast that no djinn could ever hope to escape it. All right, that was probably exaggerating the situation just a bit, but I would take Julia's words to heart all the same.

Whatever move I made, I would have to do it soon.

But even though I promised myself I wouldn't let the matter lie, I wasn't given much of a chance to formulate any kind of plan. The day after that, while I was off trying to teach a group of kids who looked as if they'd rather be building snow forts or going snow-boarding the importance of subject/verb agreement and why plants are green, apparently a large group of guards, directed by Captain Margolis, showed up at the justice center and hustled Jace and Natila away. They weren't going far, but they might as well have been spirited off to Alcatraz for all I could do to save them.

They had been taken to the lab facility.

"Why?" I whispered to Julia, feeling the cold clench of despair in my gut after she told me what had happened. The whispering wasn't strictly necessary, as the commander was still up at the labs, but for some reason, I couldn't help myself. The timing had to have been a coincidence, although I couldn't help wondering whether someone had overheard our conversation at Pajarito's and ratted us out. No, that couldn't be it. Otherwise, I probably would have been locked up in Jace's former cell, and Julia would have at least been questioned, if not held as well. But here we both were, collating reports for Margolis as if this was just another afternoon at the office.

"I don't know why," Julia responded, also in hushed tones. "I didn't have any advance notice. Around ten this morning, I saw a white van pull up out front, along with a couple of trucks and that yellow Hummer they use whenever they want to look intimidating. There were about ten people in uniforms, and they all came inside and went straight to the detention area, then came back out again a few minutes later. Or at least I assume they went to the jail, because when they came out, they had two people with bags over their heads with them."

Shit. *Shit*. The only two people in Los Alamos who could possibly be on the receiving end of that kind of treatment were Jace and Natila.

"And then they drove off. It looked to me as if they were heading toward the labs, as there isn't anything else in that direction." Julia paused then and gave me a sorrowful look. "I'm so sorry, Jessica. Here, maybe you would've had a chance. But at the labs?" Her shoulders lifted, and she reached out and gave me an entirely unexpected squeeze on the hand. Yes, we'd been friendly, but this was the first time she'd ever touched me, and I was moved by the gesture. Because of her past, it probably wasn't easy for her to reach out to another person. "You've been there. That facility is huge. They could be keeping your friends almost anywhere."

"Do you know it well?" I made sure to keep my tone as calm as I could. Now was not the time for me to lose it, even though inwardly I was fuming in a mixture of frustration and rage, and mostly just wanted to scream at the injustice of it all.

"The lab?" she asked, then shook her head. "No. I mean, I went up there once or twice with the commander so I could take notes during his conversations with Miles, but he stopped taking me a while back."

"Did he say why he didn't have you go with him anymore?"

"No." A brief pause then, as if she were stopping to puzzle it out. "In the beginning, when we were still communicating with other groups, Miles was trying to get the word out about the devices he'd created, and Margolis wanted me there to keep a record of those conversations."

That explanation made another question pop into my head. "Could other people make the boxes as well? They look sort of...complicated."

"Most people, no. But the group in L.A. had someone with them who'd worked at JPL—you know, the place where all the rocket scientists hang out in Pasadena?"

I nodded. Left to my own devices, I probably wouldn't have paid JPL or rocket scientists any particular attention, but my father had loved all that stuff, and if there was a launch or coverage on the news of the Mars Rover landing or whatever, he'd stop to watch it if he had the time. Remembering that about him made a little pang go through me, and right then I missed him so much that the longing might as well have been a physical pain. It was different from my need for Jace, although no less strong. I had to believe that my father would have understood why I had to rescue the man I loved, even though he was not precisely a man at all. Love was love, in whatever form it might take.

Julia went on, "Well, the guy from JPL seemed to understand what Miles was talking about, and it sounded as if the Los Angeles group was in the process of constructing their own device. That was what Miles had been dreaming of—getting every survivor group equipped with one so they could protect themselves."

If I hadn't had a vested interest in making sure one particular djinn got as far away as possible from those goddamn boxes, I would've agreed that was a great plan. The only hope for the Immune was to have the ability to defend themselves, and, as far as I knew, Miles's device was the only thing that seemed to work effectively.

Maybe too effectively.

"What's his deal, anyway?" I inquired. "That is, I understand being angry about what happened and wanting to do something about it, but this obsession of his feels almost too personal."

"For him, it is. He lost his wife and baby daughter to the Heat."

That was about the last thing I'd been expecting Julia to say. Miles Odekirk was one of those people you had a hard time imagining having sex at all, let alone procreating. But it seemed his losses had been just as profound as anyone else's.

I only managed to get one word out in response. "Damn."

She let out a tiny breath, barely enough to be called a sigh. "I know. I can't imagine what it must be like to lose a child. That is, all of us have suffered losses, but there's something particularly horrible about that. Anyway, losing his family is what's driving him. I don't think he'll ever let it go. And now that he's got two captive djinn?"

"He's never going to let *them* go," I whispered. Although the office was heated well enough, ice seemed to be filling my veins, killing all hope. I remembered too well what the lab facility had looked like—building after building, all with what had seemed like miles of corridors. Jace and Natila could be anywhere in there. Anywhere.

And if I couldn't find them, how in the world could I possibly save them?

CHAPTER THIRTEEN

As I'd anticipated, Evony didn't take the news at all well.

"Goddamn sons of bitches!" she growled as she stood at the kitchen sink, rinsing away the last of the day's grime from her hands. For someone who took as much care in her appearance as she did, she didn't seem to worry too much about her fingernails, only that they were clean. She kept them clipped short and didn't bother with polish.

"I know," I said. I was leaning up against the counter, Dutchie at my feet. It wasn't quite suppertime yet, and the dog knew better than to beg, but she kept looking up at me wistfully, hoping I'd relent and get dinner for her a few minutes early.

After she plucked a dishtowel from where it was hanging on the handle of the refrigerator door, Evony dried off her hands, then tossed the towel on the countertop. By then, I'd given up protesting every time she did that. Instead, I picked up the dishtowel and put it back where she'd gotten it. At another time, she might have smiled at my anal-retentive behavior. Right then, though, she was scowling, and didn't even seem to notice.

"So," she said at last, "what're you going to do?"

Great. Not exactly the response I was hoping for. "Actually, Evony, I kind of thought this was going to be a 'what are *we* going to do?' kind of conversation."

Still frowning, she went over to the refrigerator and got out a beer. It was the last one of the six-pack, since we wouldn't get a new allotment until the following week, and, judging by the way she tossed the empty box in the trash, I could tell the realization only made her that much more angry. True, she could buy herself drinks at Pajarito's or at one of the other bars in town in the interim, but that meant using up more of her work vouchers.

She popped the cap and took a long pull at the beer, then said, "I don't know what the hell we should do. That place is huge. Or at least, it looks huge. I've never been inside. You would know better than I do."

"I was in *one* building," I protested. "There's at least ten of them, I think. So I have no idea what they're all like."

"Probably crawling with guards."

"I don't think we have enough survivors here in Los Alamos to make the lab or anywhere else 'crawl' with guards, but yeah, I'm sure there are enough to make things difficult." I wondered then if Dan was among them. He was on the perimeter guard rotation, and I thought he'd put in a few shifts at the jail at the justice center, but of course he would never mention such a thing to me, and not just because the djinns' presence in the holding cells was supposed to be a secret. Julia's teasing aside, I knew he was interested in me, and admitting that he'd been playing prison guard to my captured djinn lover was not something he'd probably find too appealing.

But because I knew I wasn't brave enough to ask him openly, the question of whether or not Dan was now being stationed as a guard at the lab was sort of moot. About all I could hope was that any plan I did come up with wouldn't involve him directly. I'd hate to see him get blamed in case Evony and I somehow did manage to free our two djinn.

She took another large swallow of beer. Lately it seemed as if she'd been drinking way more than she should, but I wasn't her mother. I didn't think it was my place to tell her to stop. If that was her way of coping with the situation, there didn't seem to be too much I could do about it. Besides, it didn't seem to interfere with her work—she got up every morning and cheerfully headed off to the motor pool. In a way, I thought she preferred hanging out with Shawn and Brent to being with me. Maybe I reminded her too much of what she'd lost, since I'd suffered a similar loss. Or maybe being with the guys was a little bit like being back with her brothers and working on cars.

Shrugging, she told me, "I don't know what you want me to say, Jess. I mean, I wish I could come up with some brilliant plan off the top of my head, but I don't think that way. Even when Jace and Natila were only in the detention center, it would have been hard enough, but now?" Another swallow of beer. Then she said, "I think all we can do is hope this is just a temporary thing. Like, maybe they took them up to the lab or something for tests, and then they'll go back to the regular jail in a day or so."

"Tests?" I repeated. That sounded a lot worse than merely being interrogated. At the same time, I couldn't help thinking that maybe Evony was now trying to downplay this turn of events because she really didn't have any idea what we could do about it. Tone sharp, I asked, "What kind of tests?"

"How the hell should I know? Do I look like a scientist?"

"No."

Evony shot me a glare at that response, but then she only shrugged and drank some more beer. "That doesn't *have* to be why they're up there. It's just something I thought of."

"I hope you're wrong," I said. "Because a while ago, Miles Odekirk was asking me if I'd ever seen Jace get hurt or be in pain. I said I hadn't, since it was the truth, and also because I was hoping that if I made Jace sound really tough, then Odekirk would know it was impossible to do anything that really would hurt him."

Those big brown eyes of hers, with their now-familiar cat-eye liner, widened. "Is it? Impossible, I mean. I never saw Natila get hurt, either, but it wasn't like we were doing much that would put her at risk."

I looked past Evony and out the kitchen window, which was more or less oriented to the southwest, in the direction where the labs were located in relation to our house. It was dark now, so I couldn't really see much. That didn't matter, though. I knew Jace was out there somewhere.

At last I said, "I don't know whether it's impossible. I can only hope that it's not what Miles Odekirk is trying to find out."

And the nightmarish notion continued to haunt me—that Jace and Natila were now being tortured somehow, and there wasn't a single goddamn thing I could do about it. The psychic bond that he and I had shared was now broken, shattered by Odekirk's infernal little box. Jace couldn't reach out to me, and I certainly didn't have the sort of mental gifts that would allow me to reach out to him. I'd never really believed in psychics, but now I wished I was one, just so I could know was happening to him up at the labs.

At least Julia had made it sound as if Miles Odekirk didn't max out the settings on his little machines just because he could. No, he would probably get by with inflicting a little less pain if that meant the effective area of the device would be that much greater. After all, if my suspicions were correct, Dr. Odekirk had probably come up with a bunch of new ways of doling out pain. He didn't need the box to inflict his own personal world of hurt.

That realization effectively stopped my waffling. Maybe I was being crazy. Maybe I'd be caught, and then nothing Julia Innes could do or say would save me. Right then, I was willing to take the risk if I could hear Jace's voice again, could have him reassure me that he really was all right, and that yes, they were performing tests on him at the lab, but they weren't anything he couldn't endure.

Dutchie roused when I slid out of bed, since she'd been sleeping on the floor near the entrance to my room. I leaned down and stroked her behind the ears, whispering, "Stay quiet, baby. I'll be back before you know it."

That seemed to reassure her, and she settled back down, nose on her front paws, but eyes open, watching me. I didn't turn on the bedside lamp; Evony was a fairly heavy sleeper, but no point in risking waking her up at exactly the wrong moment. If this went sideways, I wanted her to be able to say with all honesty that she'd had no idea what I was up to. Luckily, my wardrobe wasn't that extensive, so even in the darkness it was easy to lay hands on my jeans and a long-sleeved T-shirt and a sweater. My boots were sitting next to the bed, and I sat down and pulled them on before tiptoeing out of my room and down the hall. Thank God the house had wall-to-wall carpet—it muffled my footsteps as I crept through the living room and headed to the coat closet. I always kept my gloves stuffed in my pockets and wound my wool scarf around the coat's hanger, so I didn't have to go hunting for any of the outdoor items I needed.

The part that worried me the most was the sound of the garage door opening, but I had to take that risk. From the house, it was a little more than two miles to the lab, a distance that would have been easily walkable in decent weather, but not something I really wanted to attempt in the middle of an icy night at the tail end of January. It had snowed about three days earlier, and the weather had been clear since. That didn't mean it wasn't still bitterly cold, with overnight temperatures dropping below zero for the past several nights. I had no choice; I had to drive.

At least Evony's room was at the very back of the house, as far from the garage as you could get and still be in the same building. There was a good chance she wouldn't hear anything, especially since she kept her bedroom door shut most nights. I think it was mostly to keep Dutchie out; Evony was friendly enough with the dog, but that didn't mean she wanted a border-collie mix snoring next to her all night. Selfishly, I didn't mind all that much. I wanted my dog in the room with me. Her presence was a comfort, something to help keep me going when I woke up in the middle of the night and realized that the Jace-sized space in the bed next to me remained empty.

My purse was still sitting on the dining room table where I'd dropped it, so I dug out my keys and then headed for the garage. It was bitterly cold even in that protected space, and I hurried inside the Cherokee, then turned the key in the ignition. At the same time, I punched the remote for the garage door and began backing out as soon as there was enough clearance for me to escape. I didn't even let the door roll up all the way, but instead pushed the button again so it would close immediately.

Right before we'd arrived in Los Alamos, Margolis had instituted a curfew...for everyone's safety, he claimed, but I knew it was more so he wouldn't have to waste manpower policing the streets. No one was supposed to be out between eleven p.m. and six a.m., except the unlucky few who pulled guard duty on the graveyard shift. Evading the guards wouldn't be too difficult, though. I'd seen the duty rosters and therefore knew that only two teams patrolled the dark, quiet streets of Los Alamos during those dead hours. It was a risk I was willing to take.

Even so, that didn't mean I wasn't being cautious. The moon was almost full, and so I really didn't need my headlights. I kept them turned off and drove along slowly, staying on the side streets as much as possible. If I did have the bad luck to run across a patrol, well, I'd tell them I'd woken up with horrible cramps and was going to see Ellen O'Dell, a nurse practitioner who was the colony's sole medical provider at the moment. Her house really was in the direction of the labs, so my lie should sound plausible enough. Driving around in the middle of the night with no headlights on was another story, but I could say I'd left them off because I didn't want to disturb anyone. That part was a little shakier, I knew. Then again, in the past I'd found that bringing up the unpleasant subject of cramps was enough to make almost any guy stop asking questions. From what I'd seen on the roster, none of the female guards ever seemed to pull the overnight rotation. I figured I was probably safe from having another woman poke holes in my story.

All my worries about getting caught seemed to have been for nothing, though. I slipped from street to street and saw no one, nothing moving. Well, that's not entirely true. As I turned onto Trinity Drive, I saw a brief flash of light reflected in a pair of golden eyes. A second or two later, two coyotes loped across the street and disappeared behind a building. Foraging for food, most likely; I couldn't think what else would have driven them out on such a bitter night. The outside temperature reading on the dashboard said it was minus two degrees.

At last I was clear of town and rising toward the Los Alamos laboratories. I couldn't risk taking the main road in, not with that guard shack positioned square in the middle of it. Possibly at night it wasn't manned, but I wouldn't chance it. When I was a little less than a quarter-mile away, I pulled over onto the side of the road and shut off the engine, then got out.

The wind hit my face in a blast that felt as if it had blown in straight from Antarctica. I gasped, but that was a mistake, as all it did was force more freezing air into my lungs.

You can do this, I told myself. *This coat is rated up to minus thirty. Now get moving—you'll warm up.*

Hands jammed in my pockets, I clicked the remote to lock the Cherokee, then began trudging up the hill. Out here, the snow was up to mid-calf, chilling my feet almost immediately, despite my thick boots and heavy socks. It would have been much easier to follow the road, as that had been plowed, but of course I couldn't do that and hope to avoid detection.

A wire fence enclosed the facility. Maybe once it had been electrified, or maybe not. And maybe they had some kind of video surveillance out here, although I didn't see any evidence of it. Miles Odekirk seemed more than a little paranoid, although it was possible he had already analyzed the current population of Los Alamos for any threats and had decided it wasn't worth wasting the electricity to keep out intruders who didn't exist. So when I put my hand on the wire fence, nothing happened, and nothing happened when I stepped down on another strand of wire, creating a gap I could slip through.

I let out a breath but remembered not to pull it back in too quickly. Already I could barely feel my toes. I needed to get out of this open, snowy spot and into the paved section of the facility as soon as I could.

Hurrying while trying to trudge through calf-high snow only made matters worse, so I took careful, deliberate strides. Unless we got another storm—which wasn't in the forecast, according to Manny Delgado, the Los Alamos group's amateur meteorologist—my tracks would be clearly visible the next morning, but there wasn't much I could do about that. The wind was picking up, creating blowing drifts of snow that looked like ghostly shapes wavering in the moonlight, and if

I were really, really lucky, the drifting snow would be enough to obscure the evidence of my passage.

Well, a girl could hope, anyway.

After what felt like an hour but was probably more like twenty minutes or so, I emerged onto the pavement, in what seemed to be the back end of one of the facility's parking lots. The building the lot was attached to seemed to be completely dark, and there were no cars around. Whether that was a good sign, I didn't know for sure. They might've been trying to hide any evidence of where they were keeping Jace and Natila, or it could simply be that the two djinn were elsewhere on the lab's campus.

Still, I had to try.

Jace? I thought with all my might. I had no idea whether I was doing this at all correctly—in the past, he had always been the one to touch my mind first, and we'd opened a dialogue from there. Now, though, I had to take the initiative, since of course he could have had no idea that I would do anything as insane as venture out to the labs on a sub-zero January night.

I heard no reply, nothing except the low howl of the wind in my ears, which seemed to come right through the knitted cap I'd pulled down tightly over my head. The moonlight was so bright that I could see the snow drifts tracing their way across the empty parking lot, even though it clearly had been plowed recently.

All right, nothing here. Time to move on to the next building. I hurried into the lee of the structure, glad for a moment's respite from the ceaseless wind. This one was mostly dark, but unlike the first building, a few lights showed on the second and third floors. I wondered how many people would be on the lab's campus during a normal workday. Miles, of course, and a few guards, but did he have any support staff of his own? Julia had never mentioned anyone performing that kind of work, and I hadn't thought to ask. During my time here, I'd made the acquaintance of quite a few people, but nowhere close to the entire population of the colony. And I had a feeling that anyone who worked up at the labs would have been instructed to stay somewhat aloof. I'd never seen Miles at Pajarito's, that was for sure.

Time to try again. *Jace?*

The answer came back almost immediately. *Jessica?*

The syllables of my name were so filled with incredulity that, despite my current precarious situation, I couldn't help smiling a little.

Yes, my darling, it's me.

How—what are you doing here?

I heard they'd brought you to the labs. Are you—are you all right?

No answer at first, which made my icy hands turn that much colder. If he really was all right, I knew he would have told me immediately.

Then at last, *I am as well as can be expected.*

What are they doing to you?

Nothing I cannot survive. At least, not yet.

Although I was so cold that I had begun to feel like a walking block of ice, a tiny flame of fury began to burn in my core. *Jace, what are they doing?*

A small, dry little sigh, like a whisper at the edge of that odd extra-sensory communication I could only share with him. *Attempting to discover our limits. I told you once that it is very difficult to kill a djinn. Well, let's just say this Dr. Odekirk is trying his best.*

It had been hours since I ate dinner, but even so, I could feel my stomach roil, and I tasted the sourness of acid at the back of my throat. My fears hadn't been for nothing, had in fact been far too correct. *I have to get you out of there. Where are you?*

My love, you've risked too much just being here. Please go back to wherever you're staying. I can endure what they're doing to me. What I cannot endure is knowing you had been caught here. There is no lie you could give them, I fear, that would allow you to walk free if that were to happen.

I would have argued, except I knew he was telling the truth. Getting caught while driving around Los Alamos after curfew was one thing. Being found out at the labs, when there was only one possible reason for me being here?

Yeah, I was pretty sure I wouldn't be able to lie my way out of that.

Please, then...at least tell me what they're doing, I pleaded. *I promise you that I'm probably imagining far worse than what's actually going on.*

That's doubtful. Jace paused, in fact hesitating for so long that I worried he would stop there, would refuse to say anything else for fear it would upset me too much. But real horrors certainly couldn't be any worse than my imagined ones...could they?

Then he said, *Small things at first—breaking a finger to see how quickly it would heal. Burning my flesh, again to see how soon I would recover. Electric shocks.*

I must have let out a small, tortured sound, even though I was doing my best not to react, because he said,

My love, these are small things. Yes, they hurt, but not for long. You've seen how quickly you heal now, and that is only as a result of being connected with me, of having a very small percentage of the sort of healing power a djinn possesses. A burn is gone within seconds, a broken leg good as new in less than a quarter-hour.

And you can heal, even with that device blocking most of your powers?

Yes. I don't know why. True, I am not healing as quickly as I normally would. Even impaired as I am, though, I still heal at a rate that would be considered miraculous in a human being. But rest assured that so far

they haven't happened upon anything that could do any permanent damage.

Is there anything that can *do permanent damage?* I hated asking the question, but some part of me wanted to know.

Of course there is. We djinn are exceptionally long-lived, but we are not immortal. Only God and his angels can lay claim to such a quality, and I am certainly no god, nor an angel.

I decided to ignore the reference to God, and the angels. Jace spoke of them so simply, as if their existence was something that should be taken for granted, and I didn't have time to get into a theological discussion. *Then...what* can *hurt you?*

A long, long pause, during which the night seemed to grow colder and the wind whistled even more shrilly in my ears. Then he said, *The thing that gives each djinn his or her power, the element we control, is also the one thing that can be our undoing. Burn me, shock me, push me off a cliff—it doesn't matter. But take away my breath, my air, choke me or smother me, and I die. Just as Natila, water elemental that she is, can be drowned, or Zahrias consumed in fire.*

Oh, my God. It made a cruel sort of sense, but at the same time, hearing this particular revelation chilled me that much more. Such a simple thing. It frightened me more than I'd thought possible, to know how his existence could be ended.

But...maybe the answer was so simple that Miles Odekirk would never figure it out. Maybe he'd keep concocting more and more elaborate tortures, and would never realize the key to destroying the djinn lay in their amazing powers, that the thing they controlled had the ultimate control over them.

But I couldn't allow Miles to keep experimenting on Jace, or on Natila. I didn't care what my lover might think—I had to get him away, get him to safety.

Again I asked, *Jace, where are they keeping you?*

I could almost see his weary smile. *Very close, beloved. It would have to be, or we would not be able to communicate in this way.*

So most likely he was being held in the building whose shelter I now used to shield myself from the wind and the drifting snow. *Is there anyone in the building?*

Two guards.

Anyone else?

Dr. Odekirk was here earlier, but he left some time back.

Is Natila close by?

I'm not sure. I know we were brought here in the same vehicle, but then we were separated, and I haven't seen or heard her since.

Damn. In my mind, I'd been imagining them in a sort of lockup similar to where they'd been held in the detention center, cells right next to each other. But from what Jace was saying, it sounded as if they were being held in different rooms...possibly, if my luck was bad enough, on two different floors. I wouldn't let myself contemplate the possibility that they could be in two entirely different buildings.

Do you remember how many flights of stairs you went up when they brought you here?

We didn't climb any stairs—there was an elevator. But if felt as if we went up two or three floors.

Two or three floors...and that was exactly where I'd noticed lights on in the building. They had to be up there. And, knowing that, I wasn't about to let this opportunity slip by.

Opportunity? I chided myself. *What opportunity? That building has to be locked, and you don't have any weapons with you.* I mourned the arsenal I'd left behind in Santa Fe, but I'd come here to Los Alamos unarmed, knowing that if I showed up with even the most innocuous .22 locked in the glove compartment of my vehicle, there would be too many questions asked. True, I could claim that I needed the guns for self-defense, but there really wasn't that much to defend against on the empty highways between Santa Fe and Los Alamos.

My kingdom for that chrome-plated Ruger....

Pining over a gun wouldn't help anything, however. I reminded myself that none of the male guards here in town were exactly what you'd called highly trained professionals. Much to Captain Margolis' dismay, he was the only one among them with actual military training. Nancy Olson had, as I'd guessed, been a cop, but as a woman, she wouldn't have nighttime guard duty. Among the rest of the Los Alamos survivors, some had been weekend shooters, and that was about it. I knew I was as good a shot as any of them. And all right, I didn't have a gun now, but if I could just get inside, I stood a fighting chance. My father had taught me how to disarm an opponent. It did require getting the jump on them, which hadn't been the case when that one man confronted me at the Walgreens back in Albuquerque. This time, though, I'd be ready.

Assuming I could get enough feeling back into my fingers to wrap them around the trigger of a gun.

Jessica, what are you planning? Jace asked, that mental voice now sounding slightly alarmed.

Nothing, I replied. *Just a bit of a rescue.*

Jessica—

Don't bother to tell me to stop. I'm not going to turn around and go back home like a good little girl. Not when I've finally found you. I'm going to get you, and then I'm going to get Natila, and then the three of us will be out of here before anyone even knows what happened. They don't have phones here, so it takes a while for word to get around.

But they have walkie-talkies, Jace pointed out. *I've seen them.*

Oh, crap. I'd forgotten about those. Well, all right, disarm and disable the guards, and then take their walkie-talkies. All in a day's work for a former grad student turned jack-of-all-trades teacher.

I'll handle it, I told him.

Jessica, please—

We're not having this argument, I said, and began inching around the perimeter of the building. My coat was dark, and my jeans and boots as well, so I assured myself that I would look like just another moon-shadow, something blurry and indistinct and not easily tracked. If the facility had infrared cameras, I was sunk, but I told myself not to borrow trouble. Besides, even if they did have those cameras, someone would still have to be looking at the monitors at the exact right moment, and I knew they didn't have the security manpower for that level of scrutiny.

I came to an entrance and stopped. All was quiet here, one downward-facing fixture on the wall opposite me providing the only lighting. Holding my breath, I pushed down on the door handle, an angular steel thing.

And the door opened. Holy shit.

I'm inside.

It was unlocked?

Yes. Crazy, huh?

Not crazy. A trap.

Why would it be a trap? No one knows I'm here.

Just because you want that to be true doesn't mean that it is.

A wave of irritation passed over me, but I brushed it away as best I could. *Jace, there's no one here. If it really was a trap, wouldn't someone have grabbed me already?*

A short silence. *Possibly.*

I think the door's unlocked because there's no reason to lock it. Hardly anyone comes up here to the lab. All the survivors in town think it's creepy. And the few who do come up here on business come in through the guard station and are already on everyone's radar.

You're doing a very good job of convincing yourself, aren't you?

By which I inferred that I had yet to convince him. Biting back the impulse to tell him, "Whatever, Jace," I only said, *The second floor?*

He sounded tired as he said, *The third, I think.*

Even I wasn't so foolhardy as to take the elevator. I crept down the corridor until I found the stairwell, then began to climb. The stairs were metal, and it was harder than I'd thought to make my way upward and not have every footfall echo off the walls around me.

Could you have made any more noise, Jessica? I scolded myself as I stepped a little too heavily on one stair. *Might as well have called ahead to tell them you were coming.*

Despite the echoing stairwell, I made it to the third floor without being stopped. I cracked the door and peeked down the hallway, first in one direction, and then the other. The place was entirely deserted, as far as I could tell.

Do you know where you are on this floor? I asked Jace.

Midway down, I think, he replied. *They placed a hood on my head when they brought me here, so I can't be completely sure.*

I burned at the thought of how they'd treated him, but I didn't have time for anger right then. *Are the guards with you now?*

No. They went out some time ago—a half-hour, I think. They don't tend to stay in the room with me. They're here when Dr. Odekirk performs his...tests.

I couldn't let myself think about those tests now. With any luck, Jace would have suffered the last of them. *What else is in your room?*

Not much. A bed—not much more than a cot, really. That's all. When Dr. Odekirk comes in to interrogate me, the guards bring in a chair and then take it away again. I think the device they are using to inhibit my powers must be somewhere close by, perhaps in one of the adjacent rooms, but it's definitely not in here.

I felt like making a Guantanamo reference, but I wasn't sure Jace would get it. Anyway, the good news was that he was alone for the moment. The bad news was that meant the guards were roaming around the building somewhere. And I might have been lucky enough to find the entrance to the building unlocked, but I kind of doubted they'd be that careless with the room where they were holding Jace.

Okay, I'll scout around a bit. I need to figure out some way to open the door.

Be careful.

I will.

As I began to make my way down the corridor, flattening myself against the wall as best I could and hoping the dim lighting would help to conceal my presence, I realized that most of the doors here were secured by keypads. The only way I could possibly get inside would be to enter the correct code. I figured the odds of that were roughly the same as my waking up and realizing this had all been a horrible dream.

Not that I wanted it to be a dream. Not Jace, anyway. I wished then for a world where the Dying had never had happened, but where I could still have Jace. Such a world didn't exist, though, and, as my grandfather used to say, wish in one hand and spit in the other, and see which one fills up first.

I squared my shoulders. *Am I getting closer?* I asked Jace.

I think so. Your voice is stronger.

Well, that was something. At least it seemed as if I was going in the right direction. I stopped in front of a door. *What about now?*

Still stronger.

After glancing down the corridor in both directions and assuring myself that it remained empty, I knocked on the door. *Did you hear that?*

No.

Okay, that wasn't it. I sidled up to the next door, then knocked again. *What about this one?*

Nothing. But your voice sounds very strong now— you must be close.

What was that about third time's the charm? I went up to yet another door and knocked.

Yes, I heard that.

Thank God. *Can you come to the door?*

No, he replied. *They tie me to the bed when they're not interrogating me.*

Son of a bitch. I inspected the keypad next to the door. A red light was blinking on and off, which I assumed meant it was armed. I didn't pretend to know too much about those sorts of things, but I guessed that it might send a signal to whoever was overseeing the building's security if the wrong code was entered too many times.

Or maybe even once.

The door is locked with a keypad system, I told Jace. *Don't suppose you know the code?*

Eight nine four three seven.

I blinked. *What?*

Eight nine four three seven, Jace repeated. This time he sounded almost amused. *I have the strongest connection with you, Jessica, but if a mortal is thinking a thought strongly enough, I can overhear it, in a manner of speaking. Especially if that thought is repeated. My guess is that the guards would repeat the code to themselves so they wouldn't forget it.*

Handy, I remarked. Fingers trembling—whether from nerves or because I was beginning to thaw out, now that I'd been inside for a while—I reached out and entered the sequence Jace had given me.

I was sure a siren was going to go off, or the emergency lights in the corridor would start flashing. Instead, the red light flipped over to green, and I heard a distinct *click*. The door moved a fraction of an inch.

Holy shit. I pushed the door open all the way and slipped in, then shut it behind me. I was in a small room that might have been someone's office once upon a time—the floor was covered in dark green industrial carpeting, and a clock hung on the wall. All the other furniture had been removed, except a narrow bed pushed up under the window. And lying on that bed was Jace.

Or rather, Jasreel. All this time, my mind had been conjuring him as the man I'd come to love, the man who wore Jason Little River's face, but the person lying on that cot didn't look like the mortal who'd died of the Heat. No, this was the harder, sterner-looking man, his dark eyes shadowed, and lines of pain cut into his face.

But I didn't care about that. He was still the man I loved, no matter who he looked like. I ran across the room and knelt next to him, fighting the tears that rose in my eyes.

"Oh, Jace," I said, and he shifted the tiniest fraction of an inch so he could look over at me. That was all the bonds holding him to the metal bunk would allow.

"Beloved," he whispered, his voice cracked, as if with thirst or disuse. Or maybe it was a little of both.

"Let me get you out of here," I told him, fishing in my coat pocket for the little Swiss Army knife I carried there. It was small, but the blade was sharp, and should be able to cut through the cords binding him.

"Hurry. In general, they don't leave me alone for more than an hour at a time."

And since he'd already said the guards had left a half hour or so earlier....

I sawed at the rope that held his left arm tied up to the metal frame of the bed. Luckily, it wasn't very thick rope, and the strands began to separate almost at once. I wondered that they didn't use something sturdier, then realized this was more a way of punishing Jace than keeping him from escaping. He had no way to do that, not with the door locked from the outside and one of Miles Odekirk's damn machines preventing him from using his djinn powers to get away.

"This is madness, Jessica." Jace's voice was soft. I heard no condemnation in it, more wonder that I would attempt something so foolhardy.

"No, it's not," I said, cutting through the last few strands of the rope and moving on to the one that held his right hand. As I did so, he lifted his left arm, flexing it as if to get the blood circulating again. "I would have done it sooner, but I only just found out where they were keeping you. And then they moved you here—"

"Shh. It's all right." The hand I had freed reached out to touch my hair, and I wanted to start crying for real then, feeling the warmth of his skin, the wave of love coming from him so palpable, it was like the first kiss of the sun after a long, cold winter.

Then his right hand was free as well, and he was pulling me against him, his mouth finding mine. I kissed him, even though I knew I should be moving on to free his feet. But I had to taste him again, glory in the sensation of those lips pressed to my lips, if only for a stolen second or two.

I did pull away, though, and began sawing through the rope that held his right foot. At the same time, he was bending down to start pulling at the knots of the other rope, the one on his left leg. In less than a minute he was free, and I stepped away so he could push himself up off the bed.

Oh, he was so gloriously tall, and although I could see the shadows of pain in his features, his confinement didn't seem to have affected the heavy muscles of his arms and chest, the strength of his back. His expression was grave as he stared down at me, and although I could tell he wanted to reach out and pull me against him again, he didn't.

"So," he said. "I am free. Now what?"

"We get the hell out of here."

"And what is the temperature outside?"

"A little below zero," I admitted. "But the cold never bothered you before—"

"When I was in full possession of my powers, no. But that device is sapping me of most of my strength, and until I am completely free of its area of effect, I can be hurt by the cold like any mortal man. Unfortunately, I am not dressed for such an outing."

As I stared at him, I realized for the first time that he wore a plain black T-shirt and a pair of black sweat pants. His feet were bare. He could probably survive a few minutes outside dressed like that, but not the long trudge back to where I'd left the Cherokee, even though it was downhill.

"We'll find something," I said. "There has to be someplace in this building where there's a spare coat or two, and maybe some boots. But we can't stay in here—we still have to find Natila first."

Jasreel watched me for a few seconds, then nodded grimly. "And perhaps if I get far enough away from the device in this building, it will not affect me as adversely, and I'll be able to endure more than I thought I could."

"Exactly," I said, keeping my tone as encouraging as possible. For all I knew, he could be right. I didn't know enough about how the boxes worked to even begin to estimate how far their effect extended.

I reached out and took his hand, and he grasped my gloved fingers. Worse come to worst, I'd give him my scarf and my knitted cap. He could never fit into my coat or my boots, but having a little extra protection from the cold would help some.

Hand in hand, we slipped away from the small room that had been his prison. The corridor was still empty, to my relief. Even so, I made sure my voice was barely above a whisper as I asked, "Do you think Natila is on this floor?"

He shook his head. "I don't think so. We djinn can sense one another. Even with the device switched on, I was aware of her presence, if she was close enough— which is how it was back at the first place they were keeping us. Once we were here, though, I lost contact."

Which meant she had to be on the second floor. Unless the light I had seen earlier had absolutely nothing to do with Odekirk's second captured djinn, and she was being held in an entirely different building after all.

I pushed the worry away. We were here now, so the logical thing to do would be to search the second floor before we started second-guessing ourselves.

"This way," I said, hurrying in the direction of the stairwell. I supposed I should be glad that Natila's likely location was only one floor below us, and not farther up in the building.

But we never got to the stairs. When we were halfway there, the doors to the elevator opened, and out stepped Miles Odekirk, flanked by not two, but four guards. The fluorescent light in the hallway glinted off his glasses, obscuring his eyes. I saw his mouth, though. It curved in a faint smile, just before he said,

"Going somewhere, Ms. Monroe?"

CHAPTER FOURTEEN

THE ROOM MIGHT HAVE BEEN A TWIN TO THE ONE where'd they'd been keeping Jace locked up—square, with ugly green carpet and a clock ticking away somewhere above my head. In this case, however, it felt far more cramped, mostly because it held Miles Odekirk, Captain Margolis, and two guards in addition to me.

I had no idea where Jace had been taken. One of the guards had spirited him off. Well, attempted to, actually. Weakened and drained by the constant influence of the device he might be, but Jace still fought back, landing a blow to the man's temple before launching himself in my direction, fear and desperation clearly etched on his face.

At once two of the other guards tackled him, wrestling him to the ground and then slapping a pair of handcuffs on him. I screamed my own protest, but with

Margolis' hand clamped around my arm like a band of steel, I knew I was powerless to help my lover. He was hauled off down the hallway—not in the direction of the room where he'd originally been imprisoned—and I was dragged into this other chamber, where I now sat on a hard little chair, hands bound behind me.

"Well," said Margolis, an unpleasant sneer on his face, "it appears that Dr. Odekirk's suspicions about you were correct."

I maintained a stony silence, since I'd decided as they brought me in here that keeping my mouth shut was probably the best approach. Protesting my innocence wouldn't do much good, seeing how they'd pretty much caught me red-handed.

The two men exchanged a glance, while the guards to either side were doing their best not to react. I didn't know either of them, although I thought I'd seen the taller of the two in Pajarito's once or twice. But I could tell by the not-quite smirks pulling at both their mouths that neither of them had much sympathy for me or my predicament. Well, why should they? To them I must seem like the lowest of the low, someone who had cast her lot in with the enemy.

I supposed I should be glad that no one had referred to me as a "djinn-fucker."

Not yet, anyway.

"I'd ask if the cat had your tongue," Margolis went on in conversational tones, "except I think we all know why you're not talking. There isn't much of a defense for what you did, is there?"

Mouth tight, I lifted my shoulders. I had a feeling the expression I wore was one my mother had always hated—the not-quite pout, eyes shifted to the side. It practically radiated guilt but wouldn't admit to it, although in this case I was guilty of a whole hell of a lot more than just coming home an hour after my parents' designated curfew, back when I was in high school and had stayed out too late with my friends.

"She's not going to talk," Odekirk put in. "We've seen the same thing in the other one. They fancy themselves in love with these creatures."

I stiffened. "Other one"? He had to be talking about Evony. According to the clock, I'd been in their custody for a little more than an hour. Plenty of time for them to send someone over to the house and haul Evony out of bed, then bring her here for questioning.

Despite my vow to keep silent no matter what, I burst out, "Evony Rodriguez had nothing to do with this. She doesn't even know that I left the house tonight!"

Again Margolis and Odekirk exchanged one of those sidelong glances. "Funny, she said almost exactly the same thing," the commander remarked. "Sounds a bit rehearsed, if you ask me."

"I don't give a shit what it 'sounds' like," I snapped. "She was sleeping when I left, and if she'd known what

I was planning, she would've tried to stop me." Maybe that was true...maybe it wasn't. I didn't know if she would have volunteered to come along, but I had a feeling she wouldn't have tried to keep me from going, if it meant a chance at getting Natila back.

"So, are you saying her devotion to her lover isn't as strong as yours is to this...Jasreel?" Odekirk pronounced the unfamiliar name with distaste.

"I'm not saying that at all. I'm just saying she probably has more common sense than I do."

Margolis smiled. There was no warmth in his eyes, though, and I knew he was enjoying this, liked seeing me completely in his power. Julia had told me that he liked to play the role of seducer and didn't take things any farther than that, was certainly no rapist, but now I had to wonder whether that assessment had been entirely accurate. And I got it then. What he enjoyed was baiting me. Messing with my head. I certainly wasn't anything special to him, just another female he might find a way to exploit.

In a way, even though Miles Odekirk's was not what you would generally call the most comforting presence in the world, I found myself glad that he was here. I doubted Margolis would attempt anything while the scientist was around.

"You may be right about Ms. Rodriguez," Odekirk said. "But let's test that hypothesis, shall we?"

A shiver went through me, even though the entire building was slightly overheated, and I'd begun to perspire in the heavy sweater and boots I was wearing. They'd taken my coat away, saying I wouldn't need it. Right then, I didn't. But, like Jace, I wouldn't get far without it....

"Test?"

Margolis jerked his chin at the two guards, and they came over to me and undid the ropes that had held me to the chair. It felt good to stand up, to be able to move my arms, but I doubted they'd freed me out of the kindness of their hearts.

"Building C," he instructed the guards, and they nodded briefly.

Each of them took me by an arm and marched me out of the room, then down the hallway to the elevator. Margolis and Odekirk followed us, not speaking as we descended to the ground floor. From there we headed outside, the bitter wind literally taking my breath away as it hit me. In that moment, my thick wool sweater felt like the world's thinnest chiffon.

But I didn't have time to worry about frostbite, because almost as quickly as we'd gone outside, we entered another building, this one a low, sprawling single-story structure. Something about it felt squat, evil, although I tried to tell myself that was just my fear talking. Buildings couldn't be evil.

What people did in them, on the other hand....

We moved through one corridor, then turned down another, and another. Overhead, more fluorescent fixtures glowed, and I wondered how much of the colony's energy was being wasted here on keeping this place lit when everyone else's power was rationed, and it was strictly lights out after ten o'clock for all the rest of us plebeians.

I told myself it didn't matter. I knew I was letting my mind run here and there so I wouldn't let myself worry about where they were taking me, what kind of test they were referencing. About what might lie ahead.

The distraction wasn't working very well.

After turning down yet another corridor, a short one this time, the guards stopped in front of a large industrial-looking door. One of them reached out to open it, and the other pushed me inside.

The room was big, with high ceilings and a cement floor. It looked as if it might have been a workshop at one time; metal tables lined the walls, but any equipment they had possibly once held now appeared to be long gone. Now the space was empty.

Well, almost empty.

On the other side of the room, not quite placed up against the wall, were two heavy chairs. Tied to those chairs were Jace and a woman I didn't recognize, but guessed must be Natila. Like him, she looked tired, with smudged-looking shadows under her big blue eyes. Somehow, though, that didn't diminish her beauty, the perfection of her ivory skin and the fine bones of her face. Her lips were rosy and full, and pale, wavy hair flowed almost to her waist. No wonder Evony had fallen for her, had thought she must be something right out of a dream.

Evony. I realized then that she was there as well, standing off to one side with her hands tied behind her back and two more guards flanking her. They were none other than Mitch and Butch, and, judging by the grins they wore, they were enjoying this immensely.

The guards accompanying me pushed me forward until I was more or less lined up with Evony. She shot me a look of pure venom and snarled, "What the *fuck* were you thinking?"

"I'm so sorry—" I began, but one of my guards, the man on the right, clamped his fingers on my upper arm in warning.

Margolis stepped forward, lips twitching oddly. I couldn't figure out what the hell his problem was, until I realized he was fighting to keep back a smile. Like Butch and Mitch, he was probably having a good old time tonight, but didn't want to look undignified.

Too late for that, asshole.

He said, "We'd been planning to perform this little experiment anyway, but Ms. Monroe's stunt this evening made us realize it really required an audience. Dr. Odekirk and I agree that it will also be an interesting test of your...love...to see how the two of you react."

Evony made a growling sound, but I could tell both Mitch and Butch must have clamped down on her arms as well, because she winced and fell silent. The whole time, though, her gaze was fixed on Natila, and I knew the longing and fear on Evony's face had to be mirrored in my own.

I forced myself to stand still, though, to not react any more than I already had. The bastard looking gloating enough as it was, and I didn't want to give him any additional satisfaction.

Margolis' jaw hardened, and he nodded at Dr. Odekirk. "Proceed."

He stepped forward, saying, "We've performed various tests on the two prisoners, both of whom exhibit exceptional powers of healing. After discussing the situation with Captain Margolis, I've decided to move on to more traditional, but no less effective, means of gathering information."

In other words, torture. I wanted to yank my arms away from the men who held them, run to Jace and Natila. But I knew I wouldn't get more than a foot. I could only stand there, cold dread coiling in my stomach. Jace had already spoken of broken fingers, electric shocks. What the hell were they going to try this time?

Margolis unclipped the walkie-talkie from his belt and said, "We're ready."

A door on the other side of the room opened, and three more guards entered. The first one held one of

Miles Odekirk's devices, while the other two were lugging heavy buckets with them. Some water slopped over, and a horrible suspicion began to grow in me. No, they couldn't....

Evony seemed to get it at the same time. Pulling against the men who held her, she burst out, "You can't do this! It's—it's un-American!"

A look of pure irritation passed over Odekirk's thin features. "Actually, not to be pedantic, Ms. Rodriguez, but the United States utilized this form of interrogation on many occasions. Besides, one can argue that effectively, there is no America any longer, and therefore our actions can't be labeled un-American." His gaze flicked over to Margolis. "Proceed when you're ready."

The commander nodded. "Oh, we're ready now. Williams, D'Olivo, go ahead."

And the guards tilted the chairs backward so both Jace's and Natila's heads were angled downward toward the floor. It looked supremely uncomfortable, but I knew their current position wasn't the worst of it. Not by a long shot. I wanted to be relieved that this wasn't a traditional waterboarding—neither of their faces had been covered, and they were only secured to chairs and not a slab of plywood or something—but I had a feeling this was going to be bad enough.

Then the two men lifted their buckets and began pouring water onto their captives' faces. I wanted to scream, to kick back at the guards who held me. But even if I somehow managed to get away from them, there was still Captain Margolis to contend with, or Butch and Mitch, or even the guard who held the djinn-control box. There was nothing I could do to stop the scenario playing out before me.

Jace spluttered, water spraying up and away from his mouth. In her chair, Natila was twisting and writhing, attempting to turn her face to one side so the water would splash off her cheek and not go into her nose and mouth. She was only partially successful, however, and when the man assaulting her realized what she was doing, he grasped her by the chin and held her in place so she couldn't move.

I wished I could look away. But I had a feeling my guards would do the same thing to me—grab my head and force me to watch, and I wouldn't allow them to manhandle me any more than they already had. Instead, I looked on grimly, knowing this was horrible, but that Jace and Natila would survive it, just as they'd already survived every other torture Margolis and Odekirk had thrown at them.

But then Jace's words came back to me: ...*take away my breath, my air, choke me or smother me, and I die. Just as Natila, water elemental that she is, can be drowned....*

Oh, my God.

I risked a quick glance over at Evony, and although she was straining against Mitch's and Butch's cruel grip on her arms, I saw more anger than fear in her face. She didn't know. Natila must never have revealed to her how she could die.

Natila was gasping, horrible gargling sounds coming from her throat. Margolis looked on, satisfaction clear in every line of his smug features, while Dr. Odekirk was tapping away on that goddamn iPad of his. It was obvious that neither one of them was going to put a stop to this. No, they were going to watch and, if not precisely enjoy it, in Odekirk's case, then learn everything they could from it.

If Natila died, and he put two and two together....

I lunged forward, breaking the grip the guards had on my arms. Right then I wasn't even sure what I intended to do—knock the buckets of water away from the men's hands, I supposed—but it didn't matter that I had no clear plan. I had to stop this. Not just for Natila's and Evony's sakes, but for Jace's as well.

But Margolis was in the way, and as soon as he saw me tear myself out of the guards' grasp, he was moving, snaking one arm around my throat and pulling me against him. I struggled, but he tightened his grip.

"Don't make me," he murmured in my ear, and I stopped, knowing that he was capable of choking me then and there. After all, who would stop him? Certainly none of the guards, and I doubted Miles

Odekirk would lift a hand to save me. After all, to him I was just another djinn-fucker, although I doubted he would ever use such a crude epithet himself.

The horrible choking noises Natila had been making halted abruptly. I saw her slump in her chair, although the ropes that bound her in place kept her from slipping to the ground. The guard who had been performing the waterboarding procedure set down his bucket, and the first flicker of uncertainty that I'd seen in any of these men passed over his features.

"Captain?" he said. "I'm not sure, but I think this one might be dead."

Evony screamed and struggled to break free of the grip Mitch and Butch had on her arms. Tears streamed down her face, but I knew she wouldn't be able to get away. Tough she might be, but they each outweighed her by probably a hundred pounds or so.

"I'll check, Captain," Miles Odekirk said, his gaze resting on me where I was still being held by the commander. "It looks as if you might be somewhat... occupied."

By then the second waterboarder had stopped torturing Jace, and tilted him back in place so he was more or less upright. He sat there and blinked, and then seemed to realize what had happened, anguish twisting his features.

"Oh, no. God, no."

"Do you believe in God, then?" Odekirk asked in mildly interested tones as he stepped over to examine Natila's limp form. "I have to say that's rather surprising."

"You'll find out the day you drop dead, and He sends you straight to Hell for what you've done today." This was a Jace I'd never seen before, dark eyes blazing, black hair dripping lank against his cheeks and throat, an expression on his face that said he would gladly reach out and snap Odekirk's neck if he could just be freed for a few seconds.

"Hmm...an Old Testament God, then." Odekirk laid two fingers against Natila's damp throat and waited a few seconds. Then he moved those same fingers to her wrist and tried again. "It does appear that she's dead. Interesting. We'll need to move her to a morgue—there's one at the funeral home down on Spruce Street. Then I'll perform an autopsy."

Evony screamed again, redoubling her struggles. Not that it made any difference; the two goons holding her only tightened their grip that much further. At the same time, Jace made a sound of incoherent rage and began struggling in his chair, so much so that he lost his balance and toppled to the side, hitting the cement floor with a sharp *crack*. Mitch and Butch began to laugh, but stopped abruptly when the scientist lifted an eyebrow at them.

"Get him up," Odekirk snapped. "We might as well take these three back to the justice center. Clearly, our security here isn't as good as I'd hoped, whereas this djinn and the woman were held there for weeks without incident."

"Are you sure?" Margolis began, but Odekirk sent him a quelling look.

"The evidence suggests that they'll be more secure there."

"Right," the commander replied, and for the briefest second I felt him increase the pressure on my throat before he let go altogether and pushed me toward the two guards who had originally held me. "Keep an eye on that one," he said, his tone casual. "She's a bit slippery."

They flanked me, their grips beyond iron this time...more like case-hardened steel. I knew I wasn't getting away.

And so I was marched out of there, a weeping Evony right behind me, while I heard them gather up Jace as well and have him bring up the rear. Just outside the entrance to the building, the white unmarked van Julia had described to me was waiting. How it had gotten there so quickly, I didn't know, but I supposed one of the guards must have radioed for it to come pick us up.

I hadn't rescued Jace. All I'd succeeded in doing was getting Natila killed, and Evony made prisoner. What the hell I was supposed to do now, I didn't have a goddamn clue.

CHAPTER FIFTEEN

Since I'd never seen the cells where Jace and Natila had been imprisoned, I wasn't sure what to expect. But they were more or less standard-issue, I supposed—enclosed in bars, with a hard little cot in each one. The bathroom facilities were down a short hallway, and you had to ask a guard to take you. I supposed it was better than having to do it out in front of everyone, but still, not the most dignified thing in the world.

Evony had retreated to her cot and was huddled in a corner, knees drawn up to her chest, face buried in her arms. When I'd tried to call out softly to her, she'd shot me a glare of such fury that I recoiled.

Let her grieve, Jace told me. He'd been silent the whole way here, and also while we were shoved into our individual cells, with me next to Evony and him across the narrow walkway that separated the pairs of cells. Of course they had to put him in a cell where I could see him but not touch him. I had to believe that was done on purpose.

He went on, *When she wishes to speak to you, she will.*

I couldn't even be relieved that we still had this strange power of mental speech, despite one of Odekirk's boxes sitting in plain sight on the guard desk only a few yards away. If Jace had been any farther from me, he probably couldn't have communicated in that manner, simply because I could tell they had cranked the damn thing up pretty high—he was shivering, and I could see the way his chest rose and fell too rapidly.

Sitting at that desk was one of the guards who'd performed the waterboarding, a ruddy-faced man I vaguely recalled was named Jeff or John or Jack. Something like that. I supposed it didn't matter. What did matter was that Jace and I could carry on a conversation like this right under his nose, and he wouldn't be able to tell.

It's all my fault, I said. *If I hadn't gone off all half-cocked, Natila would still be alive.*

That's not true. Jace had assumed a position similar to Evony's, arms wrapped around his knees, although in his case I knew it was more in an attempt to keep himself from shivering too badly. My heart ached for him, for how he must be suffering now, although

I knew he'd survived weeks of such treatment and doubtless could survive a bit longer. *You heard what Margolis said. They'd planned to test this particular torture at some point anyway. Your presence merely gave them an audience.*

That was more or less what the commander had told me, and yet I couldn't find myself too relieved to hear it. All right, so he had claimed that they were going to do the waterboarding sooner or later. But what if it had been later? Maybe if I'd really stopped to formulate a concrete plan, rather than allowing my desperation and fear to drive me to attempt a rescue before I was ready, then Natila might still be alive.

Wracked with guilt, I argued, *You don't know that for sure.*

Jace's shoulders lifted the merest fraction before he stilled again. Even that small movement was enough for the guard to give him a suspicious glance, but as Jace was quiet enough after that, the man gave a shrug of his own before returning his attention to the tablet on the table in front of him. It looked like he might be playing Candy Crush. Strange, the artifacts from before that still hung on. I supposed the games already downloaded on the tablet would continue to function until the device itself broke down.

No, I don't know when they would have finally tried that particular torture, Jace replied. *But you cannot take this responsibility on yourself. You did not kill Natila.*

Margolis, who gave the order, and Odekirk, who probably planned it, and the guard who actually drowned her—they are all guilty. Not you.

My mental voice was very small as I said, *Evony will never forgive me.*

She may not, Jace said frankly, and I had to stop myself from flinching. *That is something only she can decide. You cannot force forgiveness. You can only wait to see if it is offered to you freely.*

In which case I had a feeling I'd be waiting an awfully long time. But he was right. This wasn't about me. This was about Evony and her loss, and she needed to work her way through it on her own terms, whatever those might be. I nodded and leaned back against the wall, wondering how long they planned to keep us here, and whether they would torture all three of us on the next go-round, or only Jace.

Down the hall, I could hear the creak of a door opening, and footsteps echoing on the polished cement floors. I didn't know what time it was, but it felt as if we'd been in here forever. In reality, though, the sun was probably just rising. Maybe it was time for a change in shifts. I hoped the approaching footsteps heralded something that innocuous, and weren't the sound of Margolis coming to get us and visit further tortures on Jace. If they'd already ferreted out the significance of Natila's death by drowning....

It wasn't Margolis who came into the detention area a few seconds later, however, but Dan Lowery. My cheeks burned as his gaze settled on me for a second before he turned to the other guard. "All quiet down here?"

"Like a tomb," the man responded. "Not a peep out of any of them—well, unless you count that one in the corner who won't stop sniffling."

"Good," Dan said. "The commander said I should take over for a while so you can get some rest."

"Good." The guard got up from the desk and yawned. "I'm going on thirty-six hours with no sleep now. This last hour I could barely keep my eyes open. Not that it mattered much, since none of the prisoners were doing anything except sitting there."

Dan nodded, watching as the other man pulled his coat off the back of his desk chair and shrugged into it. A bored-sounding, "'Bye," and he was gone, hurrying toward the exit.

I watched this exchange with some trepidation. There had never been anything between Dan and me, and I hadn't wanted there to be. Even so, the current situation was more than a little awkward. Would he sit quietly at the desk and ignore us, or would he come over and mock me for being an idiot?

It seemed he'd decided to do the latter, since, after waiting a few moments, he slowly approached my cell. "Come here," he said, his voice hard.

"I doubt we have anything to say to each other," I replied. Across the way, Jace's gaze sharpened at my words, and he gave Dan a probing look.

"I'll decide that."

Since I didn't know what else I could do, I slid off the cot and approached the bars of my cell with dragging steps. "What do you want?"

In response, he darted a quick look over his shoulder. Right then, I realized he was glancing at the security camera, which was mounted on the wall above the guard desk. "Here," he said in an undertone, reaching out to slip a small piece of paper into my hand.

Without thinking, I took the paper, then folded my fingers around it. I had no idea what he was doing or why he was acting this way, but now that we were standing this close to one another, I couldn't see any anger or hatred in his expression. More like... resignation.

"You're an idiot," he told me in much louder tones. "We could've been good together, but you had to waste your time on this piece of shit?" A slight jerk of his chin in Jace's direction, and Jace stared at him with narrowed eyes. As he was opening his mouth to reply, I said,

Don't, Jace. This is just an act. There's no need to defend my honor.

You're sure?

Positive.

Very well. Jace settled back against the wall of his cell, arms folded, mouth tight and angry. It was a good act. He really did look pissed off.

Well, maybe he was, but not because of anything Dan had just said.

With the barest of nods, Dan headed back to the guard desk and sat down, then made a show of fishing an old dog-eared paperback copy of The Stand out of a desk drawer and flipping open to somewhere in the middle. It took a lot for me to keep from grinning at his choice of reading material.

I settled myself back down on the cot, then adopted a position similar to both Jace's and Evony's—knees up against my chest, fingers knotted together in front of them. In my case, however, I did so because I had a good idea that I could make out whatever was on the little slip of paper without anyone else being able to see what was written on it.

Purposely staring off into what I hoped looked like the middle distance, I shifted focus for a fraction of a second so I was able to read the two words on the paper scrap.

Hang tight.

No name signed to that short note—not that I'd expected one. But even in those two words, I recognized the graceful, looping handwriting, so different from my own scrawl. I'd seen that writing on plenty of sticky notes while I was helping out at the justice center.

Julia had sent me that note.

Right then a rush of relief and gratitude went through me, so strong I thought Jace must surely sense it. And he did, apparently, because he lifted his head and sent me a piercing glance.

Good news?

I think so. But we have to be patient.

I've learned something of patience these past few weeks. He didn't smile, because I guessed that he'd seen Dan's glance at the surveillance camera, and he didn't want to do anything that might attract attention. But I could feel him relax slightly. Then he closed his eyes, as if attempting to marshal what little strength Odekirk's device permitted him.

Slowly, I unwrapped my hands from around my knees. Fingers clenched around the scrap of paper, I bent down as if to scratch my leg, then slipped the paper inside my sock. When they locked me up in here, they'd taken away my boots. I had to hope Julia would be able to return them to me, or I wouldn't get very far. Not in this weather.

The minutes ticked by. Dan read at the desk and shifted his position every once in a while. To look at him, you'd never know he was conspiring to break a group of prisoners out of the city jail. In her corner, Evony didn't move at all. Maybe she'd finally fallen asleep. I wished I could communicate with her the way I could with Jace, give her some idea of what might be coming, but of course that was impossible. All I could do was hope she'd be able to think on her feet and follow along when the moment did arrive.

Then I heard footsteps. Lighter than Dan's, hurrying down the hallway. I sat up, pulse racing, and saw that Jace had roused himself as well. Even Evony lifted her head, as if picking up on the excitement surging through me.

Julia emerged into the detention area, expression grim. A glance over at Dan, and he set down his book and then got up from behind the desk.

"Did you—" he began, and she nodded.

"It's down. We have five minutes before it manually reboots."

"What?" I asked, and Julia looked over at me.

"The security system. I disabled it, but it'll be back online soon. We have to get you out of here before then."

"Margolis—"

"He's over at the funeral home with Odekirk. They're both…occupied."

I couldn't help wincing, since I knew exactly what was keeping them busy. Where the hell did a physicist even learn how to perform an autopsy?

Evony obviously understood the meaning of that exchange as well, since she got up off her cot and wrapped her fingers around the cell bars. Her face was a study in anguish. "They're cutting her up? My Natila?"

"I'm sorry," Julia said. "There was no way I could stop them. But at least it means their attention is elsewhere. We do have to get moving, though."

While they'd been speaking, Dan had come to my cell and inserted a key in the lock. Without saying anything to me, he opened the door, then moved on to Jace's cell. He emerged and came straight to me, folding me in his arms. It felt so good to be there—and yet I could feel how he was shaking, how hard his heart was beating.

"Can you do this?" I asked him.

He nodded.

Apparently noting our exchange, Julia turned away from Evony and said, "I'll take care of that." She went to the device and moved her hands over it. Almost at once, Jace's heart beat began to slow, and some of the tremors that wracked his body started to subside.

"Sorry I couldn't turn that down before," Dan said as he unlocked the door to Evony's cell. "But I only had one training session with it, and I was afraid I might make matters worse if I started messing with the thing."

"That's all right," Jace replied. He looked over at Julia. "What's the plan?"

"My Suburban is parked outside. I've got Dutchie locked up in the back. You're going to knock Dan and me out, and then you're going to steal the car and get the hell out of here."

Jace blinked. "I'm going to what?"

"The only way Margolis will swallow any of this is if we make it look convincing." Julia's voice was calm, as though she allowed people she'd only just met to knock her unconscious every day of the week. "The security system's been glitching for weeks, so this hiccup shouldn't raise too many eyebrows. You're going to take Dan's gun and hit him with it, and then you're going to do the same thing to me. They'll find us both here unconscious, and my car keys stolen...and you three gone."

Evony, face tracked with dark streams of runny mascara and eyeliner, crossed her arms and glared at Julia. "Where are we supposed to go?"

"To Taos," Jace said.

"I can't go there without Natila. What's a Chosen with her djinn?"

My heart constricted at the despair in her voice, but I said gently, "They'll take you in. You're still Chosen, even if—even if Natila is gone."

The only reply I got from her was a narrow-eyed glare, and I swallowed. Obviously, those fences were going to take a long time to mend.

Ignoring the tension between us, Julia said, "You have to go, and you have to go now." She glanced down at her watch. "Now you only have two and a half minutes until the security system turns back on."

"What about the rest of the people in the building?" I asked.

"Most of them are in the break room. It's Ernie Lasky's birthday, and someone made cake."

I shook my head. "You do think of everything, don't you?" One of these days Julia would stop impressing me. Maybe.

A quick smile. "I try. Now get out of here."

Evony moved past me, darting over to the desk so she could pick up Odekirk's device. "We should take this thing with us."

"Are you nuts?" I demanded. "Look at what it's doing to Jace. We can't have it in the car with us. "

"We'll turn it off," Evony said.

"No, you can't do that," Julia cut in. "Odekirk has them daisy-chained somehow...if one is shut off, an alarm light goes on in the other two. Once you're outside Los Alamos, it should be all right, since the cat will be out of the bag anyway, but doing it before then will only send out the alert that much sooner."

"It's all right," Jace said. "I've lived with it close to me for weeks. I can manage a few more minutes. Now that it's been turned down, it's bearable."

I didn't like it, but I knew arguing any further would only waste time we didn't have.

"We're running out of time," Julia said, voice tight.

"I know." A pause, then, "I should do this, I think," Jace said. With a lightning strike of a move, he pulled the gun out of Dan's holster and hit him across the temple with it. At once he collapsed on the ground, a slow trickle of blood beginning to emerge from his hairline.

"Very efficient, Jasreel," Julia remarked. "My turn, I suppose."

"I commend you for this," Jace told her. "And we will not forget what you have done for us." Before she could even reply, he struck her just the same as he'd done Dan, and she, too, tumbled to the cold cement floor.

I winced. "You sure they'll be all right?"

"I believe so. Dan may have a mild concussion—I was able to calibrate the blow better the second time. But other than a few headaches, they should be fine."

There wasn't much I could do except nod. We certainly couldn't waste the opportunity Dan and Julia had given us. I knelt and pulled a key ring out of Julia's jacket pocket, then straightened. "Let's go."

The three of us—all without footwear—padded down the hallway and then up the flight of stairs that led to the main floor of the justice center. Because I'd spent so many hours working in the building, I knew exactly which exit led to the parking lot. I headed there, Jace at my side and Evony only a pace or so behind us. As Julia had promised, the place appeared more or less deserted, and no one stopped us as we ran out the rear door and into the icy brightness of a winter morning.

At once the chill from the sidewalk rose through my sock-clad feet, but I couldn't stop to worry about that. Only a few paces to the Suburban, and then I was clicking the remote to unlock it and we were all piling in. No one protested when I got behind the wheel—maybe both Jace and Evony were used to me driving all the time, and so didn't bother to suggest that one of them should pilot the SUV.

I gunned the engine and then slid on some black ice as I was pulling out of the parking lot. Damn. I needed to back off. Maneuvering this boat of a Suburban was a lot different from my father's Cherokee.

Even though I knew I had to concentrate, I felt my throat tighten at the thought of the Jeep. I would have to leave it behind—I didn't even know where Margolis' goons had taken it after I'd left it parked by the side of the road on the way up to the lab—and that was like leaving the last memento of my father behind as well.

But then Dutchie barked from the area behind the back seat where Julia had put her, and the tears receded. The Cherokee was just a car. A good one, and it had saved me over and over again, but the most important thing was that I had everyone here with me. Jace and Evony and Dutchie, somehow miraculously safe.

We slowed to a more sedate pace once the justice center was a quarter-mile or so behind us. Yes, everyone knew Julia's Suburban, and the windows were tinted, so you'd have to get close to see who was actually behind the wheel. Despite that, I didn't want to go out of my way to attract attention. We still needed to get down the hill and away from Los Alamos.

In the passenger seat, Jace still looked tense and drained. I couldn't take my hands off the wheel, but I managed a quick glance over at him.

"Are you all right?"

A brief nod. "It is difficult, being this close to one of Dr. Odekirk's devices. I'll be fine once we're entirely away."

So would we all. Well...I didn't know about Evony, but I had to hope that eventually she'd get past the pain of losing Natila. And surely they'd have to give her refuge in Taos, even if the djinn who loved her was now gone.

We were past the town limits now, moving down Highway 502 as it wound through the mountain pass on its way into Española. Soon we'd be coming up on the checkpoint at the bottom of the hill. I had to pray that they weren't watching the outbound lanes, or at least not paying much attention to them. After all, anyone mere mortal heading out of the safety of Los Alamos was running the risk of coming up against the bad djinn, the ones who apparently had decided to make a sport of hunting humans.

But it wasn't the djinn I was worried about. Evony and I had Jace with us, and the djinn had signed a pact to leave us Chosen alone. We just had to get past that checkpoint.

I saw it now, approaching fast in the lanes ahead. No yellow Hummer this time, but a couple of dark pickup trucks. As I'd thought, the men standing next to those trucks were looking away from us, out toward Española. I wondered at the futility of such a guard when no one new had approached Los Alamos for weeks, but Captain Margolis loved routine almost as much as he loved his petty cruelties.

My foot wanted to lift from the gas, but I wouldn't let it. I'd already decided the best thing to do was blow through the checkpoint at full speed. There was plenty of room on the right to go around those trucks, and I didn't know if Julia and Dan had already been discovered, whether a warning had already been radioed ahead.

"Jessica—" Jace said, and I nodded.

"I know."

They definitely had been warned. Two shotguns were being lifted in our direction as we barreled toward the two trucks.

"Everyone down!" I cried, and Evony and Jace both ducked, even as one blast, then another, hit the Suburban. The first shot glanced off the roofline, but the second one hit the windshield square on, sending out a flurry of spiderweb cracks surrounding a hole I could've put my fist through. If Jace hadn't gotten out of the way when I warned him, the shell would've exploded right in his face.

But then we were past, although that didn't keep them from continuing to fire at us. Another shell hit the rear window, and Dutchie yowled.

I felt as if that shell had struck me. Oh, God, if those bastards had hit her....

"Evony, check on Dutchie!" I screamed, sock-clad foot jammed on the accelerator as I manhandled the Suburban down the highway. The worst of the damage was on the right side of the windshield, but it was still hard for me to see.

I wanted to pull over so badly that the compulsion was like a physical ache, but I forced myself to keep driving, to make myself breathe, until I heard Evony say, "She's okay, Jessica. Some glass from the window exploded on her, and I think it scared her. But she's okay."

The relief flooding through me was so intense that for a moment I worried I was about to pass out. I risked the briefest look possible into the back seat, saw Evony clinging to Dutchie, arms around the dog's neck while Dutchie whuffled happily into Evony's chest. Then I felt Jace's fingers cover mine on top of the steering wheel. His flesh was still cold.

As Julia had said, the cat was definitely out of the bag now. No point in being cautious anymore. "Evony, please turn that fucking thing off. The switch is somewhere on the bottom."

A few seconds passed while she fumbled with the device. Then she said, "Okay."

I glanced over at Jace, and he nodded.

"It's off," he said quietly. "My powers are back. I can feel them."

In that moment, I could tell he looked better. I wanted to stare, but I knew I had to keep my attention on the road. However, even that brief glance had told me that the shadows were disappearing from under his eyes, and color had returned to his cheeks. His voice sounded stronger, too, firm and calm. This was the Jace I'd feared I would never see again.

"What now?" I asked. "Can we ditch the Suburban? Can you just—I don't know—blink us back to Taos?"

An amused smile touched his lips. "If it were just you and me, I would say yes. But to take you and Evony, and the dog, after so many weeks of having the power drained from me...no, I don't think it's possible. We'll have to get there the old-fashioned way."

It figured. Distance-wise, Taos really wasn't so far from where we were now. An hour's drive on a good day. But the highway was already starting to look snowy, now that we were past the area protected by Odekirk's devices, and we had a long way to go before we got to the parts of Taos that the djinn deemed worthy of clearing.

Then I had a thought. "All right, maybe taking all of us is asking a bit much. But up in Taos the djinn were clearing the roads. Can you use your powers to do that? It would make the rest of the drive go much quicker."

He nodded at once. "I should have thought of that myself. That is simple enough, since I can have the air do my bidding."

And then…the drifted snow that had covered the highway began to blow away, as if an unseen wind had come along to clear our path. It was no natural wind, of course, but one Jace had created for us, not blowing from one direction, but pushing the snow to either side so the center of our lane was as clean and dry as it would be in the heat of summer. I increased my speed, inching up to forty, and then fifty. If there had once been any abandoned vehicles on this stretch of highway, Margolis' crews must have cleared them away, probably taking the most useful trucks and SUVs back up to Los Alamos.

There was no pursuit that I could see in the rearview mirrors. Maybe now that they knew the djinn were actively hunting unprotected mortals, the survivors in Los Alamos didn't dare to come after us, past the safety of the field projected by Odekirk's little boxes. How much had we weakened that field by taking one of the devices away with us?

I supposed I would never know. Right then, it didn't seem to matter too much.

We were away. We were safe.

CHAPTER SIXTEEN

"So," Zahrias said, a frown pulling at his brows, "this is the cause of all our troubles."

We stood in the conference room he seemed to be using as his audience chamber. A fire crackled in the hearth, and Lauren had brought us all mulled wine, even though it was only late morning and not really an hour I would have considered appropriate for wine-drinking. Not that I minded; after that escape from Los Alamos, I definitely needed a drink. It just amused me slightly that the djinn didn't seem to pay much attention to human notions of time and the customs associated with them.

On the surface, our setting appeared warm and inviting enough, and definitely a welcome relief after the chilly drive we'd just endured, with the frigid air blowing in through the Suburban's shot-up windows. But I could tell Zahrias was not pleased that we'd brought one of Dr. Odekirk's boxes with us. Not at all.

Evony had begged off from this meeting, saying she only wanted to rest, and Zahrias hadn't protested, had said that of course she must take as much time as she needed. Learning of Natila's death hadn't seemed to upset the djinn leader much; he'd only shaken his head and then moved on, saying that we would all have sanctuary here, and that Evony should take the room where she'd stayed during our first time in town.

Jace and I were given a more luxurious suite than the one I'd had before, and somehow clean clothes were miraculously provided for us. Both of us bone-weary, we changed and freshened up as best we could, and then came to speak with Zahrias. Apparently, he was unwilling to give us anything more than that half hour or so of downtime.

"I thought we might study the device," Jace said. "Evony's idea that we should bring it here was a good one. If we can learn its secrets, then we can also learn how to keep it from being used against us."

"Hmm." Zahrias crossed to the table that held the mulled wine and picked up his glass. His gaze flickered to me for a second. "I will admit, Ms. Monroe, that I did not expect to see you again...especially with Jasreel at your side."

Thanks for the vote of confidence, I thought. Actually, though, I really couldn't blame Zahrias for thinking that way. If someone had asked me to lay odds on my chances of success, I wouldn't have given myself anything over fifty to one. "We had help," I told him. "Some very brave people put their lives on the line for us."

From the surprised expression that flitted across his swarthy features, I guessed Zahrias hadn't expected that any mortal who wasn't Chosen would have lifted a finger to help a djinn. "Is this true, Jasreel?"

"Yes," Jace responded. "They follow a man named Margolis, and although most in the town do his bidding, there are some who don't believe his actions are just, who didn't think Natila and I should have been hunted down and imprisoned. Two of them—Julia Innes and Dan Lowery—helped us to get away. I might have suffered a fate similar to Natila's if they hadn't engineered our escape."

For a second or two, Zahrias didn't respond, only stood there with his hands wrapped around his glass, as if to re-warm the mulled wine it contained. "So it was at this Margolis man's orders that you were imprisoned in the first place?"

Jace nodded.

"And what of the Chosen who were missing?" Zahrias asked then. "Did you have any word of them?"

"No," I said, wondering yet again what could have possibly happened to those four men and women. "I couldn't ask outright, but it was fairly obvious that

Margolis' people hadn't captured anyone like that, or had anyone matching their descriptions come to Los Alamos at all. It's as if they vanished into thin air."

The djinn leader didn't like my reply, I could tell; his dark eyes narrowed, and angry orange-red flames flickered into existence around his head before disappearing again. "How can you be sure this Julia woman wasn't concealing the fact that the missing Chosen were there all along?"

"Because I would trust Julia with my life," I said simply. "I already have, really. She had no reason to risk herself to save us, but she did, just because she knew it was the right thing to do. I suppose there's a very remote chance that Margolis somehow slipped the Chosen in under her nose, but I doubt it. She's his— well, I suppose she's like Lauren here. She keeps everything running."

"And yet this Margolis doesn't realize that she's betraying him?" Zahrias didn't quite sniff, but it was obvious that he wasn't too impressed with what he'd heard about the commander of Los Alamos.

"I wouldn't be too quick to dismiss him," Jace put in, finally going over and retrieving his own glass of mulled wine so he could take a drink from it. "Yes, so far Julia has been able to fool him, but that is only because she is a formidable person in her own right. But Margolis' word appears to be law, and he has a sizable group of men who follow him without question. Their numbers are far greater than ours."

"Normally, I would say that is of no account, but for these things." Zahrias shot a disgusted glance at the box before looking back over at me. "While I suppose I can see the logic in wanting to know how they work, I don't see what you think we can do about it. We are djinn, not scientists or engineers. The things of this world bend to our will, and so we have no need of gadgets in the way that you mortals do."

His dismissive tone made my hackles go up. All right, so some of our science hadn't ended up doing a lot for our planet. But we'd also achieved great things, and I wasn't about to let it go that easily. "Fine, so the djinn don't need to know how to change the timing belt on a Subaru. But what about the Chosen here? Isn't there one of them with any kind of scientific knowledge? Anyone who could at least try to take a look at this device?"

A shrug, the shining fabric of his robe glinting in the warm reflected firelight. "Perhaps. I will admit that I have not familiarized myself with the particular talents and skills of most of them. That is their partners' concern, save where they can be useful to the group here—like Lauren, or Aidan and David, who enjoy watching the roads for us. But I will have Lauren make inquiries."

That was a start at least, although I could tell that Zahrias didn't think it particularly important to know how the boxes worked, as long as they weren't being used directly against anyone in his group here. "Did you know that the other djinn have been hunting the rest of the survivors?" I asked.

He didn't reply immediately, but instead looked over at Jace, who nodded and said,

"Yes, it seems the final purge has begun. You've heard nothing of this?"

"I have not been in communication with them lately, no. But we knew this was inevitable. It's the entire reason why you have Chosen, is it not?"

The indifference in his tone chilled me. I was beginning to wonder if I'd ever be able to figure out this man...this djinn. He didn't seem to care at all what happened to the rest of humanity's survivors, and yet he did appear to be concerned about the Chosen in his community, especially when it came to the four who had disappeared so mysteriously. Was that only because their disappearance affected djinn he knew?

I had no idea. Again I puzzled at his role of leader here, when he himself was with no one, whether Chosen or djinn. Had he somehow been given this assignment, or had he volunteered for it?

Jace said, voice tight, "True, this is what was agreed upon. But you know my feelings on this matter...and the feelings of the rest of us here."

A pause as Zahrias drank the rest of his mulled wine, then set the glass down on the table. When he turned back toward us, his eyes were hooded, revealing little, but something in the set of his mouth seemed to indicate that this was an argument he had had before, and didn't want to have again.

When he spoke, however, he sounded more weary than angry. "Yes, I know those feelings very well, as you've made them abundantly clear on more than one occasion. I have not had speech with the others, and see no reason to. They are set on their course, and we are protected here, and that is all we need to concern ourselves with. For now, I would advise you to enjoy this reunion with your beloved, and to let the rest of this go. I should think you would be eager to be together, rather than belaboring the same point over and over again."

Well, that was one thing Zahrias and I could agree on. While I understood the need for this debriefing, for lack of a better term, what I wanted most was to be with Jace, to hide ourselves away in our suite for a while so we could rediscover one another. Or, in my case, discover him for the first time. We had made love many times, but that was when I'd thought he was Jason Little River. I needed to be with him now, in his true form, so I could fall in love with him all over again.

Something of these thoughts seemed to have communicated themselves to Jace, because he nodded at

Zahrias and said, "That is true enough. I suppose we can discuss the device more tomorrow."

"I will have Lauren see if there is anyone in the group who can contribute to that conversation."

Those words had the tone of a dismissal. Jace said, "Until tomorrow, then," and I chimed in,

"Thank you, Zahrias."

He seemed somewhat surprised that I'd thanked him, but recovered enough to incline his head and say gravely, "You are very welcome, Jessica Monroe."

That seemed as good a time as any to make our escape.

We didn't go immediately to our suite, however, but to the dining hall to see what we could scrounge up. By then it was almost noon, and so Phillip, the former chef turned cook for the djinn/Chosen colony, was in the kitchens overseeing lunch preparations. Although he startled upon seeing us—it seemed as if word hadn't yet begun to spread regarding Jace's and my return—when Phillip heard we hadn't had a proper meal for some time, he put together a wonderful lunch together for us and set it all on one of the resort's room service carts.

"Just leave it outside your door when you're done, and someone will come along to get it," he told us, blue eyes glinting slightly. That glint seemed to indicate he understood that we probably wouldn't be all that eager to leave our suite anytime soon.

Both Jace and I thanked him and headed off to our room. We'd left a fire burning in the hearth, and the pleasant scent of wood smoke greeted us as we opened the door. I trundled the room service cart in while Jace shut the door. To my surprise, he didn't follow me as I went over to the little table for two by the window, but remained standing where he was, surveying the space.

"Is something wrong?" I asked. Maybe he didn't like the room, for some reason. It was done in a vaguely Native American motif, with a kiva fireplace and neutral tones. I thought it was beautiful, but....

"Nothing's wrong," he said at once. "It's just...this. Being here with you. Those weeks I was being held captive, I didn't think I would ever see you again, let alone have the chance to be with you like this. I think I'm trying to tell myself that this is real, and not a dream I conjured to comfort myself while enduring Margolis' torments."

Something about his words brought home to me more than anything else everything he'd gone through. I let go of the cart's handles and crossed the room to him, took his hands in mine. At least his fingers were warm, which meant he had recovered...physically, if nothing else. I pulled him closer, whispering, "I'm so sorry. I should have tried to get you out sooner. I was trying to blend in, get them to trust me. I knew if I got caught, I'd never be able to get you away from there. But I got caught anyway, so I shouldn't have wasted all that time."

He brought my fingers to his lips, kissing them, and a tremulous sort of warmth went over me. I wanted him so badly, and yet this still felt so strange. This was Jace—I recognized the intonation of his voice, even if it was slightly deeper than the voice he'd used as Jason Little River. And those dark eyes were the same shape, more or less, although they now showed more laugh lines when he smiled. The lines of the mouth, so close, but subtly different, enough that when I kissed him, I had to remind myself that this was Jace, but also Jasreel, and that they were one and the same, even if my eyes weren't still entirely convinced of that fact.

"Beloved," he said, the word making my heart turn over. I didn't think I would ever get tired of hearing him call me that. "Please, if you love me, do not berate yourself. You did what you thought best. I truly believe it was the best strategy, because you're right—if you had simply shown up and immediately tried to go where you were not allowed, I have no doubt that Margolis would have apprehended you at once. It was bad luck that you were caught when you finally did have the opportunity to find me. We were very close to getting away, after all."

Not close enough, I thought, but I knew better than to utter those words out loud. Jace and I had already been over this, and I knew he wanted me to let the matter go. Sometimes that was hard for me; I wanted to work at a problem until it was resolved to my satisfaction. Some things couldn't be fixed, however. I didn't have a time machine; I couldn't turn back the clock and head another direction down that corridor at the labs, and possibly elude capture that way. Besides, even if the two of us had gotten safely off that floor, we still would have had to attempt to rescue Natila, and we could have gotten caught just as easily doing that.

"I suppose so," I said reluctantly, and he pulled me to him then, brought his mouth against mine. I could taste the sweet-spice of the mulled wine on his tongue, and in that moment regret was forgotten, worry cast aside. There was only Jace...Jasreel...this amazing man whose lips seemed to fit so perfectly with mine, even if they were a slightly different shape from the lips of the Jace I had first kissed.

We held the kiss for a long moment. At length he pulled away, though, sending me an apologetic look. "Beloved, I want you...more than you can possibly know. But I also know I won't be able to love you properly without eating something first."

I wanted to laugh, just because he seemed so worried that I would be offended. How could I be, though? For all I knew, he hadn't eaten a decent meal in weeks. Smiling, I replied, "Jace, I think I can manage to wait another fifteen minutes or so. Besides, I'm hungry, too."

He seemed to relax then, going over to the cart and picking up one of the smoked turkey and provolone sandwiches Phillip had made for us. One bite, and Jace's eyes widened. I had to fight back a smile, since I'd had roughly the same reaction when I first tasted Phillip's cooking.

Although he must have been ravenous, and probably could have devoured the whole thing in just a minute or so, Jace stopped and set down the sandwich. "Aren't you going to eat?"

"Yes," I said. I hadn't been lying when I'd told him I was hungry, but there was something oddly satisfying about standing there and watching him eat, knowing it had been a very long while since he'd had any real food. But since it appeared he intended to wait until I began to eat as well, I went to the room service cart and retrieved my own sandwich. As I'd thought, that widening of the eyes hadn't merely been from satisfying what must have been a raging hunger—those sandwiches would have been amazing even to someone who didn't feel like eating. Smoked turkey, and thick slices of provolone, and roasted red pepper and fresh-baked ciabatta rolls...I wasn't sure how Phillip managed it all, except that Taos was apparently like Los Alamos in that it had never suffered a loss of power, and so all the food in the various restaurant freezers and so forth had survived more or less unscathed.

Jace and I took our food over to the little table by the window and sat down, eating in companionable silence while we watched a playful wind blow through the courtyard outside, sending little flurries of snow fluttering into the air. The meal had something of the feeling of a ritual. We'd eaten together many times before, but this particular breaking of bread seemed to renew and reestablish our relationship, to bring us back together, sealing the djinn and Chosen bond.

Once he'd finished his sandwich, and the small bowl of sliced apples that had gone with it, Jace wiped his mouth with a napkin. "And you don't mind?"

"Don't mind what?" I asked, wondering what he was driving at. I'd been about to pick up a slice of apple but paused, something in his expression stopping me.

"That I am...not the man you fell in love with. Not precisely, anyway."

I met his gaze squarely. Yes, there were many similarities in his appearance to Jason Little River, but Jasreel was not the same person. I'd already begun to catalogue the differences, to recognize them for what they were, and then to put them aside. So what if the shape of his jaw was slightly different, or the arch of his brows? Those were all trivialities. They weren't Jace. I'd never known Jason Little River, not the real one. I'd only known Jace, wearing Jason's appearance. But the person inside?

That hadn't changed.

"You are exactly the man I fell in love with, Jasreel." My voice was calm, the use of his full name deliberate. Despite my going to Los Alamos to find him, despite everything we'd both been through, it seemed he still had his doubts.

I could think of only one way to convince him that nothing between us had changed. Not really.

Rising from my seat, I reached out to him, and he took my hands and stood as well. Now that he was no longer under the influence of one of Miles Odekirk's devices, his fingers were as warm as I remembered, strong and sure as they closed around mine.

He had to be just a little taller in his true form; I realized that I had to go up on my tiptoes to touch my lips to his. And God, the taste of him, sweetness of apples, the heat of his mouth, the strength and power in that body as it pressed against mine. The clothes he'd been given were djinn garments, loose robe and full pants, and through the silky fabric I could feel the hardness of his arousal, the size of him. That seemed to be a little larger as well.

I decided I needed to find out for myself.

The pants had a drawstring, and I loosened it as I sank down on my knees, taking him into my mouth, knowing somehow that this was the best way to show him exactly how much I wanted him, that I felt no need to restrain myself. His hands knotted in my hair as he let out a groan, and I moaned a little as well, a soft guttural sound low in my throat that reverberated against his shaft, awakening an echo in his own chest. Then he sighed.

"Jessica...."

Warm heat pulsed between my legs as I suckled him. Yes, he was bigger. Not by a lot, but enough that I noticed. Enough that I shivered at the thought of him inside me.

He must have felt that tremor, because he gently withdrew from my mouth and took me by the arms, raising me so he could kiss me again, his lips closing on my tongue in an echo of the way I'd been sucking him just a moment earlier. And then my feet left the floor as he held me and we hovered in the air, which felt far warmer than it should have, even with a fire blazing away in the hearth.

"Is this how the djinn make love?" I whispered. Maybe I should have been frightened, floating several feet above the ground like that, but somehow I couldn't be. Not with Jace holding me.

"It's how I want to make love to you," he said.

Warm winds seemed to wrap around me, caressing me, and somehow my clothes were pulled away, drifting down to the floor. The silky heat of Jace's flesh touched my bare skin, and just that brush of body against body was enough to make me cry out.

But of course that was only the beginning. His mouth closed on my nipple, and his hand stroked its way up my thigh, fingers at last sinking into me, stroking me, touching me in that way only he knew how.

The orgasm came hard and fast. I clenched around him, moaning, and while the tremors were still shivering their way through my body, he pushed himself into me. I gasped, clutching the heavy muscles of his arms to steady myself, feeling how he filled me, so thick, so strong. And we found our rhythm again, floating there, no bed to constrain us, no gravity to tell us which position we should assume next, only the need driving us together, hanging on to one another as if the other person was the only real thing in the universe.

I could tell when he was close, as the gentle, warm winds blowing around us increased their speed, whipping at my hair even as he thrust into me. And then a groan so deep it could have been a rumble of thunder, and he let go, the heat of his orgasm spilling into me, while I came as well, my legs wrapped around his rock-hard thighs, pushing him even deeper as I cried out in a release I'd been craving for weeks, one I wasn't sure I would ever have again.

Softly we descended, landing on the bed. For a long while we only held one another, neither of us wanting to let go of the moment, to suffer yet another separation. But at last I pulled away just a little, mostly so I could look into his face, stare at Jasreel's features in the aftermath of his climax, and memorize his expression just as I'd memorized Jace's before.

He reached out to cup my cheek, fingers tracing the contours of my face. "You are so very real," he said. "So beautiful. So strong."

"No," I demurred, but he shook his head.

"You are, Jessica. To me, you are perfection itself. While they were keeping me prisoner, I kept thinking of you. Remembering you, our time together...it's what kept me sane. From time to time I did wonder if my memory was turning you into something you were not, but now that you're here with me, I realize those memories were only a pale imitation of the woman you truly are."

Heat flooded my cheeks. I wasn't used to being praised in such a fashion, and I didn't know what to say in response. A crack—"you're not so bad yourself"—would have been a reply the old Jessica might have made, but I couldn't do that now. Not when he was staring at me with those earnest dark eyes, his soul seemingly laid bare to me.

"I love you, Jace," I said. "I never—I never thought I could feel this way about someone. Those people in Los Alamos...they think I'm a traitor to my own kind. But they don't know you. If they did, they'd know how good you are, how amazing. How perfect."

He pulled me against him, his mouth brushing against mine. Need pulsed in me again, but I ignored it. We'd had our moment, and would have another soon enough, I was sure. Now, though, I wanted to be here, held in his arms, feeling safe and comforted in a way I'd thought I never would be again, as he laid his cheek against mine and stroked my hair.

For some reason, I blurted, "I gave our goats away."

His hand stilled on my hair. "What?"

"When I went to Los Alamos. Evony and I thought maybe they'd be more likely to take us in if we brought them gifts, so we took the goats and the chickens. I'm sorry."

For a long moment, Jasreel didn't reply, and I worried that I might have upset him with that revelation. After all, he'd put a lot of work into taking care of the animals, building shelters for them, feeding them. But then he said, voice amused, "Beloved, I doubt those were the only goats and chickens in New Mexico."

"Well, true, but—"

"And they would not have survived on their own. At least now they're someplace where they're valued and taken care of."

I had to hope that was the case. The goats were worth far more as milk producers than as meat animals, and maybe the chickens were, too. I had a feeling that Captain Margolis wouldn't scruple at chopping the head off a hen if she stopped laying, though.

"Thank you, Jace," I said simply, but he seemed to understand.

"I can't fault you for doing what you thought was best. And no doubt they have plenty of animals here in Taos, so perhaps they're doing more good in Los Alamos anyway."

Smiling, I shifted in his arms so I was gazing up into those dark, dark eyes of his. "Are you sure you're a djinn?"

An eyebrow lifted. "What else would I be?"

"Well, when you make statements like that, I have to start wondering whether you're some sort of saint instead."

The crinkles around his eyes deepened as he smiled back at me. "No, Jessica, I am most assuredly not a saint. And I realize that most of the people in Los Alamos probably have no idea what Margolis has actually been doing. They just want to live, to be someplace where they can feel safe after the world they knew was torn from them so suddenly. I can't begrudge them something that might help them to live, not when we have plenty here in Taos."

I hadn't thought I could love him more than I already did, but in that moment it felt as if something inside me gave way, aching for him, for all that he'd given me...and others, if they would just let him. How he could even be of the same race as those who'd destroyed most of humanity, I didn't know. Certainly Zahrias hadn't exhibited many of the same characteristics. And as for the djinn who were out hunting down the human race's few remaining members...well, I'd count myself lucky if I never had to encounter any of them.

"You're being a lot more charitable than I would if our situations were reversed," I said after a long pause. "Especially considering what they did to Natila."

Jasreel shut his eyes for a few seconds, long black lashes sweeping against his high cheekbones. Then he opened them and gave me a piercing look. "'They' did not do that to Natila. Captain Margolis and Miles Odekirk...and their henchmen...did. Rest assured that if I should ever encounter either of those two again, they will be made to pay the price for the crime they committed."

Strong words, said with conviction. I didn't bother to point out that if Odekirk's devices were still operating, then Jace wouldn't have a lot of options when it came to giving the two men some frontier justice. Still, it was possible he might still get satisfaction one day. After all, we'd managed to capture one of those boxes, and if we were able to get it to give up some of its secrets...well, then the tables might turn for sure.

But that was all in the future. For now, I only wanted to be with Jace, think of Jace. I pushed myself up on one arm so I could kiss him again, and he seemed to understand, because he bent and brought his mouth to mine. Then it was just the two of us, the world shut away for the moment, so we could find healing in one another.

Right then, it was enough.

CHAPTER SEVENTEEN

WE STAYED IN OUR SUITE FOR HOURS, EXPLORING one another, reacquainting ourselves with the way the other person touched, kissed, caressed. I'd been so caught up in the heat of our reunion that I hadn't even stopped to think that I hadn't taken one of my birth-control pills for several days now. They'd been left behind, along with the rest of my belongings, at the Los Alamos house.

I told Jace, and added in halting tones, "But maybe it doesn't matter—maybe djinn and humans can't have children?"

At once he folded me into his arms and kissed the top of my head. "It is a very rare thing, but it has happened several times over the centuries. Also, among djinn, a conscious choice to have a child must be made. It is not something that happens by accident. So you need have no fears on that account—we would have to decide together to have a child, and even then...." He left the words trail off.

"I don't have fears," I protested, although as the words left my mouth, I tried not to think too hard about what that unfinished sentence meant. Was he trying to say that we might not have children, even sometime in the future, when the time was right? Better to leave that alone for now. My tone firm, I added, "I'd love to have a family with you, Jace. Only... maybe not just now."

A blazing smile, and he kissed me again, this time on the mouth. "I could wish for nothing more. And we will make that decision together when the time comes. For now, though, you need have no worries about becoming with child unexpectedly."

His kisses were enough to have me pull him close again, our bodies joining once more. It seemed that no matter what I did, I could never get enough of the sensation of his flesh against mine. Eventually, though, it was time for us to emerge, if for no other reason than it was almost past dinnertime, and we needed to see what we could scrounge from the kitchens.

"And I'd better check on Evony," I told Jace after I'd gotten some food and fresh water for Dutchie. Luckily, the dog was used to our intimacies, and had slept by the fire through the whole thing, occasionally opening one eye to see whether we were done yet. "I don't want her to think we've abandoned her."

He only nodded, his expression somewhat distracted and grim. I could tell he was thinking that Evony probably wasn't much in the mood to talk to me.

It seemed he was right, because when we stopped at the door to her suite and knocked, the only response I got was a muffled "go away." Turning toward Jace, I sent him an imploring look.

He took the hint and said to the door, "Evony, we just wanted to make sure you were all right."

A long silence, during which I shifted my weight from one foot to the other and wondered how long we should wait out here before carefully tiptoeing away. But then the door banged open and Evony stood there, looking tear-stained and tragic. "No, I'm not all right. So glad you could stop in and check on me once you were done with your afternoon-long fuck-fest."

The door slammed shut again. I stayed rooted in place, shocked, even as one hand slid up to my neck, to the telltale marks Jasreel had left there. I'd been provided with clothes and a few toiletries, but no makeup other than some lip gloss, and so I hadn't really been able to cover up the marks he'd made on my throat.

Not wanting to leave things where they stood, I lifted my hand to knock again, but Jace caught my wrist in gentle fingers.

"Leave it for now, beloved," he said. "The wounds are very fresh for her, and they will take time to heal. I'll make sure someone comes to check on her, bring her something to eat."

"One step ahead of you," came Lauren's voice, and we both turned to see her approaching down the corridor as she pushed a room service cart in front of her. "I don't know if she'll eat any of this, but I thought we should make the gesture."

"Thanks, Lauren," I said, then hesitated before asking, "Have you talked to her?"

"Just briefly. I wanted to tell her again that she had a safe place here, that she didn't have to worry about not being a part of our settlement just because—well, just because she'd lost Natila." Lauren's shoulders lifted, and she shook her head. "That actually didn't go over too well. She's grieving, I know. So right now, I just want to make sure she at least eats something, and I suppose the rest will start to mend eventually."

That was very close to what Jace had said as well, but I couldn't help wondering. Was Evony's the sort of loss you could ever come back from? My bond with Jace was so intense, so intimate, that I couldn't imagine ever recovering if I somehow lost him. But that wouldn't happen. I'd come close to having him taken from me—too close—but he was with me now, and here in this stronghold of the djinn, neither Margolis nor Miles Odekirk could do anything to hurt him.

But because I didn't want to discourage Lauren, I only nodded and said, "I hope so."

Her expression was somber. "Me, too." Then her features lightened a bit. "The hordes have gone through, but there's still some food left over. Phillip's keeping it in warming trays for all you stragglers."

"Thank you, Lauren," Jace said. "Come, Jessica—I have a feeling it would be better if we weren't here when Lauren attempts to coax Evony out."

I couldn't argue with that logic. After flashing a quick smile at Lauren, I followed Jace down the hall toward the restaurant. He seemed to know where he was going, prompting me to ask, "You've been here before?"

"Yes," he said briefly. After I slanted him an inquiring glance, he added, "Zahrias designated this hotel as the group's gathering place, should it turn out that it wasn't safe or feasible to have our people scattered all over town and in some of the outlying neighborhoods. So we all spent some time here. But this has always been the place he intended to stay, even though most of the others chose to live in various houses or hotel suites in and around Taos."

"Oh," I replied, thinking it over. "So did you have a house picked out here?"

Jace shook his head. "Not really. I'd thought I could stay with you down in Santa Fe. At the time, it seemed safe enough, although Zahrias thought me strange for not wanting to be with my own kind. Eventually, perhaps, but I wanted time alone with you."

Time we'd had, although not nearly enough. Those days with Jace—even though I had thought he was Jason Little River back then—had begun to take on a hazy, idyllic quality, giving them a perfection I knew couldn't be quite accurate. We'd worked hard, spent long days looking after the animals and preparing food and doing the thousand and one things life in this post-Dying world required. But we'd had each other, and that had been enough. I would have been very happy to live a long time without any intrusions from outside.

The outside had intruded, though, and now here we were. I reflected there were worse fates than to be relegated to a luxury suite in a five-star resort for the rest of my days, but even so, I wanted to go home.

Home. Funny how a house I'd lived in for just a scant three months now seemed like the only home I could imagine. But to me it *was* home, because Jace had been there with me.

As Lauren had said, the restaurant that the djinn colony now used as a communal dining room was mostly empty by the time we arrived. It seemed the djinn weren't the demonstrative type; the few who were still there—accompanied by their Chosen—only nodded briefly at Jace before returning to their meals.

After we'd gotten our own dinner, which was herb-roasted chicken and wild rice and a wonderful vegetable dish of sautéed mushrooms and red onions and asparagus, Jace and I sat down at a secluded table off in a corner. Because live trees and plants were used as natural dividers in the space, I almost felt as if we were eating on a patio on a mild summer day, rather than indoors in the dead of winter. I was so looking forward to spring and summer with Jace—maybe we would be home in Santa Fe by then. But first things first.

I cocked an eyebrow at him. "Okay, I wasn't exactly expecting a welcome-home party with balloons and stuff, but you'd think people would look a little happier to have you back."

He poured me some wine from the bottle he'd snagged. "Believe me, they are all relieved that I've returned safely. However, it's not our nature to indulge in public displays of enthusiasm. And some are grieving for Natila."

"Only some?" I inquired, then took a sip of chardonnay.

Some people might have looked away, but Jace met my gaze squarely. "Djinn society is not as different from human as some might wish to believe. Let's just say that there are those who didn't approve of Natila's... tastes."

"Ah." In my mind, that explained a lot. At the very least, it told me why Natila had lingered with Evony in Española, rather than coming back to Taos right away. A quick glance at the few couples remaining in the dining area told me they all seemed to be straight, although I knew I recalled seeing a few male same-sex couples at the Christmas gathering more than a month earlier. "And what about the guys?"

Jasreel's mouth twitched. "Well, I suppose one would say they are more tolerated. They are greater in number, for one thing—Natila was the only female djinn in this group who had a taste for women."

That would make things difficult. And all that much worse for Evony, who had no hope of finding someone else as long as she remained here. Did she know? Had Natila told her that she was the only one of her kind in the Taos settlement? No wonder Evony acted as if she didn't have much to look forward to. Here, she really didn't.

And even if there might have been future prospects for her in Los Alamos, it wasn't as if she could have stayed there. Not after what happened to Natila.

My expression must have sunk, because Jace reached across the table and took my hand, giving it a reassuring squeeze. "It will be difficult," he said gently. "You will need to be her friend, even if she pushes you away. I have to hope that eventually she will—"

"She'll what?" I cut in, my tone bitter now that I understood the true extent of Evony's loss. "Get over it? Switch sides so she can get laid? I know—we can get her to hook up with Aldair. Maybe that'll cure her of the gay."

Something in Jace's features shifted subtly. "You've met Aldair?"

"Yes," I said. The other djinn was a subject that would have come up eventually, so I figured I might as well tell Jasreel the truth. It wasn't as if anything had happened between us...even if Zahrias had hoped it might. Not that he seemed to have a vested interest in my or Aldair's happiness...more that he just didn't appear to like loose ends. "Zahrias was trying to play matchmaker with the two of us, until I told him I wasn't interested."

I'd thought Jace would show some sign of surprise at this revelation, but instead he nodded grimly and said, "I suppose that was to be expected."

"Um...excuse me?" Something wasn't tracking here. True, Jace had known that a group of the Chosen had gone missing, but he'd never indicated that he knew who they were, or which djinn they'd been associated with.

He smiled then, but it was a mere upturn of his lips, not anything that reached his eyes. "Back...before, when those of us in the One Thousand were making our selections as to who among the Immune would be our Chosen, Aldair and I had a bit of a run-in."

"Why?"

"Because we both chose the same person. You."

There was an answer I hadn't been expecting. I sat back in my chair and stared at him blankly. "You... *what?*"

Jace still wore a smile, but now it seemed amused rather than ironic. "You're surprised by this?"

"Well, yes." This was the first hint I'd gotten that the selection of a djinn's Chosen wasn't a pure soul-to-soul connection. True, Aldair hadn't looked all that broken up about losing the woman he'd picked. Was that because she'd been his second choice?

"It has happened once or twice." With a shrug, Jasreel reached for his glass of wine and drank a large swallow.

"So...how did you solve the problem?" Although I was discomfited by the realization that I could have been with Aldair all this time, rather than Jasreel, I couldn't help quipping, "What, did you two fight a duel over me or something?"

But Jace's smile abruptly disappeared. "Not exactly. However, we did have to engage in a...contest of wills, for lack of a better term. If two djinn need to seek a resolution on something like this, then their talents are pitted against one another."

I had a wild vision of Jace and Aldair flinging gusts of wind and tornadoes and whatever other wind-borne mayhem they could think of at each other. And all because of me? Of all the survivors, there wasn't anyone else Aldair could have chosen?

Well, obviously there was, or she wouldn't have been around to volunteer to go and spy on the Los Alamos community. Whether she'd put herself forward for that venture partly because things weren't rosy between her and her djinn lover, I had no idea, but the idea seemed plausible enough.

Right then, I was just very, very glad that Jace had proved himself to be the stronger of the two. The thought of two men fighting over me seemed completely far-fetched, but I could tell Jace wasn't joking about any of this.

I let out a sigh. "This could be awkward."

"It could, if Aldair decides to be difficult. I suppose we should do our best to stay out of his way as much as possible."

Precisely how easy that would be, with all of us camping out in this resort, I had no idea. At least I hadn't seen any sign of the other djinn since Jace and I had come here, so maybe it wouldn't be horribly difficult. I hoped.

"Sounds like a plan," I said. "And if we're really lucky, maybe things will settle down enough that you and I can get out of Taos soon, and go back to Santa Fe."

"That would be wonderful," Jace replied. "I will wish for that as well, but unless we know for sure that Margolis' people won't try to hunt us down there, it will be safer for us to remain here."

True enough. I didn't know how much of a blow we'd dealt to Miles Odekirk and the Los Alamos colony as a whole by taking one of the devices, but I hoped it was significant enough that they wouldn't be thinking of going on any more djinn-hunting expeditions in the near future. There was also the possibility that we could attempt to reverse-engineer the box, figure out a way to make its powers affect the other devices so they were useless against us.

Yeah, right, I thought. *And after that, we'll build a rocket ship and fly to the moon.*

Actually, for all I knew, the djinn could fly to the moon without the aid of any technology. They weren't quite of this world, and I still didn't have a very clear idea of everything their powers entailed. Maybe someday soon, Jace would explain all that to me.

Now, though, he was watching me with worried eyes, clearly concerned that I would try to pursue the idea of getting away from here and going back to Santa Fe. As much as I wanted that, though, I knew he was right. We wouldn't be safe there.

I smiled at him, then reached out to lay my hand on his where it rested on the tabletop. "Well, I guess that means the best thing we can do is spend a lot of time in our suite. That way, we won't have as much of a chance of bumping into Aldair."

And I was gratified to see Jace return that smile, this time with his dark eyes lighting up at the prospect of all those hours alone with me. He twined his fingers with mine and squeezed gently.

"I think, Jessica, that I would like that very much."

We did spend a good deal of time in our suite, but not all, because Jace and I were called in to brief the engineering team—for lack of a better word—on any insights we could provide as to how Miles Odekirk's devices functioned. It wasn't a lot, but at least Jace had been in close proximity to one of the things for weeks and lived to tell the tale, and I'd seen Julia and Miles operate it, although that was a little bit like saying I knew how to drive a race car just because I'd watched the Indianapolis 500 with my father on a few occasions.

"I figured out some of the basic mechanics," Lindsay Adarian said, turning the box over in her hands. She was about a year older than I, and had been getting her master's in engineering when the Heat cut her education off at the knees, just as it had mine. Zahrias had put her in charge of this little task force, an appointment her consort, an earth elemental named Rafi, hadn't seemed too thrilled about. However, around here it seemed that Zahrias' word was law, and so Lindsay was spearheading the effort to delve into the device's mysteries. "But *how* it does what it does?" She lifted her shoulders, and her dark blonde hair slipped down her back. Like every other Chosen I'd met, she was gorgeous, her warm skin echoing the shade of her hair, and her eyes a startling green. "I don't have any idea. This is an order of magnitude beyond anything I was studying. This Miles Odekirk must be a genius."

"That's one word for it," I muttered, and Jace sent me a warning glance before saying,

"Jessica told me that this Los Alamos place was a center for research, some of it quite advanced. So it makes sense that Dr. Odekirk would be able to invent something quite outside the scope of your studies."

Amazing that Jace could still be so formal, so correct when referring to Miles Odekirk, the man who'd concocted a series of increasingly painful "tests" to be used on his captives and who had overseen the death of a fellow djinn. Although maybe that wasn't exactly the truth. I'd gotten the impression that Margolis had engineered that particular piece of torture, and Miles Odekirk had gone along with it so he could observe the effects of the waterboarding. Then again, he hadn't seemed too broken up over Natila's death, more intrigued that he would have a dead djinn to study.

I shivered, then sent a surreptitious glance under my lashes toward Evony, who was sitting on a stool in the corner of the auto repair shop we'd more or less turned into the local equivalent of a lab. Lindsay and a few others, including Aidan, who'd admitted that he taken "a few" physics classes in college, looted the high school for whatever useful equipment they could find, and so the workbenches were now covered with microscopes and oscilloscopes and soldering irons and a few other pieces of equipment I didn't recognize.

Although Evony knew less about physics and electrical and mechanical engineering than I did, she'd been granted a seat at the table, so to speak, just because it had been her idea to steal the device in the first place. She still wasn't speaking to me. That is, if there was absolutely no way around it, she'd reply to a question with a nod or a monosyllabic answer, but she clearly had no interest in having a real conversation, obviously still thought Natila's death was my fault because I'd gone and gotten myself caught by Margolis and his goons.

And you know, I really couldn't blame her much. Jace kept insisting that Margolis would have gotten to that particular torture sooner or later anyway, but it was the "later" part of his protests that bothered me. Yes, maybe Margolis would have gone ahead with the waterboarding, but if he'd done it a week later, or even more, it was possible that in the meantime I would have come up with a more coherent plan than "I've got to save Jace now!"

Or maybe Margolis would have managed to kill both Natila and Jace while I waited to come up with the perfect escape scenario. I'd never know, and that was was probably the worst of it all.

Lindsay was frowning, turning the box over and over in her hands. Standing a few feet away, Aidan looked on with interest but didn't seem to have anything useful to offer. Then again, why would he? This was a thrown-together group of people who might have a smattering of technical knowledge. Really, the idea that any of them could crack something put together by a mad genius with a couple of Ph.D.s and years of research experience under his belt was pretty laughable.

But they were all we had.

"The surface is like one big touch pad," Lindsay said. "It's off now, so my handling it can't affect you, Jace."

"Thank you for that," he replied. One corner of his mouth twitched, and I could tell he was trying not to smile.

She seemed to note his amusement. One eyebrow—several shades darker than her hair—went up, and she added, "Evony figured that out for us, and she showed me how it works. The switch is a small recessed button on the underside, here." Flipping the box over, she held it up so we could all get a better look. There was a dimple, for lack of a better word, in one corner of the box, and in that dimple was a button, black against black. It would be hard to find if you didn't know where to look, which I guessed had been Odekirk's intention all along.

At least now, even if we didn't know how the device functioned, we could turn it off if necessary.

And that meant we knew how to turn off the boxes that were still back in Los Alamos. Julia had said she thought there were three altogether, so now the survivors were left with two. Maybe Miles had had time to make another, maybe not.

"Luckily, I've had a couple of volunteers to help me with testing the area of effect. I wasn't going to ask you to do it, Jace, not after you had to live with one of these things practically in your lap for almost a month, but Dani offered to be a guinea pig, and so did Reyna and Tivon."

"That was generous of them," Jace said.

Lindsay shrugged. "I think they were more curious than anything else. Stories have been circulating, and they wanted to experience it for themselves. I think they believed it couldn't really have the effect you'd described."

"I assume they changed their minds after a little demonstration," I remarked, and Jasreel nodded.

"Oh, yeah," Lindsay said, obviously trying hard not to smile. "They were...well, 'shaken' isn't exactly a word I'd generally use to describe a djinn, but I think that sums it up pretty well. Anyway, I was able to determine that the more concentrated the field, the smaller it is... but you already knew that, right?"

Jace gave a single somber nod. "Yes, that's in line with what I experienced."

"At its greatest attenuation—a level where all the djinns' powers seemed to be blocked, but they experienced far reduced physical discomfort—it looks as if the field has a diameter of around a mile." She set the box down on the worktable and finally allowed herself a grin. "Good thing we'd decided to do our testing away from here, out on the road to the pueblo, or I think I would've had a bunch of pissed-off djinn on my hands."

"That's for damn sure," Evony put in, her mouth twisting. "They probably would've all gone crying to Zahrias."

That remark earned her a very sharp look from Jace, but he didn't say anything. Since he was the only djinn currently in attendance, that left the rest of us mere mortals to not-quite look one another in the eye. It was clear enough that no one appreciated Evony's comment. At the same time, we were all probably telling ourselves that she was speaking from a place of grief, and so it was best to let it go without comment.

After an awkward pause, Lindsay continued, "So I'm guessing that two of these devices aren't quite enough to protect all of Los Alamos. Jessica, Evony, do you know if the survivors were living all over town, or if they were concentrated more toward the town center?"

Evony only lifted her shoulders. Clearly, she didn't intend to contribute anything helpful.

"I'm not entirely sure," I said. "It did seem as if some neighborhoods were more populated than others. But it was more than two miles from the house they gave Evony and me to live in to the labs, so I don't see how they could have complete coverage for all that area with only two of the boxes. Then again, Julia Innes told me that Miles was getting faster at making them, so he could have replaced it already."

A few days ago, the last thing I would have wished for was to have any more of those goddamn devices in the world. But knowing we'd left innocent people vulnerable...I didn't like the idea of that at all. True, whatever else his faults, Margolis was pretty damn good at getting things done, and it was entirely possible that he'd made sure anyone outside the area of effect had relocated to a safer spot closer to the center of town. The problem was, I could tell myself that, but I didn't know for sure.

"If he keeps making more of them, do you think they'll ever get to a point where they'll come attack us here in Taos?" Aidan asked. He was fiddling with the drawstring on his hoodie and looking a little green around the gills. I couldn't blame him. The prospect of the Los Alamos survivors showing up with their own post-Dying equivalent of pitchforks and torches wasn't exactly appealing.

There was another of those uncomfortable silences, and then Jace said, "I'm sure it's what Margolis would like, but he is not so foolhardy as to attempt such a thing until they have a good number of these devices. Even if he's getting faster at making them, they're not the sort of thing that can be produced like a batch of cookies. I can't imagine he would try coming here until he had at least ten, because of course he'd have to leave several behind in Los Alamos to protect the people there."

Everyone looked relieved at that calm assessment of the situation. Of course Jace was right. Miles might be getting to the point where he could put together a box in less than a week. Even so, that would still require months for him to get up to fighting strength. I hadn't been part of the inner sanctum in Los Alamos, but I'd gotten the impression that the scientist preferred to work alone. He probably wouldn't trust the construction of the devices to anyone but himself.

"Well, good," Lindsay said in her calm, firm way. She didn't seem like the type to be easily rattled, and I wondered then how her djinn had come to her in the aftermath of the Dying. He must have announced who and what he was early on, but I would've loved to see someone with an analytical, rational mind like hers attempting to wrap itself around the idea that djinn even existed, let alone that one of that mythical race had selected her to be one of the few who survived the end of the world.

Maybe someday I'd get a chance to ask her. In the meantime, we had a lot more important things to do. Because although it would take time, I couldn't imagine Margolis letting the whole thing go and allowing an uneasy detente to settle in between the colonies in Los Alamos and in Taos. No, he thought that because of the devices, he would have the upper hand eventually, and he would bring the battle to us.

All we had to do was figure out a way to stop him.

CHAPTER EIGHTEEN

AFTER THE MEETING IN THE AUTO REPAIR SHOP-cum-lab, Aidan drove Jace and me back to the resort. The Suburban wasn't much use with its windows blown out, and we hadn't yet laid claim to a new vehicle. I found I didn't much care; even though I told myself it didn't matter, I still mourned the loss of the Cherokee, the sturdy vehicle that, almost as much as Jace, had helped me escape Albuquerque more or less unscathed.

Lauren was waiting for us, saying that Zahrias wished to speak with Jace and get a status update, since Lindsay had stayed behind at the lab to tinker with the box some more. I had a feeling her djinn consort was going to get pretty cranky at her extended absences if this went on for any amount of time, but that was between them, and I knew I'd stay well out of it.

Another part of me was irritated that Zahrias hadn't asked me to accompany Jace. I tried to put the annoyance away, telling myself that it was perfectly logical for the two of them to be talking. Even if they weren't precisely friends, they'd still known each other for a long, long time. How long, I wasn't sure I wanted to guess, but it made sense that Zahrias would feel more comfortable having an in-depth conversation alone with Jace.

It was late enough in the afternoon that I thought I could take Dutchie out for a walk to kill the time. With any luck, Jace would be back in our suite by the time I was done.

However, luck didn't seem to be with me right then. I hadn't even gotten halfway to the room before I found the corridor blocked by Aldair, who didn't seem inclined to step out of the way. Instead, he stood there, arms crossed, staring at me. This time, rather than the "civilian" clothes I'd seen him wear the last time we met, he had on the typical djinn garb of flowing, open robes and loose pants, these ones in shades of dark gray and deep blue. The amount of muscled chest those robes revealed probably would have impressed me a few months ago, but these days I only had eyes for Jace.

Had Aldair been lurking around, waiting for a moment when I was alone to intercept me? Jace and I had been more or less joined at the hip ever since we arrived in Taos, so I could see why Aldair would have been stymied up until this point. That realization didn't make me feel any better about being here alone with him. Just the opposite, actually.

"Afternoon," I said in my most casual tones, hoping that would be enough to make him move aside so I could pass.

"I see your master has let you off the leash," he returned, blue eyes narrowing between their fringe of heavy lashes.

He'd chosen those words on purpose to provoke me, or at least, that's what I guessed, and so I told myself that the last thing I should do was show any kind of reaction.

"Jace is talking with Zahrias, if that's what you mean," I said smoothly. "And I was just going to take my dog for a walk, so if you don't mind stepping aside—"

"I wanted to to speak with you," Aldair cut in. His arms dropped to the side, and he moved a step toward me. Not close enough that you could really say he was getting in my personal space, but certainly close enough that I felt my heart beat begin to speed up. I thought this would be a really good time for someone—anyone—to come along and rescue me, but as was typical of such situations, the corridor remained empty except for the two of us.

I let out a breath. "We've already spoken. You know I'm with Jace, and that's not going to change. I'm sorry you lost your Chosen—that's a terrible thing—but I can't help you. Not in the way you want, that is."

His jaw hardened. "And has Jasreel even bothered to tell you the truth of what happened?"

"As a matter of fact, he did." I lifted my own chin, adding, "It seems as if the whole thing was settled according to your people's rules, which is just another reason why you need to let it go."

"Settled?" The glitter in Aldair's harsh blue eyes seemed to indicate that he didn't think anything had been settled. "He would say that, when he twisted our contest so he would emerge the victor. Do you enjoy bestowing your loyalty on someone who's a cheat and a liar?"

Those two terms were so far removed from everything I knew about Jace that all I could do right then was shake my head and try my best not to laugh right in Aldair's face. "Jace has done everything he can to protect me, and I know he's an honorable man. So whatever you're trying to do, whatever you're trying to tell me—it's not going to work."

"Indeed it's not," came Jace's voice, tight and angry. He approached us from the direction where Zahrias' conference room was located, then stopped by my side and glared at Aldair. The two of them were nearly the same height, Jace perhaps a hair taller. I wondered if their djinn gifts were just as equally matched. Not completely equal, I supposed, or Jace wouldn't have beaten

Aldair in their fight over me. That still seemed like such a strange concept, to have these two beings dueling over the right to claim me as their Chosen.

Annoyed as I was with Aldair for attempting to force another confrontation, I knew I didn't want things to escalate any more than they already had. I moved closer to Jace and looped my arm through his. "It's okay," I murmured. "Let's just go."

But the arm I held might have been made of rock, as inflexible as it felt against mine. "No, Jessica, it is not okay. This matter was settled. That Aldair keeps attempting to stir it up again—well, that is something I will not stand for."

"Oh, you won't?" sneered Aldair. His eyes reminded me of the blue-hot hue at the center of a gas flame, burning, angry. Right then, he seemed far more like a being of fire than the air elemental I knew he actually was. "Perhaps we should have a rematch? I don't think things will go as well for you a second time."

"Enough!" The word cracked through the air like a whip, and I turned to see Zahrias striding down the hallway toward us, flames burning in the air all around him. If the intensity of that virtual fire was any indication of his mood, then he was one royally pissed-off djinn. He stopped a few feet away and crossed his arms. "Aldair, you are done here. I will waste no more breath on this issue, for you know that I did put in a word for you when you requested it, and nothing came of that. Jessica is Jasreel's Chosen, and that is the end of it. Do you understand?"

The hot blue of Aldair's eyes was almost obscured by his lashes as he scowled at Zahrias. For a second he said nothing, only glared at his leader. Then he snapped, "Oh, I understand. But do not think that is the end of it."

A rush of air, so violent it tugged at the ends of my hair and sent the loose strands stinging into my eyes, and then he was gone, disappearing in that disconcerting way the djinn had.

For a second or two, neither Jace nor Zahrias said anything, and I thought it best to keep my mouth shut as well. At last Jace released a short gust of breath. "I knew he would be a problem."

Zahrias didn't bother to argue. "Yes, things were much better when you and Jessica were safely off in Santa Fe. But we will all have to live with one another, and the sooner he accepts the situation, the better."

I privately doubted whether Aldair would ever accept the situation, but I had a feeling neither Jace nor Zahrias would appreciate my pointing out the obvious. Even though Aldair had taken himself off in a rather spectacular fashion, dark blood still suffused Jace's cheeks, and the flames dancing around Zahrias hadn't subsided, although they did appear to have moved closer to his body, hugging him almost like a second skin.

"Go back to your suite," he told us. "I think it better that you dine in your rooms this evening. I'll make sure Lauren has something sent up to you."

"That 'something' had better include a good bottle of wine," Jace all but growled, and the faintest hint of a smile tugged at the corner of the other djinn's mouth.

"I believe I can arrange that," Zahrias said, and he, too disappeared, leaving Jace and me alone.

He turned in my direction and appeared to inspect my expression closely. "Are you all right, beloved?"

"I'm fine," I replied. "He didn't do anything. Just talked."

"Sometimes that can be enough," Jace said darkly.

While I was considering that remark, he took my arm in his and began to lead me toward our suite. Although I didn't mind lying low, I did mind if our movements were restricted to the point where we couldn't even walk Dutchie. Why should Jace and I be the ones under house arrest when Aldair was the person causing all the trouble?

Then again, we were both much more cooperative than that wayward elemental....

We did walk the dog, and saw no sign of Aldair. I actually had no idea which room here at the resort was even his. Probably a good thing. After that, the wind picked up, bringing with it the scent of snow, and big white flakes began to fall just as the sun set.

It was a good evening to be under house arrest, all things considered. Jace built a healthy fire in the hearth, and we drank an amazing Bordeaux that had to have come from some private reserve room in the resort's cellars.

We sat and watched the snow fall, and fed Dutchie some choice bits of our beef bourgignon while we talked about Lindsay's work with Miles Odekirk's box and whether we'd see any real results from it. Jace didn't seem inclined to discuss Aldair, and I wasn't sure how to broach the subject. I certainly didn't want to make it seem as if I was interested in the other djinn, because I wasn't. On the other hand, I found it hard to believe that I could be the only source of what appeared to be some very bad blood between the two. I didn't think I was all that important.

So after we'd more or less scraped our dishes clean, then put everything back on the room service cart and covered it up with the tablecloth that had also been provided, I finally got the courage to ask, "Do you want to tell me what all this is really about?"

Jace had been tending the fire djinn-style, which meant using currents of air to stoke it up and shift the logs so they burned hotter. It was strange to watch, even stranger to realize that he'd had these sorts of gifts all along, and only hid them while we were in Santa Fe so he wouldn't tip his hand too soon. At my question, he paused, then turned toward me, dark eyes searching mine. Otherwise, his face was blank, and I couldn't begin to guess what he might be thinking.

A liar and a cheat. Aldair's words surfaced then, and I pushed them away. All right, Jace hadn't been truthful with me from the start, but I'd forgiven him that. I'd been so terrified and bereft after the loss of my family and friends...of everyone and everything... that I knew I couldn't have handled the truth of Jace's existence, of the djinn, of why the world had ended. Not until some time had passed, anyway. He'd wanted to shield me, and I couldn't blame him. I doubted I would have done any differently.

"Beyond Aldair being a stubborn fool?" he replied.

"Yes, beyond that. I'm not Helen of Troy—I kind of doubt I'm worth all this fuss."

At those words, Jace smiled, but at the same time, he shook his head. "You hold yourself in too little esteem. I think you compare very favorably to the fabled Helen."

I just stared at him. He'd never revealed to me how old he really was, so I supposed he *could* have been around to see the real Helen of Troy. But my brain didn't want to try wrapping itself around that concept, so I said, "Be serious."

"I am serious. Deadly serious."

In answer, I lifted an eyebrow at him and settled back in my chair, waiting. Two could play at that game.

He appeared to relent then, and came back over to the table and sat down. There was a little bit of Bordeaux left in the bottle, so he poured half of the remainder into my glass and the rest in his. Then he lifted the glass and held it up, appearing to inspect the color of the liquid, deep garnet when backlit by the fire leaping in the hearth.

"Let us just say that Aldair and I have never gotten along very well. This dispute over who would have you for his Chosen—that seemed to be the final blow. He is not the sort to accept defeat easily."

I picked up my own glass and swirled the wine in it, but didn't drink. "I'm surprised you both ended up here. I mean, didn't you all have the whole world to choose from when it came to where you would settle down...after?"

"Not exactly." He took a swallow of the Bordeaux and closed his eyes briefly, as if savoring the taste. "We came to the places where our Chosen had lived, more or less. We thought it would be less of a shock that way, since at least your surroundings wouldn't be completely unfamiliar. And since the woman Aldair took as your substitute was also from New Mexico, albeit farther south, in Roswell, it was necessary that he stay in this region."

"Was that why you were so reluctant to come here to Taos?" I asked. "Because of Aldair?"

"I would have preferred to avoid him, yes. But also...being with you in our house in Santa Fe, being together like that, was more than I could have ever dreamed of having. I didn't want that to end. I feared for the way things might change, once you knew what I was, and once you were around others like me."

How ironic that a being of such amazing powers, such age and worldliness, could experience some old-fashioned, very human insecurity. I set down my wine glass, and reached over and took his hands in mine. "I love you, Jace," I said simply. "I loved you in Santa Fe, and I love you here in Taos. Where we are doesn't matter, only that we're together."

His fingers tightened against my flesh, warm, strong. How I'd missed the feel of him, the heat of his skin. Even though we'd been back together for a few days, it still seemed like a miracle. Or maybe it was simply that everything about him was a bit more precious, now that I knew what it was like to have him torn from my life.

Our eyes met, and I saw the need there, a need echoed by my own body. We made love several times a day, and yet it still didn't seem enough to satisfy my longing for him. Maybe I was just trying to make up for all those weeks when I'd slept in an empty bed.

By some unspoken signal, we both stood at the same time. He pulled me against him, his mouth finding mine, tasting me, as I pressed against him and claimed some of his warmth for my own. Piece by piece, our clothing fell away, until we were both naked, our bodies heated by the fire and our need for one another.

We sank down on the rug, not even wanting to take the few steps getting to the bed required, touching and stroking, flesh pressed against flesh. He lifted me so I sank down on him, finding our rhythm once more, as his hands caressed me, fingers closing over my breasts.

It was perfection. He was perfection. We sighed through our climaxes together, and afterward he lifted me to the bed so we might fall asleep in each other's arms. Everything in the world was forgotten—Aldair, Miles Odekirk's devices, even Evony's grief—as I clung to Jace. How could anything possibly go wrong, when everything felt so right?

"He has gone," Zahrias said flatly.

This morning, the djinn leader had summoned both Jace and me to his conference room. That summons had come a bit earlier than I would have preferred, considering our activities of the night before. I fought back a yawn as Jace asked,

"Aldair?"

"Yes. He did not appear at breakfast this morning, and when I sent Lauren to check on him, his suite was empty, his things missing."

That made me blink the sleep out of my eyes and focus more closely on Zahrias. "Wait—you mean he just took off? Where would he go?"

Neither of them said anything at first. Then, the words coming slowly, as if he really didn't want to utter them, Jace replied, "He would have gone...to them."

"Them?" I said blankly.

"The other djinn," Zahrias responded. His tone was neutral enough, but a flicker in his eyes told me he was less than pleased by this turn of events.

"Can he do that?"

The djinn leader's brows pulled together. "He has free will. He can do what he likes."

Jace added, "It is not as if any of us was forced to be here. We chose this life, chose to save what we could of humanity. But that choice does not preclude returning to the others, for whatever reason. With his Chosen gone, and no real candidate for another anywhere close by, Aldair had no reason to stay here."

On the surface, I supposed that made sense. But I couldn't quite reconcile having enough belief in your convictions to rebel against what the majority of your race wanted, only to turn around and decide they weren't so bad after all. It was like a conscientious objector of the '60s putting down his flowers and picking up that M16 because hey, maybe shooting at innocent Vietnamese villagers wasn't as bad as he first thought.

"So...what are you going to do about it?" I asked.

"Nothing," Zahrias said. "Even if I wanted to, I could not have stopped Aldair, and I most certainly don't have the authority to go after him and force him to come back to us. We can only hope that his leaving will be the end of it."

"Why wouldn't it be?"

The two djinn exchanged a glance. They were silent for a time, for so long, actually, that I wondered if they were sharing a subvocal conversation the way Jace and I so often had.

At last Jace said, "I am sure all is well. We have an agreement with the other djinn, and Aldair going to them changes nothing at all, except that you and I will not have to skulk in our suite in an attempt to avoid him."

He sounded breezy and unruffled, and yet I wasn't sure I quite believed him. Something had passed between Jasreel and Zahrias, some unspoken communication neither of them wanted to share with me. Fine, I'd let it go for now.

But I wouldn't forget.

A day passed, and then another. I began to think that my worries had been for nothing. After all, Aldair was gone, but nothing had happened. Lindsay continued to tinker with the box—or rather, conduct minor experiments with it.

"I know one of these days I'll have to open it up and really start trying to figure out how it works," she told me one morning, almost a week after Aldair had left. "But I'm so scared I'm going to screw it up that I keep coming up with new ways to procrastinate."

"Well, that's understandable," I replied. We were alone in the "lab" that morning, as Aidan had gone out on a hunting expedition with several other people in the Taos group, and Jace and Zahrias were having yet another of their "talks" in the conference room. For all Jace's claim, once upon a time, that he and Zahrias really weren't friends, his behavior seemed to tell a different story.

It was all right, though. Even though I loved him more with every passing day and wanted to be with him as much as possible, I also knew there was a point where you could be with a person too much. Hanging out with Lindsay gave us both a chance for a little separation here and there. I would've done the same with Evony, but every single friendly overture I'd made to her had been rebuffed. At least she'd begun venturing from her room now and then, and even ate in the dining hall a few times, but she always did so at the table where Lauren and Dani sat. From all appearances, Lauren was her new best friend. I couldn't say it didn't hurt. On the other hand, at least she was being friendly with someone, even if that person wasn't me.

Lindsay sighed and set the box down on the workbench next to her. "Oh, yeah, everyone's been very understanding. But I know I should be doing more. It's just—I was good at what I was learning. I knew one day I'd make a great mechanical engineer. That thing, though?" She cast a baleful glance at the little black box. "It's so far beyond anything I've ever worked with, I don't even know where to start. I feel like one of those guys at Roswell who was asked to reverse-engineer a crashed alien spaceship."

"You believe in that stuff?" I asked, surprised. She'd always seemed way too level-headed for any of that UFO conspiracy crap.

"No," she replied, reassuring me. "I just meant it as a hypothetical example. You know?"

I nodded. A shadow seemed to pass over the sun right then, darkening the light beyond the window, and I couldn't help glancing outside. We'd had a forecast for several clear days in a row, which was part of the reason why the hunters had gone out today.

"What is it?" Lindsay asked, appearing to note my distraction.

"I don't know. I guess I wasn't expecting it to cloud up, but it feels like it's getting darker."

"Hmm." Probably glad of the chance to ignore the box for a few minutes, she hopped off the stool she'd been sitting on and went over to the door, cracking it open so she could peer outside. Good idea, since the windows in the auto repair shop weren't exactly what you could call clean.

But then she said, "Oh, my God," and something in her tone made me get off my own stool and go see what she was looking at. As I stood in the doorway and craned my head upward, every drop of blood in my veins suddenly felt as if it had turned to ice water. The breath caught in my throat, and I had to grab hold of the doorjamb to keep my knees from giving out right then and there.

The skies above us swirled in shades of black and gray and livid purple. But those weren't clouds...not exactly. As I tried to focus, I could see shapes in those strange formations, see them moving in distinct patterns. And while I stared, they began to wheel and pivot, moving toward us, gaining resolution.

Those weren't clouds. Those were djinn, an entire army of them.

The others. They shouldn't be coming here. There was a truce. An agreement.

But agreements were made to be broken, apparently.

"Shut the door!" I screamed at Lindsay, even though I knew a door would hold back a djinn approximately the same way a sheet of tissue paper would hold back a rampaging bull. Even having that flimsy door protecting us seemed better than standing out in the open like a couple of targets just waiting to be hit.

She obeyed without question, running inside and slamming the door. Then she locked it. Terrified green eyes fixed on my face. "It's—it's *them*, isn't it?"

"I think so."

"But—"

"I know. I don't understand, either." *Aldair,* I thought frantically. *It must have something to do with Aldair.*

What had he told them?

At the moment, it didn't matter. The only thing that mattered was that thousands of angry djinn were about to descend on an unprotected population.

Unprotected....

My gaze fell on Miles Odekirk's device, and I ran to it and picked it up, then turned it over in my hands.

"Jessica, what are you doing?"

"Saving us," I said, and pushed the button to activate it. I knew that Lindsay had kept it set at the level where it would cover the greatest area and yet still deprive the djinn of their powers. The automotive shop we occupied now was about a quarter-mile from the resort where most of the Taos contingent was congregated, and so we should all be covered, theoretically speaking. Yes, the device would also affect our own djinn, but better weak and tired than dead.

Or at least, I had to hope they would all feel that way.

From overhead there came a horrible shrieking noise. Still holding the device, I hurried to the window and peered out through the dirt-grimed glass. The hordes above us seemed to be retreating, moving back out of range of the box's area of effect. They grew smaller and smaller, and as they went, daylight returned.

"Holy shit," Lindsay breathed. "It worked. They're gone."

"Yes," I said, fingers clenched around the device, the sharp edges biting into my flesh. "But for how long?"

She looked at me soberly, and didn't reply.

It was a question neither of us wanted to answer.

———

The Djinn Wars continue in *Fallen*.

www.ingramcontent.com/pod-product-compliance
Lightning Source LLC
Chambersburg PA
CBHW030552260626
47157CB00006B/2292